GETTING CLOSER

"Did I say something wrong?" Annie asked Dalton.

"No."

"Then why the sudden cold shoulder?"

"I don't know what you're talking about."

She studied him in silence for a moment, then removed her hand from his arm. "Fine by me."

"What's that supposed to mean?"

"That means," she replied, giving him her best teacher's glare, "you don't want to talk about whatever I did or said that turned you into an iceman."

His eyebrows lifted, his eyes turning an even chiller shade of gray. "You think I'm an iceman?"

She shrugged. "Whatever."

Before Annie could anticipate his next move, she found her upper body pressed against the back of the couch with an irritated Dalton leaning over her.

"I'm not a damn iceman."

"Oh, yeah?"

"Don't push me, Annie. I'm warning you."

"Or what? You'll turn me into an icicle?"

He stared at her for several seconds, then a half-groan, half-growl rumbled in his chest before he swooped down to claim her mouth with his.

Though surprised he'd actually given in to the desire she'd glimpsed in his eyes, she was also secretly delighted . . .

BOOK YOUR PLACE ON OUR WEBSITE AND MAKE THE READING CONNECTION!

We've created a customized website just for our very special readers, where you can get the inside scoop on everything that's going on with Zebra, Pinnacle and Kensington books.

When you come online, you'll have the exciting opportunity to:

- View covers of upcoming books
- Read sample chapters
- Learn about our future publishing schedule (listed by publication month *and author*)
- Find out when your favorite authors will be visiting a city near you
- Search for and order backlist books from our online catalog
- Check out author bios and background information
- Send e-mail to your favorite authors
- Meet the Kensington staff online
- Join us in weekly chats with authors, readers and other guests
- Get writing guidelines
- AND MUCH MORE!

**Visit our website at
http://www.kensingtonbooks.com**

Wild For You

Suzanne Gray

ZEBRA BOOKS
Kensington Publishing Corp.
www.kensingtonbooks.com

Love is but the discovery of ourselves in others, and the delight in the recognition.

—Alexander Smith, Scottish Poet

Prologue

"Wait!" Annie Peterson said, "Don't touch that."

Jillian Morgan jerked her hand away from the pizza box on the dining room table in Annie's apartment. "Why? Did Kenny screw up our order?"

"No. It's fine, but . . ." Annie frowned, looking into the expectant faces of her two best friends, fellow teachers at a Denver high school. "Don't you realize what we're doing?"

Jillian shrugged, then flipped open the pizza box cover and picked up a slice. "I thought we were going to eat pizza, drink a few beers and watch a movie."

"Yeah," Lisa Carlyle said, "I brought *Dirty Dancing*. One of our all time favorites."

"Yum." Jillian gave a dramatic sigh. "Pizza. Beer. And Patrick Swayze in tight pants. What could be better than that?"

Annie released her breath with a huff. "Don't you get it?" At their blank stares, she said, "When I called to order the pizza, I didn't even have to tell Kenny what we wanted. He knew. Dammit, he knew exactly what I was going to order, right down to the extra sauce on the side."

"What's wrong with that?" Lisa replied with a snort, dipping her slice of pizza in that container of sauce, ordered specifically for her. "It's good business practice to remember what your best customers order."

Annie shook her head. "You're missing the point."

Jillian glanced at Lisa, who gave her a beats-me shrug in response. "Okay, Annie, I'll bite. What *is* the point?"

"The point is, we are in such a rut."

The room was silent for a moment, then Jillian cleared her throat. "I still don't get it. Kenny knew what we wanted, so you think we're in a rut."

"No, it's not just Kenny. It's this." She waved a hand to encompass the pizza box, six-pack of beer and video tape scattered across the table. "Our Saturday night ritual."

Lisa licked a drop of sauce from her fingers. "What's the big deal, Annie? We're friends who get together on Saturday night."

"Exactly," Annie replied, shoving her chair away from the table and getting to her feet. "Every Saturday night for the past year and a half. We order the same pizza. Drink the same beer. Even watch the same movies over and over again." She rubbed her forehead to ease the sudden pounding. "Not only are we in a rut, our social life sucks. Big time. I love spending time with you two but, no offense, we should have more exciting things to do with our Saturday nights." She sighed. "Let's face it, when we aren't teaching, our lives are boring."

Another long silence followed Annie's speech.

Finally, Lisa said, "My God, Annie, you're right."

"How did this happen?" Jillian looked first at Annie, then at Lisa. "How did we let our Saturday night pizza and movie get-togethers become our entire social life?"

"I'm not sure, though my breakup with Mark probably helped," Lisa replied, referring to her former fiancé and their split two years earlier.

"True," Jillian said. "The high school isn't exactly

crawling with eligible men, and the bar scene gets old really fast."

"That's not what I was suggesting," Annie said, dropping back onto her chair and grabbing a slice of pizza. "I meant we need to get out of this rut, but not by starting a manhunt. What we have to do is figure out a way to spice up our lives with something fun and exciting. Something a little bit wild."

Lisa frowned. "But legal, right?"

Annie chuckled. "Yeah, most definitely legal."

"You're right," Jillian said after a moment. "We do need to shake up our boring lives."

Lisa bobbed her head. "We should do something we normally wouldn't do."

The three ate in silence for a minute, then Jillian said, "Maybe we could get really exciting jobs for the summer."

"Hey, that's a good idea," Lisa replied, then turned to Annie. "What do you think?"

"Summer's a long ways off."

"That's true." Jillian dabbed her mouth with a napkin. "And a lot more time to stay stuck in our rut."

"Right," Annie replied. "So let's not wait till summer. Let's get jobs over Christmas break."

"But that's only two weeks away," Lisa said. "Is that enough time?"

"Absolutely." Annie smiled. "I'm sure there are lots of exciting jobs just waiting for us." She took a swallow of beer. "In fact, I already have something in mind for me."

Jillian finished her piece of pizza and reached for another slice. "Well don't keep us in suspense. Spill it, Annie."

"Nope. You'll have to come up with your own jobs."

Lisa laughed. "Okay, we get it. You don't want us to steal your idea." She chewed another bite of pizza, swallowed, then added, "I just thought of something. What if one of us turns chicken and doesn't get a job for over the holidays? Then what do we do?"

Jillian frowned. "I hadn't thought of that. Maybe we need an incentive to make sure we all hold up our end of the plan." She looked at Annie, then at Lisa. "Any suggestions?"

"How about this?" Lisa replied. "If one of us decides she likes being in a rut and chickens out on getting a job, then the wimp has to buy dinner for the other two at that new French restaurant downtown."

Annie's eyes widened. "I heard that place is really super expensive."

"Exactly." Lisa smiled. "None of us can afford to pay for one of their dinners on our salaries, let alone three, so that oughta insure we all go through with our plan, don't you think?"

"True," Jillian said. "Okay, I'm still in."

"Me, too," Annie replied, holding up her bottle of beer. "Here's to spicing up our lives over Christmas break."

First Lisa, then Jillian clinked her bottle against Annie's. With a mutual nod, followed by a swallow of beer to seal the deal, their pact was made.

As Annie opened containers of the Chinese takeout she'd picked up on her way over to Lisa's apartment, she said, "It's been a week since we made our pact. Have you two found jobs?"

"Uh-huh," Lisa replied, arranging the food on her coffee table. "When I got home from school today, I had a message telling me I got the job."

"Cool." Annie looked over at where Jillian sat sprawled in an easy chair. "What about you?"

"I've been hired, too," she said. "In fact, the guy

called to give me the news just before I left to come over here."

The three spent the next few minutes filling their plates, then settled back to eat. Then Jillian said, "Annie, you didn't tell us if you got a job."

"Yup, I sure did."

"The one you were so secretive about last week?" When Annie nodded, she said, "So tell us about it, girlfriend."

Annie smiled, then said, "Remember the couple down the hall from me, Dan and Charlene Baxter?"

"Of course," Jillian replied with a laugh. "Kinda hard to forget the Baxters."

Lisa's brow furrowed. "Wasn't there something in the newspaper about them a while back?"

"Yeah, there was," Jillian said, turning her narrowed gaze on Annie. "Don't tell me you asked Dan and Charlene for a job?"

Annie lifted one shoulder in a shrug. "Okay, I won't tell you. But I start working for them the first day of Christmas break."

"Um . . ." Lisa said, looking over at Jillian, then back at Annie. "Are you sure you want to do that? I mean, won't you have to—"

"Yeah, I will." Annie grinned. "Isn't it great?"

One

Annie squirmed on the seat of her SUV, silently cursing the creator of thong panties. In her opinion, whoever came up with the idea of wearing a strip of cloth crammed where it had no business being should be forced to wear one for eternity. Such torturous underwear had to have been the brainchild of some pathetic little kid who got picked on during recess, and the thong was retaliation for all the wedgies he'd suffered. And to think women—even some of her students—wore the damn things all day, every day. Thongs just took getting used to, they said. She huffed out a breath. *Yeah, right, like I'm going to believe—*

Her mouth dropped open, her eyes going wide at the view through the windshield. Blinking several times, she realized she wasn't seeing things. "Ohmygod," she whispered, staring in disbelief at the snow-covered road. Her berating of sadistic underwear designers had kept her from noticing the light snow flurries falling in Denver thirty minutes ago had grown much heavier since she'd headed into the foothills. And from the looks of the sky, things could turn really ugly, really fast. Tightening her grip on the steering wheel, she considered whether she should turn around or go on. Since she was closer to her destination, she chose the latter option.

Twenty minutes later, through the rapidly intensifying

snowfall, she pulled into the driveway. At least she
hoped she was on the drive. With the snow blowing
and swirling in sudden gusts of wind, visibility was de-
teriorating fast. Just as she stepped on the accelerator,
another blast of wind swept across the driveway, creat-
ing a whiteout and totally obscuring the view in front
of her. She gripped the steering wheel even harder, trying to maintain a straight heading and a steady speed.
Then without warning, the front tires hit some kind of
bump, the steering wheel was jerked out of her hands,
and with a sickening thump, the vehicle came to an
abrupt halt.

Her heart in her throat, she stared in shock at the
huge pile of snow surrounding the front of her SUV.
Putting the vehicle in reverse, she tried to ease out of
the snowbank. But even with four-wheel drive, she
wasn't going anywhere anytime soon.

"Great," she shouted, turning off the engine. "This
is just great!"

She dropped her head onto the steering wheel and
closed her eyes. *What was I thinking? This crazy idea
must've totally fried my brain.* She'd lived in the Denver
area for more than ten years, so she knew how important it was to pay attention to the weather, how quickly
conditions could change. Particularly in the winter,
and especially in the higher elevations.

She drew a deep breath, then exhaled with a long
sigh. Unless she wanted to end up a human popsicle,
she'd have to get out and walk. As much as she disliked
the idea, freezing to death appealed to her even less.
At least she had the common sense to keep boots,
heavy mittens and a scarf in her car. Lifting her head,
she pulled the key from the ignition, then turned to
grab her tote off the back seat. Her movement made
the thong even more uncomfortable—if that was possible.

She muttered a curse even her high school students would find shocking, then gave her head a shake. "I've lost my mind. That's all there is to it."

As she stepped out of her car, her boot sank into snow that nearly reached her knee. Biting back another curse, she heaved a sigh, settled the strap of her tote bag onto her shoulder, then grabbed her purse and closed the door. After pressing the Lock button on the small remote, she slipped the key ring inside her purse and filled her lungs with the cold air. The white plume of her exhaled breath mixed with the heavy snowfall, before being snatched away by another gust of wind. Tucking her chin into the collar of her coat, she started up the driveway—at least she hoped she was heading in the right direction—thinking about how she'd ended up on foot in a snowstorm.

The pact she'd made with Jillian and Lisa. Agreeing to get exciting jobs over their Christmas break was the reason she was getting so up close and personal with a snowstorm that had all the markings of turning into a real doozy. But when she'd suggested the idea to her friends, she hadn't envisioned getting stuck in a snowbank, then having to trudge through knee-deep snow in a howling wind to a house she couldn't see—but hoped wouldn't be much farther ahead—on her first day of work. Even so, the unexpected turn of events hadn't tarnished her determination to carry out her assignment for the Naughty or Nice Messenger Service. Well, not much anyway.

The ringing of the doorbell, followed by the excited barking of his dogs pulled Dalton Stoner from his reading. A softly spoken "Quiet" silenced the two mixed breed terriers. Setting aside the latest issue of

American Artist, he rose and headed for the front foyer, the dogs trotting along behind him.

As he opened the door, his eyes widened in surprise. A snow-dusted woman stood on his front porch, a scarf wound around her head and neck. A few golden-brown corkscrew curls had escaped the confinement of the scarf and framed a face with a delicate nose, high cheekbones and full lips painted fire-engine red. He'd always liked red lipstick. There was something about such a bold color on a woman's mouth, something enticing, something flat-out sexy that— Realizing his thoughts had taken a wrong turn, he snapped back to the present.

"Can I help you?"

"Are you Dalton Stoner?"

"I am. So what—" His gaze narrowed as the familiar voice registered. "You're the woman who called earlier."

Her cheeks, already bright pink from the wind, darkened even more. "Yes, and if you remember correctly, I called to tell you I had a delivery to make and wanted to be sure you'd be home. Or don't you recall that part of our conversation?"

Dalton arched a brow at the sarcasm in her voice. "I remember our conversation perfectly. But when the storm hit, I figured . . ." He shook his head. "Why would you try to make a delivery during a snowstorm?"

Annie lifted her head to meet his gaze, then wished she hadn't. Though he probably wouldn't be considered classically handsome, there was no denying that the combination of long narrow nose, wide sensual mouth, and square jaw with a small cleft in his chin added up to one powerfully attractive male. She wasn't sure what she expected Dalton Stoner to look like, but the man staring down at her through heavily lashed, blue-gray eyes definitely was not it.

She swallowed hard, then gave him her best school teacher glare. "Well, I'm here," she said, trying to keep her teeth from chattering.

For a moment Dalton couldn't respond. He was about to drown in the greenest eyes he'd ever seen, eyes currently ablaze with temper aimed directly at him. Letting her obvious anger feed his, he scowled. "Just what are you delivering that's worth the risk of driving in weather like this?"

"Um . . . could we get to that in a few minutes? I'd really like to warm up first. So . . . may I come in?"

He nodded, glancing past her to what he could see of his driveway. Not much was visible through the thick curtain of snow. "How'd you get here?"

"I drove. My car is . . . um . . . down the drive, stuck in a snowbank. With it snowing so hard, I guess I missed a curve."

He shoved a hand through his hair, muttering a crude response.

"My sentiments exactly, Mr. Stoner," Annie said, dragging her gaze from the blunt-tipped fingers pushing through his jet-black hair. "Now, if you don't mind, I'd really like to get inside."

"Oh, yeah, sure." He opened the door wider, then stepped aside. "Come in, Miss . . ."

"Peterson. Annie Peterson."

"The living room is to the left. You can warm up in front of the fireplace."

She nodded, then moved past him while pulling off her mittens. Dropping her tote bag and purse on the floor, she reached down to tug off her boots. At that moment, his dogs, who'd waited patiently a few feet away, came forward to investigate the visitor.

"Oh, what cuties," she said, crouching and holding out a hand for the dogs to sniff.

When Annie glanced up at him, the smile on her

face hit him like a punch in the gut. Resisting the urge to rub his belly to ease the strange sensation, he drew a deep breath and shifted his gaze to the dogs.

"These two rascals are Data, the one with more brown, and his brother Worf. They're usually wary of strangers, but"—he frowned, puzzled by his pets' behavior—"for some reason they seem taken with you."

"They just know I love dogs," she replied, then turned her attention to Data and Worf. "Hi, guys." She rubbed the wiry hair on one neck, then gave equal attention to the other, making their docked tails wiggle with excitement. "With names like yours"—she looked up at Dalton, a smile curving her lips and amusement sparkling in her eyes—"your owner must be a trekker."

"Not exactly," he replied, stuffing his hands in the front pockets of his jeans. "I never watched the original *Star Trek,* but when I was in college, my roommate and I—" He coughed. "We sorta got hooked on *The Next Generation.*"

"Really? Well, you must still be a fan. I mean, naming your dogs after two of the characters on a series that's been in reruns for what . . . ten years?"

"Nine," he said before he could stop himself, irritated by the blush creeping up his neck. No way would he tell her he'd named his previous dogs Picard and Riker.

"In case you're not aware of it," she said, giving the dogs a final pat, "one of the local channels broadcasts *Next Generation* reruns every night."

"Yeah, I know. I watch them every—" He coughed again, the burning on his neck inching higher to sting his ears. "Whenever I can."

"Hey, you're a grown man," she said, giving him a quick once-over. "You're entitled to watch whatever you want, whenever you want." Flashing him another smile, she finished removing her boots, then headed for his living room.

He released a shaky breath, then wiped a hand over his face. What the hell? He didn't care what anybody thought about his TV watching habits, or that his "whenever I can" really meant almost every night. But for some reason, he hadn't been able to tell the truth to the foolhardy Annie Peterson. And the way she'd raked an assessing gaze over him with those gorgeous green eyes had made him damn uncomfortable.

As Annie entered the living room, she tried not to think about the good-looking man she'd left in the foyer. Crossing to the impressive stone fireplace, she noticed a large Christmas tree tucked into one corner, then turned her attention to the rest of the room, glancing around with open curiosity. One wall had three large windows opening onto a deck, which on any other day probably offered a spectacular view of the mountains, but with the heavy snow, she couldn't see anything beyond the deck's railing. Shifting her gaze back to the interior of the room, she took a closer look. The eclectic mix of furniture styles worked well together, the pieces undoubtedly of high quality—not a surprise since the man owned a museum and art gallery—but there was also a slightly messy, well-lived-in quality she hadn't expected. A coffee table cluttered with books and magazines. Brightly colored throws on the cushions of a pair of leather couches—no doubt for the dogs. A mug and plate sat on one end table. She pulled her brows together in a frown.

She'd had the idea that the Stoner home would be more, well, artsy fartsy. Like a page out of *Architectural Digest*, filled with elegant but totally impractical and horribly uncomfortable furniture, everything perfectly arranged, and not a dirty dish, a speck of dust or, God forbid, a dog hair anywhere. She wrinkled her nose at the thought. She much preferred this room, with its hominess, clean lines and comfortable— Scowling at the direction of her thoughts, she unwrapped the wool scarf from around her neck, then freed her hair from inside her collar.

As she attempted to finger comb the tangle of curls with the hope of somehow subduing the wild mass, she glanced toward the hall she assumed led to the rest of the house. Maybe the living room was an anomaly. Maybe the other rooms were decorated exactly as she'd imagined. Maybe they—

Stop it! What are you thinking? You won't be seeing the rest of the house, so quit obsessing about it.

Determined not to think about how Dalton Stoner had furnished the other rooms in his house, she gave up on her hair and held her hands toward the fire. As the warmth seeped into her chilled fingers, her thoughts shifted to her reason for being in the man's home.

She still couldn't believe how she'd ended up here. His sister Daphne had hired the messenger service to make a delivery to him, provided Annie was given the assignment. She'd met Daphne Stoner six months earlier while shopping for a birthday present for her mother. She had nearly given up and gone home when she discovered Charmed, Daphne's small shop on Larimer Square.

Annie had loved the store immediately, as well as everything Daphne sold there. The huge selection of candles in every imaginable size, color and scent. The wonderful variety of bath salts and body lotions. The large assortment of small glass figurines and lovely sun catchers. Even the crystals Daphne claimed could be used to read the future. After their initial meeting,

Annie made Charmed a frequent stop, and a friendship had developed between the two women.

When Annie told Daphne about her holiday job—though she left out the part about making a pact with her friends—and admitted how nervous she was, Daphne insisted her reaction was nothing more than first performance jitters. Once she got her feet wet, her friend told her, she'd be fine. But when Annie didn't seem convinced, Daphne came up with an idea. What better way to get that first delivery out of the way than by delivering a message to Daphne's brother?

Annie wasn't so sure. Maybe delivering her first message shouldn't be to someone she knew—though technically she didn't actually know Daphne's brother, since she'd never met the man.

But after thinking about Daphne's proposal, Annie finally acknowledged the logic of the idea. She definitely would feel safer delivering a message to a relative of a friend—especially since Daphne's brother owned a museum and art gallery. Though she hadn't told Daphne, she figured a museum owner had to be one really boring man. Soft, delicate hands. Snooty attitude. Walking on the balls of his feet like he had a stick up his butt.

Based on her preconceived notions about Dalton Stoner, and her conclusion that going to the house of such a man would pose no threat, Annie had finally agreed to Daphne's plan. But now that she stood in his home, the moment fast approaching when she'd actually have to complete the delivery, she wasn't sure she could go through with it.

The thought had never crossed her mind that Dalton would be a real hottie, with such incredible blue-gray eyes and a sexy little cleft in his chin. Or that he'd make her insides tremble with— Squeezing her eyes closed, she refused to finish that thought. No point in going there. Once she delivered Daphne's message, she'd be out of his house in a flash. Remembering the snowstorm, her stomach pitched like a rowboat bobbing in choppy water. *Please let me be able to get back to town.*

Twirling a curl of hair around her fingers, she stared into the fire, her teeth clenched to stop a new round of chattering—this one having nothing to do with being cold. Damn. Talk about ridiculous! She handled a roomful of rowdy teenagers every day, so how hard could it be to deal with one man?

Dalton paused in the arched doorway to his living room, wanting a few moments to watch Annie covertly. When she removed the scarf and revealed her hair, he'd been mesmerized, his fingers twitching at the sight of the thick cascade of curls trailing down to her shoulders. He suddenly forgot to breathe, the overwhelming urge to touch those curls, to feel their silkiness against his bare skin catching him totally off guard.

He jerked his gaze away from her, swallowing hard. What the hell was wrong with him? He didn't even know this woman. She just showed up on his doorstep, and his brain started misfiring, conjuring thoughts about those sexy red lips and that wild tangle of curly hair, and worse, causing a mild stirring in his groin.

His mother would be thrilled. She constantly told him she couldn't believe she'd given birth to a son who had such a pathetic sex life. But then she always softened her statement by adding that he just hadn't found the right woman. He would, she assured him, and when he did—she'd give him an exaggerated wink and a knowing smile—things would definitely change.

He bit back a grin. There weren't many mothers

who would talk to their sons with such frankness. But then there weren't many women like his mother.

Widowed ten years ago at age forty-five, Dolly Stoner was independent, witty, open-minded and outspoken. A year after her husband's sudden death, she'd told Dalton and his two sisters she planned to revive her pre-motherhood dream of pursuing a career in writing. The siblings had been thrilled, until they learned she intended to write erotic fiction. That part of her announcement had come as a huge shock. Even after she became a highly successful author, Dalton and his sisters still had trouble equating the ultra-sexy books bearing their mother's name with the woman who'd raised them.

Though they had grown used to Dolly's notoriety, Dalton, at least, still had trouble accepting his mother's, in her words, "extremely active and fulfilling sex life." Not that he let her share the details of her sexual forays, but he had no doubt she indulged whenever the opportunity arose. In fact, her current indulgence was a thirty-five-year-old fitness instructor named Buzz, who didn't seem the least concerned about the twenty-year difference in their ages.

His mother and Buzz getting it on, all hot and sweaty while engaging in the horizontal mambo. *Dammit, don't go there!* Dalton gave his head a shake, forcing such disturbing images of his mother and her much younger stud from his mind before they could fully form. They were adults, and he had no right to pass judgement. Even so, he still had difficulty acknowledging his mother's carnal appetite, or the intimate things she and Buzz did in private. But in spite of his discomfort with the whole sexuality issue, Dalton liked the guy and figured more power to him. Dolly Stoner could be a

real handful, so any man who treated her right and
made her happy had his approval.

Not wanting to spend any more time dwelling on his
mother's sex life, he shifted his concentration to a
more pressing matter. Annie Peterson.

He drew a deep breath, then pushed away from the
archway and stepped into the room.

"Are you getting thawed out?"

She gasped, then swung around to face him. She'd
opened the collar of her coat, but left the rest of the
garment buttoned. Her throat working with a swallow, she nodded. "Yes, thanks."

Dalton moved closer. "Can I get you something to
drink? Tea. Coffee. Hot chocolate?"

Annie managed a smile. "Thanks, but I'm warm
enough now to make this delivery." Trying to steady
her growing nervousness, she knew she couldn't delay
any longer. She left her spot by the fireplace and nearly
ran to the hallway. "I'll be right back," she said, rushing
past him. "I need to get something from my tote bag."

When she returned a moment later, she held a
portable CD player in one hand. She set the player
on the coffee table, took a deep breath, then pressed
the Play button. Nothing happened.

She tried again, but still nothing. After fiddling
with the machine for a minute, she glanced up at Dalton. "This is really embarrassing," she said, managing
a weak smile, "but I . . . uh . . . forgot the batteries.
Would it be possible to use your CD player?"

Dalton frowned. "Don't tell me you drove up here
to deliver a singing telegram?"

"No, that's not why I'm here. But I do need music."

He stared at her flushed face for several seconds,
then sighed. Motioning to the entertainment center
on the wall opposite the windows, he said, "It's over
here."

Annie followed him across the room, then watched while he opened the glass doors and pushed several buttons. From out of the blue she was struck with the irrational longing to have those hands touch her. The thought caused her nerve endings to go on high alert. Swallowing a groan, she drew a steadying breath. Another mistake. Dalton's scent filled her head. Woodsy with a hint of some exotic spice, totally masculine and every bit as exciting. Lord, she felt tipsy. How could this man affect her so strongly? But more important, how was she going to get through the next few minutes? She never should have listened to Daphne and agreed to do this.

"You're all set," he said, jerking her out of her mental wanderings. He took a step back. "Just put in your disc and press Play."

"Okay, thanks." The words came out in a squeak, but she kept her gaze focused on the CD player, not wanting to see Dalton's reaction. Once she was certain he'd moved back across the room, she dropped the disc into place. Squeezing her eyes closed, she waited for the pounding of her heart to calm, then exhaled slowly.

She opened her eyes, then reach toward the Play button with a slightly trembling hand. Her fingertips just a hairbreadth from their target, the lights on the CD player went dark. Glancing over her shoulder, she noticed the table lamp had also gone out. The glow from the fireplace now provided the room's only light against the growing dimness of the gray afternoon.

Oh God, what else can go wrong?

She waited several seconds, but when the power didn't come back on, she moved away from the entertainment center. "Look, this obviously isn't working out very well. So I think it would be best if I leave and come back some other time."

He pursed his lips, one eyebrow arched. "Really?" he

said in a soft voice. "And just how do you plan to get back to the city?"

She shoved her hair away from her flushed face. All of a sudden she was too warm, but there was no way she'd take off her coat now. "Darn. I forgot about my car. Would you mind if I use your phone?"

"Of course not. But if you're thinking of calling road service, forget it. The roads are probably already closed, so you won't get a tow truck up here until the storm ends."

"Then what am I supposed to do?"

"Well, Miss Peterson, until the roads are reopened, looks like you're stuck here with me."

Two

"Stuck here?" Annie shook her head. "Uh-uh. No way. That's not a good idea. I mean . . . I couldn't possibly stay here with"—she waved a hand in Dalton's direction—"you."

"Is that right?" He crossed his arms over his chest, his eyes turning a stormy gray. "Since you find the thought of staying here with me so distasteful, I take it you have something else in mind."

"No, actually," Annie replied, a sinking sensation in the pit of her stomach, "that's not what I meant. I appreciate the offer, it's just that I really need to get back to the city."

"Ah, someone is waiting for you. So just call your husband, boyfriend, roommate, whoever and explain."

"I'm not married, and I don't have a boyfriend or a roommate."

"Then you need to get home because of . . . what? A dog. A sick neighbor?"

"I don't have a pet, and my neighbors are fine."

"Then you're going to have to explain why you're in such a big hurry to leave."

Annie sighed, wishing he'd drop the subject. "The thing is, staying here with you isn't . . . well, seemly."

"Seemly." He chuckled, little crinkles appearing at the corners of his eyes—no longer their former gray, but now a tranquil blue. "Odd choice in words. Can't remember the last time I heard someone use it."

Annie blinked up at him, amazed that his eyes could change color with such ease. Realizing she was staring, she looked over to where his dogs had stretched out on one of the couches. "My grandmother is fond of the word," she said in an oddly hoarse voice, "and I thought it was appropriate in this circumstance."

"Do you share your grandmother's disapproval of a man and woman spending time together without a chaperon?"

"Uh, no." She cleared her throat, bringing her gaze back to his face. "I may be old fashioned about some things, but I'm definitely more open minded than Gran about a lot of other stuff."

Dalton studied her in silence for a moment, then said, "Well, whatever the reason, you're still not comfortable with the idea of staying here with me. And the truth is, I don't blame you. I mean, we've known each other for what, thirty minutes? If it's any consolation, this is damn awkward for me, too." He huffed out a deep breath. "Look, let me put your mind at ease. You're safe here. I have no intention of seducing you on a bearskin rug in front of a roaring fire."

She looked at the fireplace, the tip of her tongue peeking out to run over those perfect red lips.

Another ripple of sexual awareness washed over Dalton, causing his pulse to spike. His mouth practically watered to taste hers. His fingers itched to touch her skin. Dammit, what was wrong with him? This wasn't the first time he'd had an immediate physical reaction to a woman he'd just met, but he'd never experienced anything like this. The next few hours, or even days—he bit back a groan at the possibility of spending days with this woman—until the roads were reopened were going to be hell.

"You don't have a bearskin rug," Annie said, pulling him from his torturous thoughts.

His eyebrows shot up. Were her words meant as more than an observation? Had he really heard longing in her voice? No, couldn't be. Tamping down the urge to call up an image of the two of them naked, rolling around on a— He shoved that thought aside, then cleared his throat. "True," he said at last, trying for what he hoped would be a detached smile. "See there, nothing to worry about."

She nodded, then turned away, but not before he caught a flash of something in her deep-green eyes. He wasn't certain, but for an instant he could've sworn she looked disappointed. Scowling at her back, he realized this entire, unsettling situation had his imagination running wild.

After several moments of silence, he uncrossed his arms and rubbed a hand over his chin. "Ya know," he finally said, "I think it would help if we sat down and talked. Get to know each other. Take the edge off this uneasiness." And, he added silently, hopefully learn something that will halt this disconcerting attraction to her.

When she didn't respond, he added, "Unless you have another suggestion."

He watched her shoulders lift as she drew a deep breath, then heard her exhale a long sigh.

"No," she said at last. Swinging around to face him, the corners of her mouth lifted in a smile. "You're right. Getting to know each other might make our situation a little less tense."

"Exactly," he said, moving closer. "Let me take your coat, then I'll get us something to drink."

Annie took a step back, sudden panic welling up inside her. "No, that's okay. I'm fine."

"Don't be ridiculous. You'll be more comfortable without that heavy coat."

She frowned. "I don't think that would be a good idea."

He stared at her for a moment, then his eyes went wide. "Please, tell me you're not naked under there."

The heat of a blush creeping up her cheeks, she sent him an annoyed glare. "Of course I'm not naked."

"Then why are you stalling?"

"Because I . . ." She pressed her lips together, then heaved a sigh. "Okay, fine." She reached for the top button of the wool coat.

By the time she freed the final button, she had regrouped and summoned her courage. She'd faced down angry teenagers bent on fighting in the high school hallway, so she could do this. Hoping she was prepared for Dalton's reaction, she took a deep breath, then opened her coat.

Dalton had no idea what he'd expected Annie to be wearing, but the thigh-length, red velvet jacket trimmed in white fur most definitely had never crossed his mind as even a remote possibility.

Holy shit. Momentarily too stunned to speak, he swept his gaze from the deep vee of the neckline revealing a tantalizing glimpse of cleavage, to the sleek muscles of her naked thighs, then down past well-shaped calves to where she'd curled her bare toes into the carpet. His mouth bone-dry, his pulse pounding against his temples, a rhythm repeated in his groin, he forced himself to look at her face.

"Something just occurred to me," he said, inwardly wincing at the raspiness of his voice. "When you called, you didn't tell me the name of the company you work for."

"Um . . . right. We purposely do that, so we don't . . . um . . . spoil the surprise."

"Surprise, huh?" Dalton swallowed hard. "Yeah, well, you've got that part of your job down pat. I'm definitely surprised." He managed a weak smile. "So, what's the name of the company?"

"The Naughty or Nice Messenger Service." Before he could respond, she rushed on. "It's a fairly new business. The owners wanted to provide a unique type of service for a select clientele, so they started their own company."

Uh-oh, this didn't sound good. His eyes narrowed. "You said you weren't delivering a singing telegram, but you brought a CD. Just what the hell kind of messages does the company deliver? Dirty limericks recited to music?"

Annie squared her shoulders, bracing herself for his reaction. "No, we deliver strip-o-grams."

Dalton's mouth dropped open in shock, momentarily at a loss for words. Finally, he said, "Strip-o-grams? You came here, in that getup, to deliver a strip—"

"Yes." Her chin lifted, defiance glittering in her eyes.

He shoved his hands through his hair, still having a hard time grasping Annie's revelation. "Who the hell would hire you to—" A muscle jerking in his jaw, he scowled. "Dammit! My sisters are behind this, aren't they?"

"Your sisters?"

"Yeah. Darcie and Daphne. They're constantly meddling in my life. Trying to fix me up with a string of women they've taken upon themselves to decide are perfect for me. I thought I'd finally gotten through to them to quit with the matchmaking, but I guess not." He raked his gaze down to her toes, then back to her face. "And why they'd pick a woman who delivers strip-o-grams is beyond me."

Annie curled her hands into fists, resisting the urge to take a swing at him. "I don't know Darcie, but Daphne was *not* trying to fix us up. She just wanted to make my—" She bit her lip, appalled that she'd nearly revealed how she'd ended up at his house. There was no way she'd tell him that Daphne's hiring her had nothing to do with matchmaking, but had been done strictly out of pity, to get Annie initiated in her new messenger job.

"What were you going to say?"

"Nothing. It's not important." Slipping off her coat, she wadded the garment into a ball and tossed it in his direction. "I brought some other clothes, so if you'll tell me where I can change . . ."

Dalton managed to catch her coat before it hit the floor, determined not to sneak another peak at the creamy flesh hinted at above her deeply veed neckline. "There's a bathroom off the kitchen." He nodded toward the arched doorway. "Through there, then to your right."

"Fine," she replied with a bob of her head, then moved past him to retrieve her tote bag.

As he watched her go through the doorway a moment later, he called after her. "I'm going to have a drink. Can I get you something?"

"Whatever you're having is fine," she replied, not turning around.

Then he heard the bathroom door click shut, leaving him with a coat that gave off her scent, and a head full of way-too-enticing images. Annie's full lips shiny with dark red lipstick. Those extraordinary green eyes. The wild tangle of curly, golden-brown hair. That sexy little velvet jacket. The white fur hem swishing against the backs of her thighs.

As he hung her coat in the hall closet, he wondered if a man's head could explode from an overload of provocative stimuli. He shut the closet, then dropped his forehead against the oak door, struggling to convince his body not to react to the erotic thoughts dancing around in his mind.

He exhaled a deep breath then pushed away from the door, disgusted to realize his mother was right. His sex life was pathetic. If he had a woman in his life, one he slept with on a regular basis, then he wouldn't be in this predicament. He wouldn't find Annie Peterson so incredibly appealing, or have to fight to keep his physical reaction in check.

And to make matters worse, the woman who'd sparked such an immediate interest was an unexpected houseguest—probably sent by his sisters—requiring him to play the gracious host for God-only-knew how long.

Not a good combination.

As he stepped into the kitchen, he flipped the light switch, then cursed under his breath. He'd forgotten about the power outage. Thank God for the fireplace and the large supply of firewood stacked out back. Even though the house was well insulated, the heat would dissipate fairly fast, especially if the wind didn't calm and the outside temperature continued to drop.

He glanced at the clock. The power had been out for only a few minutes, which meant he wouldn't have to bring in more firewood for at least an hour. Though, on second thought, hauling in more wood right now might be the smart thing to do, since the frigid air definitely would cool his lustful thoughts. But then he dismissed the idea. He doubted even running naked through the snow would help. Not when Annie would still be here when he came back in—

"Is something wrong?"

He jerked, then spun around to find the woman filling his thoughts standing a few feet behind him. "Christ, you nearly gave me a heart attack."

"Sorry. But you were standing in the middle of the room, just staring off in space."

"Yeah, well, I have a lot on my mind." Even without

decent lighting, he could see she'd changed into a baggy University of Colorado sweatshirt, gray leggings and a pair of thick white socks. Though she couldn't have worn anything less sexy, she still made his pulse race. Gritting his teeth against another unwanted surge of desire, he moved to the refrigerator and opened the door.

Grateful for the blast of cold air, he took his time pulling out two bottles of beer, then set them on the counter. "Do you want a glass?"

"Nope. The bottle is fine."

Annie watched him twist off the caps, still having trouble reconciling this man, in a flannel shirt over a dark tee shirt, and no belt through the loops of a pair of well-worn jeans, with the impeccably dressed, slightly snobbish Dalton Stoner she'd expected. Not only did his house and clothes not fit her mental image of a museum and art gallery owner, the real Dalton drank beer. And not some fancy imported brand, but the one brewed locally.

She took the bottle he handed her. "I never would have guessed you'd be a beer man," she said, surprised she'd actually given voice to her thoughts.

As he raised his bottle to his mouth, he said, "Why's that?"

She lifted one shoulder in what she hoped would pass as a casual shrug. "I don't know. I guess I figured you'd be a wine connoisseur."

He made a snorting sound. "Hardly. I like wine, but I don't know a whole lot about the different kinds."

"Neither do I." She took a swallow of beer, then said, "But I do know I can't drink red wine." She turned and headed for the living room. "Just one glass gives me a horrible headache."

Dalton nearly said "Me, too," but held his tongue.

For some reason, he didn't want to verbally admit they had something in common.

As he took another long pull on his beer, he forced himself to look at the situation with his usual clear-headed logic. The two of them being together was only temporary. Once the storm died and the roads had been cleared, he would send Annie Peterson on her way. And he'd never see her again. He scowled in the direction of the living room, wondering why that last thought gave him no satisfaction. Never seeing her again was what he wanted, wasn't it?

Of course it was, he told himself, following her out of the kitchen. The woman delivered strip-o-grams, for God's sake.

Though he had never judged anyone by what they did for a living, he couldn't stop himself from think-ing there was no way a stripper and a gallery owner could have any kind of relationship. The slight twitch beneath the fly of his jeans reminded him that he was a healthy man with a normal libido, who hadn't been with a woman in a long time, and who found Annie extremely attractive. So okay, the truth was, he and Annie could have a physical relationship—a really hot one, unless he missed his guess. But once the ini-tial flare of lust burned off, they would drift apart, and then she'd be out of his life for good.

As he dropped onto one of the couches next to a curled-up Data, something still nagged at him. If not seeing Annie again was truly what he wanted, then why did the idea of her becoming nothing more than a memory leave him with a hollowness in his chest? Lifting the beer bottle to his mouth, he took a big swallow, once again wondering what the hell was going on with him.

He glanced over to where Annie sat in an over-stuffed chair, hoping she could provide the answer.

In spite of her claim to the contrary, her appearance on his doorstep in that skimpy little red velvet number was exactly the kind of thing one of his sisters would do. Especially Daphne. *Dammit, Daf, if this is more of your hocus-pocus crap, I'll have your hide.*

Daphne Stoner's afternoon passed quickly, thanks to heavy Christmas traffic. Probably half of the shoppers who came into Charmed did so because they planned to make a purchase. The rest came in for the free coffee Daphne always provided, or simply to warm up before continuing their Christmas shopping. But she'd always encouraged everyone to look around while drinking coffee or warming their hands and feet, knowing that her carefully arranged displays could entice even the most determined "just-looking" shopper to pull out their credit card. Of the three people who'd left without at least one Charmed shopping bag in their hands, two promised to return the following week, and Daphne felt certain the third, a woman who'd eyed a stunning pair of emerald earrings while sipping a cup of coffee, would also return.

After locking the front door and turning the Closed sign to face the street, Daphne sighed with satisfaction. Though the hectic pace had left her tired, she knew when she added up the receipts, the total would be one of her best. What a great day! Well, except for one thing. She didn't know how Annie's delivery to her brother had turned out.

She'd been too busy to give more than a passing thought to what was happening up in Dalton's mountain home, but now that she'd closed her store, she wondered how her brother had reacted to her little surprise.

She frowned. Probably not well at first. Dalton

would have been angry, though too much a gentleman to take it out on Annie. No, her brother would
save the lecture for when he spoke to her. That was
the reason she didn't plan on calling him until he'd
had a chance to cool down. Her mood brightened.
But she could call Annie.

As soon as Daphne entered the apartment above her
store, she set down her purse then reached for the
phone and dialed Annie's number. Surprised the answering machine picked up after two rings, she left a
message for Annie to call with a full report when she
got home.

When her phone hadn't rung by the time Daphne
had eaten and cleaned up the kitchen, she tried
Annie's apartment again. Like the first time, two
rings and the answering machine.

As the passing minutes dragged into an hour,
Daphne began to pace. Maybe Annie had decided
not to deliver the message to Dalton after all. But if
that were the case, why wasn't Annie home? The two
of them weren't close friends, but Daphne had gotten to know Annie well enough to discover the
woman didn't date much. In fact, the only people
Annie socialized with, as far as Daphne knew, were
some of her teacher friends. Is that where she was
tonight, or had she broken her pattern and actually
gone out on a date? Daphne hoped it wasn't the latter. Another man entering Annie's life right now
would definitely complicate matters.

Finally, the waiting and not knowing were more than
Daphne could stand, so she went into the small bedroom she used as an office. The timing for a reading
wasn't good, she realized. Sunset would have been
best, and the waxing phase of the moon had passed.
Plus, Annie might not appreciate some uninvited

snooping into her life, but she just had to find out what was going on.

A few minutes later, she was nearly ready to begin. After making sure the blinds and curtains were closed tight, she lit a fat candle, then turned off the desk lamp. Once her eyes adjusted to near-darkness, she moved the candle to the corner of her desk, then took a seat at a small round table, her back toward the desk to eliminate any reflections the candle might cast onto the table in front of her.

She smoothed one corner of the dark blue velvet she'd draped over the table, then made a minor adjustment in the position of the wooden stand sitting in the center of the cloth. The stand held her most prized possession. A crystal ball made of real quartz.

Satisfied everything was ready, she took a deep breath and exhaled slowly, then repeated the procedure twice more. Each time, she imagined filling her lungs with good energy then blowing out the bad. Now completely relaxed, she gazed into the center of the crystal ball, allowing her mind to drift into a dreamlike state.

Nothing appeared deep in the ball's center for several moments, then the crystal turned a milky color, which soon cleared to reveal a wavering image floating into view.

A fireplace, a pair of leather couches, a man sitting on one couch, a dog sprawled beside him, its head resting on the man's thigh. As the man stroked a hand over the dog's neck, Daphne's brow furrowed, wondering why concentrating on Annie had resulted in the crystal ball giving her a view of her brother.

"Interesting," she murmured.

She moved her gaze away from the center of the crystal, allowing more details in the scene to become visible. Just as a camera does when it pulls back from a close-up shot, more of Dalton's living room came into view. Now she could see that both dogs were on the couch, the second terrier curled up against a pair of white socks, his dark soulful eyes staring up at—

She chuckled. "Well, well, Annie. So that's why you haven't called me."

Daphne knew she should end the reading now. If Dalton found out what she'd done, he'd be furious with her for poking her psychic nose into his privacy—even though that hadn't been her intent when she'd started the reading. But now that she knew Annie and Dalton were together, she couldn't resist watching just a moment longer.

She narrowed her eyes, concentrating even harder on the image in the crystal ball. Fascinated, she watched her brother and Annie drinking beer and engaging in what looked to be friendly conversation. But what fascinated her even more were the expressions on their faces when they thought the other person wasn't watching. Those glances appeared downright sizzling, and most definitely promising.

Daphne sat back with a contented sigh. Running a fingertip over the smooth surface of her crystal ball, she smiled then whispered, "Perfect."

Three

Annie watched Dalton moving around the kitchen, a room where he obviously felt comfortable. Thank goodness the electricity was back on . . . at least for the moment. The power had flickered on twice before, but lasted only a few seconds each time. After it stayed on a full five minutes, Dalton turned up the thermostat, then announced he'd make them something to eat.

"This will have to be something quick," he said, opening the refrigerator door, "in case the power goes out again."

"Anything is fine. Can I help?"

"Thanks, but I can handle it." He bent over to sort through the refrigerator's contents. "Grilled ham and cheese okay?"

"Sure," she replied, admiring the great view of soft denim pulled taut over a pair of really nice male buns.

After arranging everything he needed on the counter, he washed his hands, then set a griddle on the stove and turned on a burner. As he piled layers of deli ham and cheese on thick slices of bread, Annie watched in admiration.

He seemed totally at ease with the chore, as if he'd done this a thousand times. She smiled at the thought of either of her brothers in a similar circumstance. Both men definitely were throwbacks to the old school, believing women should do the cooking. Except for the "manly" art of grilling steaks in the backyard. She loved her brothers dearly, but they were such bull-headed traditionalists. Even though all three of them had been taught the basics of cooking and keeping house—because their mother insisted all three of her children needed to be able to fend for themselves—her brothers put their lessons to use only when absolutely necessary. And that wasn't often.

Ryan and Joey were such fools. But she knew the day of reckoning for their sexist attitudes would come. Sooner or later, one or both of them would fall head-over-heels for a woman who wanted no part of an old-fashioned relationship, and that's when the shit would hit that proverbial fan. Annie chuckled at the thought.

Dalton arched a brow at her. "What's so funny?"

"Nothing really," she replied, clearing her throat. "I was just thinking about my brothers."

"What about them?"

"I was imagining them cooking. When they come in from the barn or the range, the only food they want to deal with is already cooked and sitting on the table."

"They live on a ranch?"

Annie nodded. "With our parents, on the ranch started by my great-grandfather."

"In Wyoming?"

"Mmm-hmm," she replied, surprised he remembered her telling him earlier that she was originally from Wyoming.

"Beautiful country."

"Yeah, if you like living in the middle of nowhere."

"I take it you don't."

"No way. Living on the ranch was the pits. Totally boring, and so isolated. We were miles from the closest town, and then that was just a little Podunk place. I couldn't wait to graduate from high school so I could get away."

"Is that when you came down here?"

"Yeah, but technically, Boulder first. I moved to Denver after I finished college. I love it here. Lots of things to see and do. I can't imagine living anywhere but a big city."

Dalton dropped the sandwiches onto the heated griddle, contemplating what she'd revealed. Just his luck. The only woman he'd been attracted to in months was another damn excitement junkie. One more reason to want her out of his house as soon as— Annie's voice pulled him back to the present.

He glanced up to find her staring at him, her eyebrows beetled in a frown.

She studied him in silence for a moment longer, then said, "Are you okay?"

"Yeah, I was just— Never mind, what were you saying?"

"I said, we've talked enough about me, so tell me more about you."

"Like what?" He took a large bowl from a cabinet, then began tearing lettuce for a salad.

"Well . . . you mentioned your sisters earlier. What's the deal with all the Ds?"

He glanced at her, his expression blank.

"Your names?" she said. "They all start with D."

"Blame that on our mother. She had some warped idea about wanting all her kids to have names starting with the same letter as hers." He made a face. "A confusing pain in the ass, if you ask me."

"I can imagine," she replied. "Did your mother teach you to cook?"

"Hardly," Dalton said with a laugh. "I doubt my mother has cooked a meal in years. She used to before my dad died, but since then she's been too busy with her—" He frowned.

"Too busy with her . . . what?"

"She's just too busy," he replied, reaching for a carrot. "My wife taught me the basics about cooking, the rest I learned on my own."

"Your wife?"

"Ex," he said, a note of bitterness creeping into his voice. "Maureen was a good cook, and while we were dating, we spent a lot of time fixing meals together. Then after we got married, things . . . changed."

Annie waited several seconds for him to go on, but when he didn't she said, "I'm sorry." Though she'd spoken sincerely, she wasn't sorry to learn he was divorced. Being attracted to a married man would be a complication she didn't need.

He shrugged. "Live and learn." He slipped a spatula under one sandwich and flipped it over with a deft twist of his wrist.

Not certain how to respond to his statement, she merely nodded, watching him flip the other sandwich, then finish the salad by slicing the carrot and adding broccoli florets and grape tomatoes.

His hands really did fascinate her. Agile fingers, nails cut short, a sprinkling of dark hairs, and marred by several faded scars on his knuckles. Very masculine hands. Very capable hands. Before she could stop the thought, she allowed herself to imagine what those hands would feel like running over her bare skin. A delicious shiver raced up her back.

She wanted some spice in her life, that was the reason she and her friends had concocted the crazy idea to find exciting jobs over the holidays, but this wasn't what she'd had in mind. Getting snowbound with the owner of a museum and art gallery, even one as attractive as Dalton Stoner, didn't fit into the Christmas break she'd envisioned for herself. She already led a boring life, so the last thing she needed was the addition of a boring man.

So why did her heart pound and her skin tingle whenever he got close enough for her to get a whiff of his scent, or he gave her one of his dazzling smiles? She had never reacted to a man this way, and although the experience was totally awesome, it was also just as confusing. *Jeez, you'd think I haven't been with a man in . . . Okay, so maybe it has been a really long time. Even so, why—* Realizing Dalton was talking to her, she blinked then looked up to find him giving her a quizzical stare.

"Sorry, I was—" She cleared her throat, hoping the heat in her cheeks wasn't obvious. "What did you say?"

Other than the slight narrowing of his eyes, nothing about his expression gave her reason to be concerned. "I asked if you'd mind setting the table?" He nodded to the small dining nook on the opposite side of the kitchen.

"Sure," she replied, her stomach picking that moment to make a loud rumbling noise.

He flashed another megawatt grin, a sparkle of amusement in his blue-gray eyes. "The sandwiches need a couple more minutes. You won't pass out from hunger before then, will you?"

"I think I can survive that long," she replied, striving for a teasing tone, but doubting her success. Grabbing the silverware he'd laid on the counter, she headed toward the table.

Daphne dialed her sister's cell phone number, then settled deeper into her favorite easy chair.

After three rings, she heard a click, a fumbling sound, then a slightly breathless, "Darcie Stoner."

"Hey, sis, you sound like you've been running. Are you okay?"

"Fine." Darcie drew a ragged breath. "What do you want, Daf?"

Daphne heard the rumble of a male voice in the background. "I can't believe it," she said with a laugh. "My workaholic attorney sister is actually spending a Saturday night with a man. So, who is he?"

"None of your business."

Daphne knew she'd get the information out of her younger sister eventually, so she didn't press the issue. "Sorry to call at such an inopportune moment, sis, but I had no idea I would catch you . . . well, *flagrante delicto*. I'm not very good at Latin, so I do hope I said that—"

"You know perfectly well you said it right. Now tell me why the hell you called."

Daphne smiled at the exasperation in Darcie's voice. "Don't get your panties in a twist." She chuckled. "Oh, I forgot, you're probably not wearing—"

"Daphne Marie Stoner, so help me. You'd better start talking."

"My, aren't we testy." Before Darcie could reply, Daphne said, "I called to share some good news."

"What you interrupted was pretty damn good, too, so whatever you have to say better be worth it."

"Ooh, sounds like you've found yourself a real talented lover," Daphne replied, thoroughly enjoying the banter with her sister. "Don't fret, if he's that good, he won't have any trouble getting—"

"Dammit, Daf, what do you want?"

"Okay, okay," she said, with a dramatic sigh. "I was right about Annie. She's the perfect woman for Dalton."

"And you know this . . . how?"

"They're snowed in at his house right now. And from the looks on their faces, they're really hitting it off."

"Looks on their faces—" Darcie's voice dropped to a whisper. "Don't tell me you hauled out your crystal ball?"

"I had to, all right," she replied with a huff. "Annie wasn't home and I got worried. I was only trying to find out where she was, so it isn't my fault that I found her with our brother."

Darcie groaned. "If Dalton finds out, he'll skin you alive."

"I know how he'd react. That's why I don't intend to tell him. And neither will you. Got it?"

"I won't say a word. But if he asks me point blank, I won't lie."

"Ya know, Darcie, sometimes you take this ethical lawyer crap too far. We're talking about our brother's future."

"I'm aware of that. But I still won't lie to cover up your psychic snooping."

Daphne sighed. "I know. I'll just have to hope Dalton doesn't ask you a direct question."

"Yeah, me, too."

"So how long have you known lover boy?"

"Not long."

"Really? I could always do a reading. Find out more about—"

"No!" Darcie practically shouted, then lowered her voice to add, "Daphne, so help me God, if you do, I'll—"

"Okay, I won't." Daphne grinned, pleased she could still get to her sister so easily. "Just tell me if he's someone I know."

"I doubt it." Darcie's low groan vibrated through the phone line. "I really have to"—she sucked in a sharp breath—"go. Now."

"Yeah, I can tell you've got other things on your mind. Call me when you've got more time. Oh, and tell what's-his-name I said hi." Not waiting for her sister's response, Daphne pushed the Off button on her phone.

Annie rubbed under Worf's chin, then chuckled when the dog groaned, his eyes glazing over with pleasure. "Ooh, I found a good spot, huh, boy?"

"You're spoiling him," Dalton said from the other couch, annoyed to realize he was jealous of the attention Annie gave his dogs. What a ludicrous thought!

Annie glanced over at where Data lay sprawled next to Dalton. "From what I've seen, it's obvious these two have pretty cushy lives."

Dalton frowned, knowing there was no point in trying to deny the truth. Finally, he said, "If you could've seen these guys when I first brought 'em home, you'd spoil them, too."

"What do you mean?"

"They'd been neglected, practically nothing but skin and bones, their coats matted and filthy. Data had a really nasty, infected cut on one hip." He swallowed hard, stroking a hand over the dog's head. "I wasn't sure he'd make it, but thank God, my vet pulled him through."

Annie's throat tightened. "You're right, they deserved to be pampered, and you're right about me. I'd have spoiled them too. Not just because they'd been neglected, but because I think dogs are one of the best creatures on earth."

Dalton nodded. "I agree. So if you like dogs so much, why don't you have one?

"An apartment is no place for a dog. If I ever have a house, then I'll get one"—she looked over at Dalton and smiled—"or a dozen."

"Two's enough for me," he replied. "Especially

when they were younger. What one didn't think of, the other one did. I never knew what I was going to find when I got home. One day, they managed to get into one of the kitchen cabinets and broke open a bag of flour."

Annie bit her lip to hold back a laugh. "Let me guess," she said. "White paw prints all over the house."

"Yup. Thought I never would get all the flour vacuumed up." He scowled down at Data. "I was up half the damn night."

This time Annie couldn't stop her laughter. "At least they didn't get into the garbage."

"That was another day. The same day I bought childproof latches for the base cabinet doors."

"Well, they're good boys now, I bet."

Dalton's scowl softened. "Yeah. They know if they don't behave they won't get their favorite treat."

Both Worf and Data raised their heads, all four ears perked toward their owner.

Annie grinned. "They obviously know what that means."

"They understand too damn much." He rose from the couch. "Come on, you two," he said, heading for the kitchen. "Treat time."

A moment later, he called to Annie. "Want another beer?"

She hesitated responding, knowing she probably shouldn't. She'd already had two beers before they ate. Then remembering she wouldn't be driving, she figured why not. "Yes, please."

He returned to the living room soon afterward and handed her a bottle of beer, but he didn't sit down.

As she took a sip, she looked toward the kitchen but didn't see Worf or Data. "What'd you do? Lock the dogs in a closet?"

Dalton shook his head, smiling. "I put popcorn in

the microwave. Another of their favorites. They're staring up at the microwave right now, waiting for the popping to stop. When I open the pouch and pour the popcorn into a bowl, I always drop a couple pieces on the floor. It started out as an accident, but now it's a ritual."

Annie groaned. "You're such a softy. Those dogs have you right where they want you."

"Yeah, I know. Right by the balls . . . uh . . . sorry." Dalton ran a hand through his hair, a dull flush creeping up his cheeks.

Annie waved a hand in a dismissive gesture. "Pretty accurate description, I'd say," she said, amused by his obvious discomfort. "And I wasn't suggesting you need to change. The way you love and care for your dogs is wonderful, and as long as you and your dogs are happy—which you all obviously are—that's the only thing that matters."

"Not everyone agrees with you," he said in a low voice.

Annie waited for him to continue, but when he didn't, she said, "Well in my opinion, whoever disagrees with me is a real dork."

That comment brought a deep male chuckle. "Maureen would be mortified, but yes, she definitely is a dork." Turning to look into the fire, he added a murmured, "Among other things."

Before Annie could ask what he meant, the microwave beeped, followed by two quick barks.

He smiled in Annie's direction. "I'm being paged," he said, heading back to the kitchen. "I'll be right back."

A few minutes later, he returned with two bowls of popcorn. After handing one to Annie, he took a seat at the opposite end of the same couch, making Worf and Data stay on the floor. The dogs obeyed his order to sit, their heads swivelling back and forth, watching every move their human companions made, their dark eyes silently begging for a handout.

Annie chewed some popcorn, swallowed, then took a sip of beer to wash it down. Glancing over at Dalton, she bit back a smile. This was so great. She never would have thought sitting around, eating popcorn while a blizzard raged outside could be fun. Frowning at the direction of her thoughts, she decided she must've had too much beer. Why else would she mistake something so mundane, so utterly boring as fun?

"You don't like the popcorn?"

Startled from her thoughts, she turned her head and met his gaze. "No, it's fine."

He studied her in silence for several seconds, then said, "Tell me about your brothers."

"Ryan and Joey? What do you want to know?"

"Are they older, younger?"

"Both. Ryan is the oldest. I'm a year and a half younger, and Joey is the baby of the family. Though at twenty-seven, I'm sure he wouldn't appreciate me calling him that."

"Either of them married?"

"God, no," she replied with a laugh. "At their ages they should be married and on their own, but they're both still single and living at home. Don't get me wrong, they're nice guys, even though they can be real pains in the ass sometimes."

"I know the feeling," Dalton said, thinking of his own two meddling sisters. "Your brothers must like ranch life."

"Yeah, they do. You'd think they'd want their own places by now. But I guess they figure why move out as long as Mom's willing to keep doing everything for them."

"Sounds like they're not very self-sufficient."

"They could be. They just don't want to. Growing up, we all had household chores, plus our cooking lessons. So Ryan and Joey wouldn't starve, and they could sew on a button if necessary. Maybe even use the washing machine in an emergency, though the result might be really scary."

Dalton grinned. "That bad, huh?"

"Worse," she replied, returning his smile. "But they're still my brothers, and I love them."

"You heading up to Wyoming for the holidays? Or can't you stand being isolated on the ranch that long?"

"Very funny," she said with a mock scowl. "I love seeing my family, so I can handle a couple of days. But this year I'm not sure when I'll leave. If my job keeps me too busy, I might not be able to drive up until Christmas morning."

Her job. Damn, how could he have forgotten what she did for a living? All during supper, while cleaning up the kitchen together, and since they came back into the living room, he'd never given a thought to the reason for her ending up in his house. She delivered strip-o-grams, a fact he couldn't let himself forget again. Which reminded him of something else. His sister's part in Annie's arrival at his house.

"How well do you know Daphne?"

Annie blinked at the sudden change in topics. "We're not best buds," she said. "But I consider us friends."

"So you've been in Charmed?"

"Sure. Lots of times."

"Then you've seen the kinds of things Daphne sells. The witch balls. The crystals."

"Of course," she said, smiling. "She told me hanging a witch ball in a window will ward off evil spirits, and people can actually see the future by looking into one of the crystals she sells. I didn't take her seriously. I just figured she was giving me her standard sales pitch to entice customers to open their wallets."

"It's more than a sales pitch."

She stared at him for a second, then her eyes went wide. "Wait a minute. Are you saying Daphne really believes all that mystical stuff?"

"Daf does more than believe."

Annie tipped her head to one side, mulling over his statement, trying to decipher his meaning. At last, she said, "Your sister's psychic?"

Four

For a moment Dalton considered whether he should have started this conversation. But if his sister had sent Annie to his house as part of another matchmaking scheme, Annie needed to know the truth. "Daphne may not appreciate my telling you," he said at last, "but yes, she's psychic. Though she says clairvoyant is a more accurate description."

"I'm stunned. That's . . . amazing."

"Yeah, well, she's not *your* sister."

"Ah, I see." Annie chuckled at his sour expression. "She uses you as a guinea pig for her psychic experiments."

"Not exactly. But she has poked around in my life with her crystal ball readings." His jaw hardened. "Something I've warned her about countless times."

"I can see how that would upset you, but you must know she's doing it out of love."

Dalton grunted. "Still pisses me off."

"I can tell," Annie said, grinning at him. "Maybe you're just upset because she can see into the future and you can't."

He contemplated her words for a moment. "Could be. She did tell me not to marry Maureen, that the marriage was doomed." He sighed. "Turns out she was right. Anyway, between my sisters and me, Daf's the only one who inherited our grandmother's psychic powers."

Annie finished her popcorn, then set the empty bowl on the coffee table. She stared at the twinkling lights on the Christmas tree for several seconds before returning her gaze to him. "Do you really think Daphne was trying to set us up?"

"Probably." He split the last few kernels of his popcorn between Worf and Data, then placed his bowl inside hers. "It's exactly the kind of thing Daf would do. During my first year back in Denver, my sisters constantly shoved women at me. Starting with a blind date that I reluctantly agreed to. What a fiasco! After that, I flat out told them to knock it off. Like they'd listen. That's when they started with the supposed chance meetings. You know, bumping into one of them somewhere, and she just happened to have a new female friend with her. Then there were dinner invitations where I was seated beside another candidate." He made a rude noise. "It's like they're obsessed."

"Why are they so interested in your love life?"

"My guess is they think the only way for me to wash away the taint of Maureen is with a new woman. And since I haven't made the effort, they took over the job."

"Maureen did a real number on you, huh?"

He stared across the room, his mouth pulled into a scowl. "Yeah, big time."

Though Annie wanted to ask what happened, the details of his marriage and divorce were none of her business. Instead, she said, "So you think your sister's hiring me is another of her schemes."

His lips twitched. "I admit a strip-o-gram messenger is an unconventional approach. But I wouldn't put anything past my sisters. Especially Daf."

"Well, you obviously know Daphne better than I do.

But in the time I've known her, she rarely talked about herself or her family. I only knew about you because I said something about Ryan and Joey, and she mentioned having a brother. Anyway, we always talked about other things. The merchandise in her store, mostly. Or what I like to do when I'm not teaching."

"Teaching?"

"Uh, yeah. I'm a teacher. High school math."

"Really?" Dalton's eyebrows lifted. "So what's with the messenger job?"

Annie shifted on the couch, uneasy with the direction their conversation had taken. Not seeing the need to admit her social life sucked, she settled on a true, although in this case not accurate, statement. "Teachers' salaries aren't great, so lots of us find temporary work over Christmas break and during the summer."

"And you took a job with the Naughty or Nice Messenger Service."

She nodded.

Dalton stared at her in silence for a moment, then said, "I sympathize with what teachers get paid, but delivering strip-o-grams doesn't seem like—" He rubbed a hand over his jaw. "Look, this really isn't any of my business, but why that job?"

"The owners live in my building. They needed help, and the pay is good. Besides, it's the perfect job to—" Annie swallowed, uncertain if she should say any more.

"Perfect to . . . what?"

She cleared her throat. "Um, it's perfect to add some excitement to my holidays."

Excitement. The word caused a buzzing in Dalton's head and transported him back in time. Back to New York and Maureen, and hearing again why she'd gotten high for the first time. They'd only been married six months, and already she was bored with being his wife and needed some excitement.

Damn, was it possible Annie was another Maureen? Stripping for strangers sure as hell fit the profile of the always-looking-for-a-thrill personality. Whoa, hold it right there. He shouldn't be drawing conclusions about a woman he barely knew. The disaster of his marriage had naturally left him overly cynical where the opposite sex was concerned, but there were times—like now—when he had to force himself to remember that not all women were ball-busters like his ex-wife. Some would be content with the quiet, calm life he preferred, though finding the right woman—the one he could trust enough to risk laying his heart on the line again—would take some time. But as he'd repeatedly told his sisters, he was in no hurry.

The creak of the leather sofa pulled Dalton from his disturbing thoughts. He blinked, then focused on Annie's face. A slight furrow appeared above those gorgeous green eyes, and a curl of golden-brown hair had fallen forward to tease one high cheekbone.

His fingers itched to test the softness of that curl, to smooth the wrinkle from her forehead, but he fisted his hand on his thigh instead. "Is something wrong?"

"Uh, no, I was just—" She released a deep breath. "Listen, don't feel like you have to entertain me. If there's something you need to do, go ahead."

He stared at her for a moment, then rose from the sofa. "Actually, I do have a couple of things I need to take care of. Make yourself at home." He waved a hand toward the entertainment center. "Listen to music. Watch TV."

She nodded. "Thanks, I think I'll do that. Maybe I can find out the latest on this storm."

"Good idea," he replied, then turned toward the hall. "I shouldn't be long."

* * *

An hour later, Dalton clicked Send, closed the e-mail program, then turned off his computer and sat back in his chair. Time to get back to his guest. Just the thought of her sent anticipation humming through his veins. For reasons he didn't understand, he felt drawn to the woman in a way he couldn't remember experiencing.

Dammit. He didn't want to be attracted to Annie, a woman who wouldn't be happy with a man like him. A man who didn't want to spend every weekend getting drunk or high, and doing God-only-knew what. According to Maureen, that made him the worst thing a man could be. Boring. A word she never tired of throwing in his face. But he'd refused to be lured into his wife's network of jet-setting friends, into the world of booze, drugs and probably every type of depraved behavior imaginable. And Maureen ignored his efforts to convince her she should give up the lifestyle she'd come to crave. Finally, he'd had no choice except ending their sham of a marriage.

Not even his family knew all the details. He'd never been able to tell his mother and sisters the entire story about what his wife had done to him. Saying the words aloud and seeing the pity in their eyes would've been too painful.

A wave of bitterness washed over him at the hurt and humiliation he'd suffered because of Maureen. Clenching his teeth, he silently renewed the vow he'd made after divorcing her. No one would use him like that again. If a woman didn't want him for who and what he was, then to hell with her. He flat out refused to be something he wasn't.

Dalton heaved a sigh, trying to push aside the painful memories of his disastrous marriage. Until the snowstorm ended and the roads reopened, he had enough to contend with: Annie Peterson.

As he entered the living room and spotted Annie watching TV from where she sat tucked in the corner of one of the leather couches, an odd sensation fluttered in his chest. The wild tangle of her golden-brown curls once again made his fingers itch to test their softness, and her lush mouth caused a shockingly intense stirring of male interest beneath the fly of his jeans. Jesus, he was losing it!

Determined to ignore his body's reaction, he walked into the room. "What's on?"

She glanced up at him and smiled. *"Next Generation.* You only missed the first few minutes." She patted the cushion next to her. "Come on. Sit."

Though he had no intention of following her instructions, he took a seat beside her before he realized what he'd done. Keeping his gaze on the television screen, he said, "Which episode is this?"

"Captain Picard needed a break from the pressure of getting ready for a big meeting with the Jarada, so he went to the holodeck. Now he's in San Francisco, dressed like some gangster."

Dalton chuckled. "Actually he's Dixon Hill, a private investigator from the '40s."

"You remember this one, I suppose."

"Yup."

"Figured you would," Annie replied, flashing him another smile.

They watched the show in silence for a few minutes, with Annie interrupting only long enough to ask him about characters she wasn't familiar with. During a commercial, she dropped her head onto the back of the couch and sighed. "Do you think there'll ever be a real holodeck?"

"Computers are continually doing more and more, but to totally recreate a fully interactive specific time and place . . ." He shook his head. "Doesn't sound possible now, but who knows how far technology will advance."

"I think it would be great. Having a computer create all kinds of wonderful places to visit." She rolled her head to the side, meeting his gaze with sparkling eyes. "Just think about all the exciting things it would allow you to do."

Dalton turned his attention back to the television, away from Annie's glowing face. She'd used that damn word again. He drew a calming breath, then said, "I take it you like excitement."

"Well, sure. Who doesn't? That's one of the reasons I took the strip-o-gram job. And it's always fun to visit new places. Meet new people. Especially when—"

"Commercial's over." He knew cutting her off that way was rude, but he didn't care. He'd heard enough.

Annie blinked at his harsh tone but didn't respond. Instead, she shifted her gaze back to the television screen. Though she pretended to be engrossed in Picard's efforts to get away from the gangsters, her mind was elsewhere. Filled with thoughts of the man beside her, sitting as still as stone.

When the show ended and he started to get up, she grabbed his arm.

"Dalton?"

He turned to look at her through eyes that had again turned stormy gray, but he didn't speak.

"Did I say something wrong?"

"No."

"Then why the sudden cold shoulder?"

"I don't know what you're talking about."

She studied him in silence for a moment, then removed her hand from his arm. "Fine by me."

"What's that supposed to mean?"

"That means," she replied, giving him her best

teacher's glare, "you don't want to talk about whatever I did or said that turned you into an iceman."

His eyebrows lifted, his eyes turning an even chiller shade of gray. "You think I'm an iceman?"

She shrugged. "Whatever."

Before Annie could anticipate his next move, she found her upper body pressed against the back of the couch with an irritated Dalton leaning over her, his hands gripping her upper arms, and his face just inches above hers.

"I'm not a damn iceman."

She licked her lips, strangely not frightened by his abrupt show of masculine strength. Lifting her chin, she said, "Oh, yeah?" Mentally wincing at her childish response, she continued glaring at him.

"Don't push me, Annie. I'm warning you."

"Or what? You'll turn me into an icicle?" she whispered, startled by her own bravado.

He stared at her for several seconds, then a half-groan, half-growl rumbled in his chest before he swooped down to claim her mouth with his.

Though surprised he'd actually given in to the desire she'd glimpsed in his eyes, she was also secretly delighted. But her initial reaction quickly changed to shock. She felt as if the heat of his kiss had burrowed deep beneath her skin, scorching her from the inside out. Breathless, pulse spiking, body afire with need, she wrapped her arms around his neck and pulled him closer, wanting, needing the fire to burn even hotter. When he drew her bottom lip into his mouth, suckling gently, the sensation streaked through her body to a place much lower. Pressing her knees together to ease the ache between her thighs, a moan vibrated in her throat.

He pulled back enough to whisper, "Yes," then started another foray of her mouth. This time he applied a series of gentle nibbles across her upper lip. When she gasped, he slid his tongue past her lips, sending another flicker of flame over her already overheated skin.

Wow! The man sure knew how to kiss.

Annie certainly had been kissed before. In fact, she was far from innocent. A two year affair during college then a couple of long-terms relationships—one had come close to marriage—plus a one night stand she wasn't particularly proud of. She'd had too much to drink that night and the guy hitting on her had been so damn hot. Too bad his good looks hadn't carried over to his skill in the sack. Since then, she'd dated a few men—some she slept with, others she couldn't imagine getting naked with—though none of the relationships had survived long enough to progress to anything remotely serious. But not one of her previous experiences had ever affected her the way Dalton did with a single kiss.

Dalton lifted his mouth from Annie's long enough to say, "Still think I'm an iceman?"

She managed a brief shake of her head before he claimed her mouth again and sent his senses spinning even more.

Never had he tasted anything as good as the sweetness of Annie's lips, or experienced anything more arousing than the kick of her kiss. And based on the way she clutched his neck, pressed herself against him, and the little noises she made in her throat, he wasn't the only one experiencing such a strong reaction.

The whimper of one of his dogs, ensnared in a canine dream, startled him back to the present. Easing away from Annie until he sat beside her again, he struggled to catch his breath. His pulse pounding in his ears, he stared into her flushed face and started to sink into her mesmerizing eyes. Fearful he was about to drown in those glorious pools of green, he jerked his gaze away before he did something really stupid—like toss her over his shoulder and head for his bedroom—then rose from the couch.

He ran his fingers through his hair, wincing at the shaking in his hand. Exhaling a deep breath, he knew he had to say something.

"Listen, I'm sorry. I shouldn't have done that."

He heard her draw a shaky breath. "It was my fault," she said, her voice low, slightly raspy and sexy as hell. "I shouldn't have goaded you the way I did. Calling you an iceman was childish, and I'm—"

"We both made mistakes," he said, turning to face her, "so let's just forget the whole thing." Her swollen lips snagged his attention, beckoning him for another taste. Forcing himself to ignore the quick jab of desire surging to his groin, he summoned a smile. "You'd think we were a couple of horny teenagers."

She chuckled, defusing the last of the sexually-charged air still humming between them. "Maybe, but I've seen high school kids making out in the hall, and I have to tell you, I never saw any of them kissing like we just did."

"Yeah? Well, thanks, I think. But what about when teachers can't see them? I bet when they're off somewhere private, their kisses are a whole lot different."

"No doubt," she said, her expression sobering. "I'd rather not know what goes on when they leave school."

Dalton nodded, grateful the uncomfortable moment had passed. He took a seat on the opposite couch, away from the temptation of Annie, then after a moment said, "Do you enjoy teaching?"

"Yeah, I do." She flashed a quick smile. "Today's kids are a definite challenge, and some days I'd like nothing better than to knock their heads together.

But when I see the ah-ha moment on my students' faces and know they finally get something I've been trying to teach them, well . . . that's still a major thrill for me. Knowing my efforts paid off makes all the other crap I put up with worthwhile."

"I imagine making teens toe the line is a definite challenge."

"That's an understatement."

"If it's that bad, maybe you'll keep the messenger job after your Christmas break."

Annie shook her head. "Nope, I agreed to work two weeks. That's it." The doubt she saw in his face made her add, "Obviously you disagree. Why would I work longer?"

"The excitement," he replied. "You said that's why you took the job. So I figured once you got a taste, the temptation would be too much to resist."

"Look, teaching may not be a thrill-a-minute type job, but I still love it. And even if delivering strip-o-grams is exciting, that doesn't mean I'll continue doing it."

Dalton didn't reply, but simply stared at her, something in his expression catching Annie's attention. The tightening of his mouth, the furrowing of his forehead, the slight narrowing of his eyes told her just as plainly as if he'd spoken the words aloud. He didn't believe her.

She lifted her chin. Though she nearly told him she didn't give a damn what he believed, she held her tongue.

After a few tense moments, Dalton shrugged, then looked away. Though he kept his eyes focused on the television news broadcast, his mind was not on whatever the reporter was saying. Annie's last statement kept running through his head. Yeah, sure, he thought with a mental sneer, that's what Maureen said about needing something to break up the boredom of her life. Didn't take her long to decide her new circle of thrill-seeking friends was more important than anything else. First her career as a research assistant became secondary to the booze, drugs and weekend parties, then her marriage followed suit.

He squeezed his eyes closed, trying to banish the painful memories. Reliving the past served no purpose. He knew that, and had made progress in keeping what Maureen did to him out of his mind. In fact, he hadn't given her or their marriage more than a fleeting thought in a long time. But then he'd opened his front door to find Annie Peterson standing on his porch, and all the memories of his ex-wife came bobbing to the surface.

Needing to clear his head, he rose and glanced over at Annie. She looked as tired as he felt.

"I'm going to take the dogs out for a run, then I'm gonna turn in. Whenever you're ready for bed, the guestrooms are down the hall. Take whichever one you want. And if you'd like to take a shower, you should find everything you need in the bathrooms. My sisters use those rooms when they stay the night, and they keep the bathrooms stocked with shampoo and other toiletries so they don't have to pack all that stuff each time they visit."

Annie nodded. Stifling a yawn, she pushed the Power button on the remote, then got to her feet.

He looked over at his dogs. "Come on, guys, time to go outside."

As the terriers jumped off the couch and headed for the kitchen, Dalton started to follow them then stopped. "Oh, when I come back in," he said, turning to face Annie, "I'll see if I can find you a new toothbrush."

She gave him a weary smile. "Thanks, but you don't have to go to any bother. You've already—"

"No bother." He moved across the room. "I'll be back in a few minutes."

When Dalton reentered the house twenty minutes later, he was half frozen and more than ready for a hot shower. But that would have to wait a little longer. After rifling through the drawers in his bathroom, he headed for the guestrooms with an unopened tooth-brush.

When Annie didn't answer his knock, he eased the door open and called her name. He knew he had the right room because the shower was running, which also explained why she hadn't heard him.

He crossed the room toward the partially open bathroom door, intending to leave the toothbrush on the counter then get the hell out of there.

Just as he stepped inside the bathroom, the water stopped. He froze. Dammit, now what should he do? Before he could decide, the shower door slid open. He slowly turned and met Annie's shocked expression.

"This isn't what it looks like." He stumbled back-ward, cracking his heel against the doorjamb. Biting back a curse, he said, "I wasn't trying to spy on you. I swear."

"Really?" she said, reaching for a bath towel. Water dripped off her chin and ran in rivulets over the creamy flesh of her full breasts. A drop of water clung to one rosy nipple. "So what are you doing in here?"

He swallowed hard, watching her wrap the towel around herself then tuck one end between those gor-geous breasts. Christ, he'd never been so embarrassed in his life. His neck and cheeks burning, he dragged his gaze to her face while desperately trying to push the enticing picture of that wet, peaked nipple from his mind.

Several uncomfortable seconds passed before he could pull himself together enough to speak. Finally, he said, "I . . . uh . . . thought I had plenty of time to slip in and out. I mean, my sisters are in the shower forever. When they're both here, they always use all the hot water. So I figured you'd probably be the same way. I planned to just sneak in, and—" He drew a deep breath, unable to stop himself from sneaking a quick peek at her chest. The crested tips of her breasts clearly visible where they pressed against the towel, his pulse jumped and a new round of throbbing started in his groin. "And you'd . . . uh . . . never know I was . . . here." Great! Now she probably thought he was a raving lunatic *and* a pervert.

He tried for a reassuring smile though he couldn't be certain his lips had cooperated. "Anyway"—he lifted his right arm to show her the plastic package still clutched in his hand—"I brought you a nipple."

Five

"Really?" Annie replied, regarding him with eyes sparkling with humor.

Dalton saw the slight twitch of her lips and knew she was trying hard not to laugh at his gaffe. For the first time in his life, he wished he had extrasensory abilities. If he did, maybe he could conjure a spell to wipe the memory from Annie's brain, or go back in time and re-live the moment when he'd made his embarrassing blunder. But he wasn't psychic, or a magician. He was a red-blooded man whose houseguest had turned his brain to mush because he found her too damn desirable.

"You know what I meant," he said, pivoting to leave. "I'll just leave the *toothbrush* on the night stand."

"Wait."

He stopped but didn't turn around.

"I don't have anything to sleep in. Could I borrow a tee shirt or something?"

"Yeah"— he cleared his throat—"sure."

When he returned to the guestroom a few minutes later, he'd managed to recover his composure—or most of it anyway—though he still had trouble looking Annie in the face.

After handing her a tee shirt, he said, "You

probably think I'm some kind of weirdo, trying to sneak a peek of you in the shower." He rubbed the back of his neck. "I swear that wasn't my intent."

Annie once again fought the urge to laugh. True, she'd been shocked when she opened the shower door and found him in the bathroom. But she didn't know which of them had been more stunned. And the look on his face was priceless, quickly changing her surprise to amusement. "Hey, like my brothers say, that shit happens. Besides"—she shrugged—"we're both adults, so don't worry about it."

Dalton closed his gaping mouth, then chuckled. "Thanks for being so understanding. Most women would've reamed me out for what I said and did."

"I'm not like most women."

Dalton wanted to disagree. In his experience, he'd found all women to be pretty much alike. But he didn't see the need to antagonize Annie by voicing his opinion. Instead he said, "Is there anything else I can get you?"

She shook her head. "All set, thanks."

He nodded. "Good night then."

A short time later, he turned on the shower in the master bath, then stripped off his clothes and stepped beneath the spray. As the hot water pelted his skin, he groaned with pleasure. Rolling his shoulders to ease his tight muscles, he closed his eyes, then immediately opened them again to banish the image appearing in his mind's eye. Annie wrapped in a towel, hair secured haphazardly atop her head by one of the big hair clips his sisters used, a few loose curls brushing her temples and neck. Even with her face scrubbed free of makeup she was much too appealing. His dick seconded the thought by going from limp to half a boner in record time.

Jesus Christ, Stoner! You're not fifteen, getting a hard-on every time a good-looking girl gets within ten feet of you.

He blew out a deep breath, then grabbed the shampoo bottle, determined to push both Annie and his body's reaction from his mind. If he didn't get his libido under control, it was gonna be one hell of a long night.

The barking of his dogs pulled Dalton from a restless sleep. Rolling over, he glanced at the clock on his night stand and groaned. 5:30. *Damn. What had those two so wound up this early?*

Before he could decide whether to get up and investigate or roll over and try to go back to sleep, he heard Annie's soft voice ordering Worf and Data to be quiet. What the hell?

Though he hadn't slept well—thanks to continual visions of Annie popping into his head—his curiosity propelled him out of bed to find out what she was up to. Not bothering with a shirt, he pulled on a pair of jeans then headed down the hall.

As he got closer to the living room, he heard the low beat of music. He slowly moved toward the room's arched doorway and peered inside.

Annie, clad in the tee shirt he'd loaned her, stood in front of the entertainment center. She pushed a button and the music instantly changed to a country song he recognized as a huge hit from a year or two earlier.

Fascinated, he stayed hidden in the shadows, waiting to see what she did next. When she backed away from the entertainment center and started dancing, his eyes widened.

She moved with incredible grace and ease, her bare feet moving through a complicated pattern of steps.

Her sleek legs and the provocative wiggling of her

hips kicked his pulse up a notch and sent a rush of blood to his groin. The house was still cool; the automatic thermostat wasn't programmed to turn up the heat for another hour. Yet he could've sworn the air around him just shot up fifty degrees.

He contemplated whether Annie might be playing some sort of game, another attempt to put some excitement in her life by teasing him with her dancing, trying to entice him for a repeat of the kiss they'd shared the night before. There was no denying desire had definitely sparked between them. So maybe this was her way of seeing if she could tempt him to rekindle that desire, or maybe even take it to another level.

He frowned at the direction of his thinking. If she had seduction on her mind, would she pick five-thirty in the morning to set her plan into motion? Not likely. But then maybe that was part of the plan, keeping him off guard by doing the unexpected. Well, regardless of whether her little performance was a game or not, he knew one thing with complete certainty. Watching her dance was driving him wild.

Determined to put an end to this, he stalked into the room.

"What the hell are you doing?"

Annie gasped, stumbled to a halt, then swung around to face him. A hand pressed to her chest, she said, "Jeez, do you always sneak up on people like that?"

"I do when I'm awakened before the crack of dawn and find a half-naked woman dancing in my living room."

Annie looked down at the oversize tee shirt she wore. The neck hung partially off one shoulder, and the hem barely reached her knees, but the heavy cotton covered everything in between. "I'd hardly call this half-naked."

When his only response was a grunt, she pinned him with a glare. "Are you always such a bear first thing in the morning?"

As he squeezed his eyes closed and lifted his arms to run his hands through his hair, her breath caught in her throat. Though she'd suspected he was in good physical shape, the reality momentarily stunned her. Bulging biceps, impressive pecs and the *pièce de résistance*, her personal weakness in male attributes, a patch of dark hair covering the center of his chest.

Though she knew she was being rude, she couldn't stop her perusal. Her gaze dropped lower, skimming his equally impressive abs and snug jeans slung low on his hips. He'd left the snap undone, giving her a glimpse of his navel and the narrow line of darker hair that disappeared beneath his zippered fly. She had the sudden urge to slowly lower the tab and see if he wore anything beneath the snug denim. Realizing he'd said something, she gulped in a deep shuddering breath, then looked up to find him staring at her.

"Beg pardon?" she said, hoping the sexual awareness turning her insides to liquid heat didn't show.

He huffed out a breath, crossing his arms over the chest she'd been ogling. "I said," he began in a tight voice, "I don't usually get up this early, so I have a right to be grouchy."

Annie held his stare for a moment, debating how to respond. Finally she sighed. She'd gain nothing by antagonizing the man further. After all, she was a guest—an unexpected one at that—in his house. "You're right," she said at last. "But for the record, I did try to be quiet. Unfortunately, Worf and Data thought I wanted to play when I started dancing and . . . Anyway, I'm sorry I woke you."

"Is that the reason you got up at such a god-awful hour? To dance?"

"Sure. It's great exercise. I hate fitness clubs, and spinning class"—she made a rude noise—"was a total bore. But I've always enjoyed dancing. So this way I get a good workout and do something I like."

"Okay, I get that part," he replied, his forehead furrowing. "But why at this hour? You should be in bed."

"No reason to lie around when I can make better use of the time."

He could think of a few ways to make great use of her time in bed *and* get a good workout, but he kept the thought to himself.

Instead, he said, "So, do you do this dancing exercise thing every morning?"

"Most days during the week. I have to get up early for school anyway, so another half hour isn't a big deal. Gets me charged up for a day of tackling hormone overloaded teenagers who would rather be anywhere except my classroom."

"I imagine you can use every advantage," he replied, fighting a yawn.

She nodded. "Why don't you go back to bed. I promise I'll keep the volume down."

"I probably should. I didn't sleep very well."

"Neither did I."

Dalton held her gaze for a few seconds, wondering if the reason for her restless sleep was the same as his. That kiss.

Don't go there, he warned himself. He had to forget about kissing Annie, and all the other things his imagination had tortured him with during the long hours he'd tossed and turned.

He cleared his throat, then said, "Well, staying in a strange place can do that." Before she could reply, he turned to leave. "Go ahead with your dancing. I'll make coffee."

* * *

After breakfast, Dalton took the dogs out for a run, leaving Annie to her own devices. Before he slipped out into the cold, he'd once again told her to make herself at home.

Cup of coffee in hand, she decided to explore. In case he wasn't gone long, she headed for Dalton's bedroom first, which was at the opposite end of the house. Even with his permission, looking into the master bedroom made her feel like a snoop.

As she stepped into the room, her breath caught. The walls were painted the color of cream, the bed-spread and simple window treatment made from a bold yet tasteful patterned fabric of hunter green, burgundy and cream; the light oak pieces of furniture were massive but not over-powering in the large space. Though definitely decorated for a man, the room's simple decor and color choice appealed to her. A lot. She could easily picture herself spending time here.

Startled by the thought, she made a hasty retreat. In the main hallway at the other end of the house, she found another bedroom, similar to the one where she'd slept, and then she entered the final room. The furnishings, a computer sitting atop a large desk and several filing cabinets, told her this was Dalton's home office. The thick carpet was a pale terra cotta, the color repeated in the vertical blind on the window and used again with a darker shade plus a soft turquoise in the flame stitch pattern of a pair of upholstered arm chairs.

Annie moved farther into the room, drawn to the floor-to-ceiling bookcases. Scanning the titles crammed onto one shelf, she noted a large collection of books on art history. Another shelf held a variety of books on sculpture and paintings. One title jumped out at her: *The Illustrated Kama Sutra.*

She pulled the book from the shelf and carefully flipped through the pages.

"Ohmygod," she whispered. Although familiar with the *Kama Sutra*, she'd never seen paintings depicting its teachings. Each page held a painting of a naked couple in every imaginable sexual position. She turned another page, then frowned, certain what the artist had painted would be physically impossible to duplicate. Yet strangely, even if a man and woman couldn't twist themselves into pretzels to copy the pose, she found looking at the painting . . . well, arousing.

Her curiosity piqued, she did a quick check of other books on the shelf and discovered at least another dozen titles dealing with the *Kama Sutra*. Hmm, interesting. The man obviously had a thing for the ancient love manual. A fascinating discovery. One that had her wondering if she'd been wrong in her initial assessment of the man.

The notion that Dalton Stoner, the boring, stuffy museum and gallery owner, might actually have a bad-boy side sent a spark of heat surging through her body. Definitely an intriguing idea, even if it was only her overactive imagination.

Taking a seat in one of the chairs, she rested the book on her lap then turned the page. As she stared at another equally erotic painting, her mind replaced the couple with Dalton and herself. Her nipples tightened at the mental image, the heat in her veins intensifying and pooling between her thighs.

Dalton slipped off his boots, shrugged out of his down-filled parka, then grabbed one of the old towels he kept in the mud room.

"Okay, who's first?" he said to Worf and Data. When neither dog seemed inclined to volunteer, he chuckled at the pair of woeful expressions, then pulled Data closer. "Yeah, I know, you guys hate this. But it's the price you pay for wallowing through snowbanks that are over your head."

As he rubbed the towel over Data's wiry coat, sending frozen chunks of snow bouncing across the floor, his thoughts turned to Annie, and how long before he'd be able to send her on her way. At the moment, the storm had eased up, but from the looks of the heavy clouds coming over the mountain peaks, the reprieve would be short-lived.

He loved the peaceful solitude, the quiet beauty of the mountains. And any other time, he wouldn't have minded being snowbound for a few days. In fact, he would have welcomed the time alone. But his forced confinement with Annie left him torn. One minute he wanted her gone, and the next he wanted her in his bed, warm and willing. Damn, what a hell of a mess.

Once he finished drying both dogs, he poured himself another cup of coffee then walked into the living room. Finding the room empty, he went in search of Annie. He found her sitting in a chair in his office, concentrating on a book lying open across her lap.

He watched her from the doorway for a moment, then moved into the room. Another several seconds passed before he said, "Must be a really good book."

Annie's head snapped up. "What?"

"I said, that must be a really good book. You didn't hear me come in."

"No, I didn't. I guess I was—" She cleared her throat, closing the book with a thud. "Can I ask you something?"

"Sure."

"What's with all the books on the *Kama Sutra*?"

"It's something I've been interested in for a while." He tipped his head to get a better look at the book she held. When he saw the title, he smiled. "Good choice. That's one of my favorites."

She stared up at him through widened eyes, the pupils dilated. "Why?"

"It's a spectacular book, don't you think? The paintings are—"

"That's not what I meant. Why the interest in the *Kama Sutra?*"

Dalton took a sip of coffee before replying. "Have you ever been to my museum?"

A blush crept up her neck. "No . . . um . . . I'm sorry to say, I haven't."

He waved away her obvious embarrassment. "Don't worry about it. The High Country Museum and Gallery has been open only a couple of years. Lots of folks in Denver haven't been there. But now that you've met me, maybe you'll stop in sometime."

Not giving her a chance to respond, he indicated the book lying on her thighs. "If you enjoyed looking through that, then you'll like the exhibits at my museum. We have one of the largest collections of erotic paintings and sculptures in North America."

"Are you serious?"

"Very."

"You really have paintings like"—she opened the book to the page she'd been studying before he'd come in—"this one?"

"Some," he replied. "Several are from my personal collection, but most are on loan from private collectors or other museums. And there are other paintings similar to those displayed in the gallery. They were done by talented young artists, so the style is much different."

Annie gave her head a shake, obviously trying to absorb what he'd just told her. "When Daphne said you owned a museum and an art gallery, I had no idea the exhibits were . . . well, of such an adult nature."

He stared at her for several seconds, watching her blush spread to her cheeks, and the wild throbbing of her pulse at the base of her neck. His gaze meeting hers, he said, "Would it have mattered if you had?"

"What do you mean?"

"Would you have changed your mind about coming here if you'd known about my museum's speciality?"

"Why," she said with a smile, "because I might think you're some kind of sexual deviant?"

He chuckled. "Yeah, something like that."

Her smile fading, she stared into his eyes, their color darkening to a deep, rich blue. At last, she said, "You're not, are you?"

He sobered as well, then moved closer. After holding her gaze for a tense moment, he lowered his head and brushed a light kiss on her mouth. As he straightened, he whispered, "What do you think?"

When Annie couldn't get a word through the tightness in her throat, she managed a quick, negative shake of her head. She drew a steadying breath to calm her racing heart, but instead filled her head with his scent—a blend of his shampoo, fresh air mixed with pine, and the subtlest hint of male sweat. A lethal combination, she realized, stunned at how easily she reacted to this man. With no effort at all, he had rekindled the desire smoldering inside her. She needed all her powers of concentration not to squirm in her chair in an effort to ease the ache between her tightly clenched thighs.

Hoping she appeared more composed than she felt, she said, "Have you always been interested in erotic art?"

"No. My parents were always dragging my sisters and me to museums when we were kids. At first I hated the hours wandering through long halls, from room to room, to look at boring old paintings. But eventually I developed an appreciation for the arts."

"Surely your parents didn't take you to see exhibits like the ones you have on display."

He grinned. "Well, not until I was sixteen or seventeen. Even then, they were still selective about what I was allowed to see. They didn't want to corrupt my mind, I suppose. Anyway, my parents were very open when Daf, Darcie and I were growing up. No topic was off limits, and books about sex were always in our house." He laughed. "When I got together with my friends, they always wanted to come over to my house."

Annie smiled. "So they could sneak a peek at what was probably forbidden in their homes, I'll bet."

"That's one bet you'd win," he replied, then downed the last of his coffee. "To answer your original question. My interest in art started back when I was in college, working part time in a gallery. The owner scheduled a show with several new artists. Jackson Kidd, a sculptor who did spectacular nudes, and Marisa St. Clair, a painter who was doing her own collection of paintings based on the *Kama Sutra*." He flashed another quick smile. "That show blew me away."

"And you were hooked."

He nodded. "Yeah, big time. Even after I graduated and got a job on Wall Street, I knew someday I wanted to own an art gallery. When I had the extra cash, I started buying a few pieces. And I continued to add to my collection whenever I ran across something I really liked." He stared into his empty cup. "That was something else Maureen and I argued about."

"She didn't share your love of art?"

"I thought so at first. We actually met in an art

gallery." He made a snorting sound. "Turns out everything I believed about her was a lie."

Annie wasn't sure how to respond to this last statement, so she let it pass for the moment. "So what made you decide to move back here and open a gallery?"

He moved around the room, appearing to be lost in thought. Finally, he heaved a deep sigh, then said, "My divorce. That changed everything. What I wanted to do with my life. Where I wanted to live. I realized the end of my marriage could be a chance to make my dream come true. Maybe my only chance, and if I didn't go through with it, I'd live to regret it."

She waited for him to continue. When he didn't, she said, "Tell me about Maureen." Annie wasn't sure of her reason for asking, but something inside made her want to know about the woman who had caused Dalton so much pain.

He turned, leveling his narrowed gaze on her. "What?"

"I asked you to tell me about Maureen."

"Why the hell would you want to know about her?"

Six

Annie started at Dalton's sharp tone, then shrugged. "Curiosity, I guess."

Several tense moments passed while she watched a variety of emotions play across his face as he worked through how he planned to answer her.

Finally, his shoulders lifted with a deep breath. Exhaling heavily, he turned to her. "I'd rather not talk about Maureen. She's part of my past, an unpleasant part I've put behind me."

Annie stared at him for a moment. From what she'd learned about him, she wasn't sure she agreed with his statement about having put Maureen behind him, but she didn't voice her doubts. Instead, she said, "Do you ever see her?"

"Nope. I haven't been back to New York since my divorce, and she'll never come here."

"Because of you?"

"More like she couldn't stand being in such an unrefined place. She had a hard time dealing with the fact that she'd married a man from the wilds of Colorado instead of one of the ritzy sections of New York or Connecticut like the old-money snobs filling her family tree. Hell, I couldn't even get her out here to visit my sisters."

"She still lives in New York?"

"Last I heard she was dividing her time between

London and the Hamptons, supposedly living with some washed-up British rocker." Before Annie could comment, he added, "I only know that because I have a friend on the East Coast who gets his jollies by keeping me informed about Maureen's life. I couldn't care less what she's doing or who she's doing it with, but I can't get that through my friend's thick head."

"Do you think he's trying to get you two back together?"

"God, I hope not. He knows about the months of hell she put me through. So go back for a second dose?" He gave his head a fierce shake. "I'd have to be more of a dumb ass than I already am for marrying her in the first place."

"Hey, don't be so hard on yourself. If we all knew what the future held, then nobody would marry the wrong person and allow themselves to be put through an emotional wringer." She offered him a quick smile. "Well, maybe the weirdos who get off by being miserable would do that, but not the rest of us."

The corners of his mouth lifted in a reluctant smile. "Remember, I have a sister who can see into the future." His smile faded. "If only I'd listened to her."

Annie rose, dropped the book on his desk, then approached him. "Don't," she whispered, laying a hand on his arm.

He glanced down at her hand, then lifted his head and met her gaze. The pain she saw in his eyes made her heart cramp in sympathy. When he started to speak, she pressed her fingers against his lips.

"Don't start with the what ifs," she said. "We all make mistakes. Some big. Some small. Sometimes we don't suffer at all, and other times the pain is beyond horrible. The best we can hope for is to learn something each time we mess up, and become a better person because of it." She removed her hand from his mouth, then couldn't resist running a fingertip over the small cleft in his chin. "You're not the first man who married the wrong woman. So please don't let a single mistake ruin the rest of your life."

A muscle twitching in his jaw, Dalton lowered one hip onto the edge of his desk. "You don't have to lecture me like you would one of your students."

She studied him for a moment, trying to gauge if anger had prompted his reply. Hoping she wasn't reading him wrong, she crossed her arms, lifted her chin and glared down her nose at him. "Well somebody needed to."

For several seconds he didn't react. Then he shook his head, a chuckle rumbling in his chest. "Miss Peterson, I bet you're hell on wheels in the classroom."

She blinked several times, then grinned. "You'd better believe it," she replied. "After almost eight years of teaching, I've developed a pretty impressive lecture arsenal, so watch yourself or you may be on the receiving end of another classic Peterson ass-chewing."

"Ass-chewing. Is that what your students call 'em?"

"No, actually, that's what my brothers called the talks our dad gave them when they messed up. Daddy never raised his voice, but man was he effective."

"So it wasn't just your brothers on the receiving end, huh?"

She flashed another smile. "'Fraid not. I got my share of those softly spoken lectures, too."

Dalton stared at her for several seconds, then chuckled. "I'll just bet you did."

Annie wondered what he meant by his comment, but decided she'd rather not know. Glancing around his office, she said, "If you've got work to do, I'll just make myself scarce." When he didn't respond, she started to turn away.

"Ever shoot any pool?"

"Computer game, or the real thing?"

"The *only* way to play pool is on a billiard table, with balls and cues."

"Ooo . . . kay," she replied, fighting a smile. "Gotcha."

"Does that mean you know how to play?"

"In theory. I played a little in college, but I was never very good."

"I've got a table downstairs. Maybe I can give you some tips."

"You want me to play a game of pool? With you?"

He made a big production of looking around the room. When his gaze, now filled with amusement, once again landed on hers, he said, "Must be. We're the only two in here."

Annie stood motionless, imagining Dalton helping her with a pool shot, his body brushing against hers in an almost intimate caress. She needed all her willpower not to shiver in reaction to the sensual encounter her mind had conjured.

Before she could pull herself together enough to respond, he rose from his desk. "If you don't want to play, just say so. I'm a big boy, I can take it."

"That's not—" She exhaled, struggling to slow the wild pounding of her heart. "Yes, I'd like to."

He gave her a long, considering stare, those blue-gray eyes making her already warm cheeks burn even more. Finally, he said, "Are you sure, because the look on your face just now gave me the impression you had something else on—"

"Dalton," Annie said, hoping his probing gaze hadn't succeeded in discovering what she'd been thinking about, "I'm sure."

"Okay." He smiled. "Let's go."

* * *

Annie was right, Dalton found out a while later. She wasn't very good at pool. But her lack of skill didn't bother him. Normally playing against a beginner would have been a frustrating experience, but not when Annie was that novice opponent.

As he was quickly learning, everything with her was different. The more time he spent with her, the more he enjoyed her company. Plus, the view of her sweet little ass each time she bent over the table to make a shot was a definite bonus.

"Ya know," Annie said, studying the layout of the balls on the table, "pool isn't as hard as I thought."

"Yeah, well, me telling a math whiz that pool is a game of angles wasn't one of my smarter decisions."

Annie laughed. "Who'd've thought knowing geometry would come in handy for something like this!" She leaned over the table in preparation for her next shot, then looked up at Dalton. "How's my position?"

Dalton jerked his gaze from her ass, then took a step closer. "Spread your legs a little more." She made the adjustment. "That's good. Now, keep the cue at waist level. Hold your body still. And remember, move just your arm. You only need to kiss the cue ball off the five to make this shot, so use a nice easy stroke."

She followed his instructions, sinking the five ball with respectable if not perfect form.

When she straightened, she flashed him a smile, a definite sparkle in those beautiful green eyes. "I had no idea pool was so full of"—she winked at him— "sexual innuendos."

"What?"

"Spread your legs. Kissing. Nice easy strokes." She shrugged. "Well, don't you think those add sexy overtones to the game?"

He cleared his throat. "Never thought about it," he said, stepping aside to give her room for her next shot.

"Really?" Her brow furrowed. "I would've thought you'd be like most men, finding sexual connotations in just about everything."

The hell of it was, Dalton really hadn't thought of pool in that way, but now thanks to Annie, that's all he could think about. "Yeah, well," he said after a moment, "guess I'm not like most men."

As she bent over the table, a provocative picture of her in a similar pose popped into his head, only she wasn't wearing clothes and he— *Dammit, Stoner, get your mind out of the gutter.* He wiped a less-than-steady hand over his face, certain he'd never be able to look at a pool table the way he had in the past.

Willing himself to concentrate on something besides the curves of Annie's bottom, or the X-rated images flashing through his mind, he watched her line up her shot. He could see her lips move and strained to catch her words.

"Cue at waist level," he heard her tell herself. "Body still. Move just my arm. Nice easy stroke."

Stroke. Shit, there was that word again! Closing his eyes, he willed his body not to respond. Unfortunately, his body wasn't listening.

After playing a half dozen games of 8-Ball, they decided to quit for lunch.

"So," Annie said, following him into the kitchen, "what do you think of my future as a pool player?"

"You won't be ready to join the women's pro tour any time soon." He smiled. "But if you work on your technique and learn more about strategy, you could become a pretty fair player."

"Good enough to beat you?"

"Maybe." He dried his hands, then turned to meet

her gaze. "Remember, I won a bunch of amateur tournaments back when I was in college."

"Yeah, I know." She lifted her chin. "I'm not afraid of your reputation."

"No," he replied, managing another weak smile. "I bet you're not."

"Then, will you help with my technique and teach me more about game strategy?"

He studied her in silence for a several seconds, wondering at the reason for her request. Finally, he said, "If that's really what you want, I'll teach you. But if you're yanking my chain by pretending interest in a game I enjoy just so you can get closer to me, then forget it."

A crease forming between her eyebrows, she moved closer. "Did someone do that to you? Is that why you're so skeptical of me?"

He started to deny it, then figured what the hell. Nodding, he said, "Maureen. When we first met, she pretended to enjoy the things I liked. Shooting pool. Art. Dogs." He made a snorting sound. "I knew some women played games to get a husband, even stooping to some pretty devious tactics, but I really thought she was different. I never suspected she was faking interest in—" He blew out a deep breath. "Anyway, once we were married, it didn't take long for the truth to start surfacing. Turns out, she couldn't stand any of the things I thought we had in common and suddenly had no problem telling me so."

Annie clenched her hands into fists, wishing Dalton's poor excuse for a wife was in the room. Oh, would she love to give the woman a well-deserved tongue-lashing, or better yet, a solid punch in the face for hurting this man. Forcing herself to relax, she touched his forearm, the heat of his skin making her fingers tingle. "I'm sorry. No one should have to go through that."

Dalton huffed out a deep breath. "Yeah," he said, his voice rough with the emotions bubbling beneath his outer calm. "It's ancient history now."

Annie gave his arm a squeeze, then pulled her hand away. He might call his failed marriage ancient history, but that was a smoke screen. Whether he wanted to admit it or not, he was still suffering because of what Maureen had done to him.

Daphne watched Darcie prowl the living room of her apartment. Two years apart in age, she and her sister had always been close, best friends, sharing each others' secrets, fears and hopes. Though college had separated them, they'd kept in touch as much as possible. And now that they were both settled in their careers, finding time to see each other had gotten more difficult. Determined not to drift apart as so many siblings did, they started their sister-time, getting together for a few hours every Sunday. Sometimes they went out to brunch, but more often, they spent the time in one of their apartments.

Darcie had never liked sitting still for very long, one of the reasons she'd done so well as an attorney—an endless desire to excel and a stubbornness few could match. But she'd always been able to kick back and relax when they got together on Sundays. That day, her obvious nervousness was something new.

At first Daphne hadn't said anything, hoping her sister would either settle down or start talking. When neither happened, she'd finally had enough.

"For God's sake, sis, will you park your ass in a chair. Your pacing is getting on my nerves."

Darcie swung around, a faint blush tinging her cheeks. "Sorry. I guess I'm just antsy."

Daphne studied her sister for a moment. Sometimes she forgot how much they resembled each another. There definitely was no mistaking they were sisters; the only differences were eye color—Darcie's dark blue and her own gray—and hairstyle—hers was longer and wavier than the sleek, chin-length cut Darcie preferred. Right now her sister's hair was far from its normal perfection, totally mussed as if she'd run her hands through it repeatedly.

Finally, Daphne said, "What's going on, Darcie?"

"Nothing."

"You might get someone else to believe that. But this is me, remember. I know you, and I can tell something is definitely troubling you." When Darcie didn't reply, she added, "Look, if you don't want to talk about it, okay, but at least sit down."

"Fine," Darcie replied with a huff, "I'll sit." Shooting an angry glare in her direction, she dropped onto the seat of an overstuffed chair.

Daphne stared at her sister's mutinous expression, then shifted her attention to the newspaper article she'd been trying to read. She knew from experience that continuing to push Darcie would only make her clam up even tighter. If her sister wanted to talk, it would happen only when she was ready. Not before.

After finishing the one article and moving on to another, Darcie's voice interrupted her reading.

"Daf, I think he might be the one."

Daphne carefully lowered the newspaper. "Who?"

Darcie scowled. "Don't play dumb. You know I'm talking about the man I was with when you called last night."

"Oh, that guy."

"Yeah," she replied, tracing the floral pattern of the chair's upholstery with a fingertip.

"Who is he?"

"Quinlan Jett."

"Hmm, interesting name. So how long have you been seeing him?"

"Couple of weeks."

Daphne lifted her eyebrows. "Really. And already you think he might be the one?"

"I know, it's crazy." Darcie sighed, then dropped her head against the back of the chair and closed her eyes. "But Quin is like no other man I've ever known. He makes me laugh one minute, and so angry the next I could spit nails. And then before I know what's hit me, I'm in a lather to rip his clothes off." She sighed again. "Pathetic, aren't I?"

"No. Sounds to me like you're in love."

A burst of laughter erupted from Darcie. "God, if this is love, I could've gotten along just fine without it." She opened her eyes and met her sister's gaze. "I don't know how to handle this, Daf, and I'm scared."

Daphne pushed off the sofa, moving to kneel in front of Darcie's chair. There was no mistaking the confusion swirling in her sister's dark blue eyes. "It's okay, hon," she said, clasping Darcie's hand. "This is all new for you, and being scared is only natural. But once you get used to the idea, everything will be fine."

The corners of Darcie's mouth tilted up in a wobbly smile. "Thanks, sis. I hope you're right."

Daphne returned her smile. "So does Quin know how you feel?"

"God, no! I can't tell him he's the man I want to marry, the man I want to father my children, the man I want to grow old with. Jeez, I *am* pathetic." She rubbed her forehead. "Besides, if I start spouting all that sentimental crap, I'd probably scare him off."

"Maybe he feels the same way."

Darcie sighed. "Yeah, I wish."

Daphne gave her sister's hand another squeeze, then got to her feet. After pouring each of them a fresh cup of coffee, she said, "Where did you meet him?"

"In the courthouse."

"He's an attorney?"

Darcie shook her head. "No, he said he was there on business, but . . . Actually, now that I think about it, he never did tell me what he was doing in the courthouse that day. Anyway, he bumped into me in the hallway, spilling coffee on my suit. I was ticked. I had a bail hearing in less than five minutes, and I didn't have time to go back to my office and change. But then I looked up and saw his face."

"Love at first sight, huh?"

"More like lust," Darcie replied with a chuckle. "He's absolutely the most gorgeous man I've ever seen. Not handsome in the classic sense, more of a rugged mountain man, with the most incredible topaz eyes. And hot damn, did he get my engine revving."

"So one look and you were a goner."

"Pretty much. He offered to pay to have my suit cleaned, and he wanted to take me to lunch to make up for his clumsiness. I told him I had to be in court, but he said he'd wait." She took the cup Daphne handed her. "We've been together as much as possible since."

"Well, obviously he's good in bed," Daphne said before taking a sip of coffee. When Darcie's eyes flared with temper, she held up a hand. "No, I don't want to know all the steamy details. But tell me about him."

"He's twenty-nine. Originally from South Carolina. Went to college in Texas. Austin, I think. He likes sports but isn't a fanatic. And he loves my chili."

"Really? Well then you'd better drag him in front of a judge for the 'I dos' immediately."

"Ha ha, very funny." Darcie sent her sister a blistering glance. "I know I'm not very good in the kitchen, but I do know how to make a kick-ass chili."

"Hey, as long as Quin appreciates your culinary efforts, who am I to question anything?"

"Exactly. Now, let's talk about something else. Have you heard from Dalton, or that Annie-woman you sent up to his house?"

"No, nothing from either of them. But I heard the mountain roads are all closed. Sure would like to be a mouse in our brother's house right about now."

Darcie set her coffee cup on an end table with a thunk, then leaned forward. "Daf, please don't tell me you're thinking of doing another reading."

Daphne lifted one shoulder in a shrug. "I considered the idea, but decided against it."

"Thank God," Darcie replied, sitting back and blowing out a deep breath. When her sister remained silent, she said, "You still think Annie is perfect for our brother?"

"Absolutely. I just hope he'll give her a chance."

"I wonder what Annie's gonna say when she finds out what you did, and whether she'll appreciate your efforts at matchmaking. But my main concern is our brother. You know he gets really upset when he thinks one of us is trying to set him up. So how's he gonna react to your latest stunt?"

"I suspect Annie will be angry at first, but if she likes Dalton at all, which I'm certain she will, she'll forgive me. And as for our dear brother, no big deal. Oh, I'm sure he'll rant and rave, tell me to keep my damn nose out of his life, then storm off to sulk for a while. Nothing to be concerned about."

"I don't know how you can be so blase about his reaction. I'd be shaking in my boots right about now."

"No need to worry, sis. I'm not concerned about Dalton. I just hope Annie can handle him."

Seven

Dalton rapped his knuckles against the door of the guest bedroom, then turned the knob and pushed the door open. "Annie," he called from the doorway. When she didn't stir, he moved closer to the bed, keeping the beam of his flashlight directed away from her face.

"Annie," he said again, reaching out to give her shoulder a gentle shake. "Come on, you need to get up."

"Why?" she responded, her voice groggy with sleep. "What's wrong?"

"The power went out right after we went to bed and the temperature in the house is dropping fast."

"Not cold," she murmured, burrowing deeper beneath the bedcovers.

"Maybe you aren't now. But you will be if we don't get into the living room. I've got a fire going."

He heard her sigh. "'kay, in a minute."

He smiled at the lump she formed on the bed. "No, not in a minute. Now."

When a soft snore was her only response, he turned off his flashlight, tucked it in the pocket of his sweatpants, then grabbed the covers and flipped them to the foot of the bed.

"Hey! What are you doing?" She sat up and reached for the blankets. Before her fingers found their target, he bent and scooped her into his arms. Her shocked gasp made him smile.

"Take it easy, babe. I'm going to carry you into the living room."

"This isn't necessary," she said, wiggling to free herself. "I'm perfectly capable of walking."

"Yeah, I know. But you weren't in any hurry, so I helped you along. Now, hold still and enjoy the ride."

She huffed out a breath. "Fine."

As Dalton carried her through the cold, dark house, Annie tried to relax. But being held in his arms, tucked securely against his muscular chest, one hip brushing his flat belly with each stride, was affecting her more than she wanted to admit. She was all too aware of her attraction to this man, and their current proximity made relaxing next to impossible.

In the living room, he removed his arm from beneath her knees and let her slide down his body until she stood on the sleeping bag he'd spread out in front of the fireplace.

"Get comfortable," he told her, "while I gather a few more things."

She nodded then stepped away from him, immediately missing the heat of his body pressed to hers. Taking a seat on the sleeping bag, she wrapped her arms around her up-drawn knees and stared into the fire.

He returned a few minutes later, carrying several blankets and more pillows. After dropping everything onto the floor, he sat down next to her. She glanced over at him, smiled, then shifted her gaze back to the fireplace and the dancing flames.

The only sounds in the room were the crackling of the fire and the soft tick of a clock. When Annie made no move to lie down, he said, "It's only a little after five. Don't you want to go back to sleep?"

"Maybe in a while." She suddenly turned toward him. "I'm curious about something."

"What?"

"Your interest in the *Kama Sutra*."

"What about it?"

"Did you first get interested because of that painter you mentioned, the woman who did paintings of the *Kama Sutra*?"

"Marisa St. Clair?" When she nodded, he said, "Yeah, that's when my interest started. I'd heard of the *Kama Sutra* before I saw Marisa's paintings but really didn't know much about it. At one of her showings, we had a conversation about the inspiration for her work. She talked about the *Kama Sutra* as being a lot more than what I'd always thought. Frankly, I was intrigued, so I bought some of the books she recommended. And I kept buying until"—he shrugged—"I had an entire collection. I still buy books whenever I run across one I don't have." He pursed his lips thoughtfully, then added, "What began as a casual interest has turned into one of my passions."

She smiled to herself. Hmm, with passions like erotic art and the *Kama Sutra*, maybe Dalton had a streak of bad boy in him after all.

"Nothing wrong with that," she said at last. "Living would get pretty boring if people didn't have something they're passionate about in life. So, tell me about the *Kama Sutra*."

His eyes narrowing, he studied her in silence for a moment. Finally, he said, "Are you sure you want to talk about this?"

"Absolutely. I'd like to know why it's become a passion of yours. So how about enlightening me?"

"Okay," he replied, stretching out on his side and propping himself up on one forearm. "First of all, to understand the *Kama Sutra*, you need to know some things about life in ancient India. Society banned most sexual activity outside the bonds of marriage and permanent celibacy was considered intolerable, which

made getting married a sacred duty in order to pro-
duce children and fulfill sexual desiress. And to
properly fulfill those sexual desires, society also believed instruction was needed. That's the reason the
Kama Sutra was written."

When Annie opened her mouth to speak, he held
up a hand to stop her.

"I know what you're going to say. Yes, that's why the
book has the reputation of being just a sex guide. But
that's a misconception. The *Kama Sutra* is much more
than that. It's really about manners and conduct. Sort
of a manual for living. It instructs young men on how
to find the right woman, how to entice her into a relationship that will hopefully lead to marriage, stressing
the importance of courtship and compatibility. And it
gives a list of sixty-some Arts and Sciences that cultivated
people were expected to know. Things like singing, lan-
guages, writing, chemistry. All of those were to be
studied along with the teachings in the *Kama Sutra*."

"What about the paintings in that book in your office? The ones of the couples in all those bizarre
sexual positions. They had to have been inspired by
something in the *Kama Sutra*."

"Yeah, they were. There's an entire section called
'On Sexual Union' that explains the finer points in the
art of lovemaking. Unfortunately, that's why the book
has taken the rap of being nothing more than a sex
guide, but I can understand why. Since the subject was
taboo in many parts of the world for generations, it's
only natural for people to focus on the part that deals
with erotic love and describes a variety of exotic sexual positions. Anyway, the sexual union section really is
extraordinary."

"How do you mean?"

"Even though the *Kama Sutra* is more than two

thousand years old, its teachings are still relevant today."

"Right." She rolled her eyes. "As in, people like sex as much now as back then?"

He smiled. "Sure they do. But that's not what I meant. The *Kama Sutra* urges men to seek marriage based on love, not convenience. And it emphasizes the importance of relationships as a whole, encouraging couples to strive for deep connections emotionally as well as physically."

"And that's accomplished . . . how?"

"By putting sex at the center of their relationship."

Annie's eyebrows arched. "Really?"

"Really. Sex is the ultimate communication between a man and a woman, and deepening a couple's sexual union will strengthen their relationship. The *Kama Sutra* teaches men that pleasuring their partners is as important as pleasing themselves."

"Mmm, I like the sound of that." She laughed. "Must be it was written by a woman."

"No, afraid not," he replied. "It's a collection of stories and lessons written by perhaps a dozen men. A religious scholar and educator named Vatsyayana combined them into one volume and added some of his own comments and observations. Even though the writers were men, by today's standards they definitely had some liberated views about sex. Pretty amazing for so long ago."

"I'll say." She straightened her legs and lay down, then turned her head toward Dalton. "So tell me about the sexual union section."

"If you're hoping I can recite it from memory, sorry to disappoint you."

She gave him a wide-eyed stare, one hand placed over her heart. "Aw gee, I'm crushed." Unable to keep up the charade, she smiled. "Come on, Dalton, you said the *Kama Sutra* is one of your passions. You obviously know a lot about the entire book, including the sexy part, so start talking."

He returned her smile but didn't speak, studying her face while trying to figure out her reason for asking. Was she sincere, just making conversation, or looking for a cheap thrill? When he found only genuine interest in her expression, he finally nodded.

"A lot of that section," he said, "gives instructions in what we would call foreplay. Things like touching, embracing, kissing, biting, scratching and striking."

"Ouch. Were ancient Indians into S & M?"

"No, though some of what was considered acceptable in those days might be interpreted that way in today's society. None of those things was meant to be done with the idea of maiming, but for the purpose of heightening the sexual experience."

"Yeah, well, a little nip is one thing, but scratching and striking wouldn't heighten anything for me."

He smiled. "Me either. The *Kama Sutra* didn't say couples had to do everything it described. It just offered a variety of ways to enhance their pleasure, and instructed couples to pick and choose which ones to try. If something didn't work for them, they weren't expected to do it again."

She nodded, then fell silent. After a few moments, she said, "What does it say about kissing?"

"That there are many kinds. Let's see, there's the bent kiss, the turned kiss, the pressed kiss, and lots of others. But I don't remember their names."

"Could you—" She sat up, her throat working with a swallow. "Could you demonstrate some of them?"

Dalton noted her dilated eyes and the quick rise and fall of her breasts beneath the tee shirt he'd loaned her, and felt the responding sharp tug of attraction. He knew doing as she asked wasn't a good idea, but when he opened his mouth to refuse, the words he intended to say somehow changed to, "I suppose so."

He also pushed himself to a sitting position, then lifted a hand to brush a curl away from her face. "I've never done this before," he said in a soft voice, fascinated by how her hair wrapped itself around his fingers.

"Kiss a woman?" She snickered. "Come on, slick. I know that's not true."

"No, I meant, I've never demonstrated something from the *Kama Sutra*." He untangled his fingers from her hair and withdrew his hand. "Kisses or anything else."

She cocked an eyebrow, a smile teasing her mouth. "Good, then I'm your first."

"Yeah, my first," he whispered, leaning closer. "Tip your head to the right." When she complied, he tipped his head in the opposite direction and touched his mouth to hers in a brief kiss. When he pulled back, he said, "That's the bent kiss. And this"—he grasped her chin gently with one hand and tilted her face up to his—"is the turned kiss." Once again he brushed his lips over hers.

"What's the—" She gulped in a deep breath. "What's the pressed kiss?"

"As I recall, there are two versions. One is pressing a kiss on the other person's lower lip with a lot of force. And the other, called the greatly pressed kiss, is when one of the lovers does this." He reached up and carefully took her lower lip between this thumb and index finger. "And then they do this." He leaned closer and touched his tongue to her lip. He felt the shock ricochet through her, heard her soft gasp. "And the last part is this." Still holding her lower lip, he pressed his mouth firmly to the plump flesh in another quick kiss.

When he pulled away, he realized he should've followed his initial instinct and refused Annie's request. He'd thought he could demonstrate a few kisses and remain unaffected. God, what a dumbshit he was! And now he was paying the price, with a racing pulse, ragged breathing and half a hard-on. And just from a few little kisses that weren't really kisses at all, but just teasers for the type of lip-lock he really wanted to lay on her. A kiss like the one they'd shared the other night on the couch. That memory sent another blaze of heat ripping through his veins, forcing him to clench his jaw to hold in a groan.

Annie drew a shuddering breath, then blinked several times before she could refocus her eyes on the man beside her. Wishing the pounding in her temples would ease, she said, "Well, I . . . um . . . have to say, that Vatsy-whatever guy really knew his stuff about using kisses as foreplay."

"Yeah," he replied, trying not to wince at the roughness of his voice, "he did. He also knew his stuff about a lot more than that."

"Such as?"

"He instructs couples to pay close attention to what pleases their partners. Observe each other's reactions. Talk about what gives each of them pleasure and what doesn't. And maintain an open dialogue in order to strengthen their relationship."

"Definitely good advice, don't you think?"

He nodded, staring at her through hooded eyes, his lazy perusal moving from the top of her head, down to the puckered tips of her breasts pressing against the cotton tee shirt, then back to her face. Each place his gaze touched made her skin tingle with sexual awareness and sent a shiver rippling up her spine.

He reached for one of the blankets. "You're cold. Here, put this around—"

"No, I'm not cold." She drew a ragged breath then blurted, "In fact, I'm pretty hot."

When his furrowed brow told her he hadn't caught the implication behind her words, she managed to summon up the nerve to add, "Guess it's all this talk about sex."

He blinked, clearly surprised by her statement, then studied her with an intensity that sent another lick of sexually charged heat surging through her body. Finally he nodded, his lips curved into a slow, easy smile. "The *Kama Sutra* can be pretty . . . er . . . stimulating."

Before she could tell him she agreed, he lifted a hand and ran his fingertips across her cheek. "What do you like, Annie?"

"What?"

"I know you like to be kissed, but what else?"

She frowned. "I . . . um . . . don't know what you're asking me."

"Do you like being touched?" He raked the backs of his knuckles down one side of her neck. "Here maybe." His fingers dropped to lightly graze a nipple. "Or here."

She gasped, moving restlessly, desperately wanting him to touch her again.

"Talk to me, Annie."

She swallowed hard, trying desperately to pull herself together. "Uh . . . yes, I like how you touched me."

Not giving him a chance to say anything more, she scooted even closer, then whispered, "What about you?" She touched her tongue to his ear. "Do you like me touching you this way?" She took his earlobe between her teeth and gave it a gentle nip. "Or like this?"

Dalton sucked in a sharp breath, momentarily stunned by Annie's actions. Normally, aggressive women were a big turn-off for him, but just like everything else about the woman beside him, that sure as hell wasn't the case now. He actually liked her blatant come-on. In fact, he found her behavior damned arousing.

He cleared his throat, then said, "Yeah."

She shifted away from him but couldn't bring herself to meet his gaze. "Dalton, am I the only one who feels this . . . whatever it is between us?"

"Maybe you'd better clarify what you feel."

"This"—she searched her muddled brain for the right words—"hot, tingly kinda feeling I get whenever I'm close to you. My heart starts to pound and I have this throbbing in . . . um . . . certain places." She lifted her head, making herself look into his eyes. "Do you feel anything like that?"

Do I? Jesus, she had to be kidding! Dalton forced himself to draw a slow, deep breath, trying to recoup from a sudden bout of dizziness, the blood in his head having headed south in record time. He needed a moment to recover, then he finally said, "I feel it."

Her breath came out in a rush. "Thank God."

Such an honest reaction made him chuckle. "Well, then, I think we should explore whatever is between us more thoroughly by doing as Vatsyayana suggests and find out what gives the other pleasure." He dropped onto his back on the sleeping bag, then reached up and toyed with a curl of her hair. "Would you agree?"

"Yes," she replied, her voice low and incredibly sexy. "I think we need to do a lot of exploring." She cast a quick glance down his body, her quickened breathing telling him she'd noticed the obvious bulge of his erection. When her gaze once again met his, she extended a hand toward his chest but stopped short of touching him. "Are we starting now?"

Though struck with the sudden urge to beg her to

touch him, he managed to hold back the words. He really should think this through more thoroughly. But looking into those gorgeous green eyes, that lovely flushed face surrounded by that wild tangle of hair made him realize she was the most spectacular woman he'd ever seen. And based on their recent exchange, she wanted him as much as he wanted her. Even so, allowing their sexual banter to progress to the physical wouldn't be a smart idea. He wasn't into casual affairs, especially with a woman he couldn't see as a permanent fixture in his life, but dammit, he did want her. More than he could remember ever wanting a woman. His throbbing erection twitched in agreement.

He closed his eyes, eased out a compressed breath, then made his decision. For the first time since his horny teenage years, he let his hormones overrule his brain. Opening his eyes and meeting her expectant gaze, he said, "Yeah, we're starting now."

She smiled, sending his heart into a wild gallop. "Could you . . . um"—she gave the sleeve of his sweatshirt a gentle tug—"lose the shirt?"

He sat up, pulled the shirt over his head and tossed it aside. "Anything else?" he said, flashing a wolfish grin.

She gave a quick shake of her head, making her curls bounce with the movement. "Not just yet," she replied, placing two fingers on the center of his chest and pushing him back down onto the sleeping bag.

He stared up at her, wondering what was going on behind those fascinating eyes, and hoping he wouldn't have to wait very long to find out.

Annie took a deep breath, willing her hand to remain steady while she explored his chest. The silky black hair tickled her fingers and, at the same time, sent a shot of excitement racing through her that settled into a warm ache low in her belly. His skin was warm, his muscles flexing slightly at her touch. He wasn't bulky like a contender in the Mr. Universe pageant, but still extremely muscular. As she ran her hand over his nicely developed pecs, a low hum vibrated in her throat. God, his body was to die for.

When her fingers found one flat male nipple, she heard his indrawn breath hiss through his teeth. She lifted her gaze to meet his, while brushing her thumb back and forth over the tightened nub. She watched his eyes close, saw his jaw go rigid.

Her hand stilled. "Am I hurting you?"

His eyes fluttered open, revealing a flame of deep blue burning in their depths. "No," he whispered, his voice slightly wobbly. "But I think you might be killing me."

"Do you want me to stop?"

"God, no!"

She chuckled. "I don't want to stop either, but I also want to keep you alive." Moving her hand to his other nipple and giving it the same attention, she added, "Any suggestions on how we can do that?"

"A few."

When he didn't volunteer anything more, she said, "Care to elaborate, or am I supposed to guess?" She eased her hand down his chest, past the ridges of his ribs and onto his flat belly. His stomach muscles contracted at her touch.

"You . . . uh . . . could kiss me. For starters."

"Mmm, good idea," she replied, bending lower, bringing her face close enough to his to feel the warmth of his choppy breath on her cheek. "And then what, I wonder?"

Not allowing him to answer, she pressed her lips to his, delighted by the low rumble of male pleasure in his chest and the pressure of his arms wrapping around her waist to pull her closer.

What started as a gentle kiss quickly escalated into

hot and frantic, a wild need to taste completely, to plunder thoroughly.

Annie shifted, aligning her body more firmly against his until they were pressed together from chest to thighs. One of his hands moved up to cup the back of her head, the other sliding down to grasp her bottom. Holding her tightly in place, he pushed his tongue into her mouth to explore, taste, tease, all the while grinding his erection against her belly.

There was no mistaking the message his body was sending hers, and heaven help her, her body was responding with astounding speed. She couldn't believe what was happening, had never wanted a man more than she wanted Dalton at that exact moment.

In spite of the intense physical attraction zinging between them and the overwhelming need clawing at her insides, a moment of sanity told her giving in to that need would not be the smart thing to do. Yes, he was great looking, yes, she enjoyed talking to him, and yes, the sexual chemistry between them went beyond phenomenal. But maybe her attraction stemmed from the forced closeness of being snowbound in his house—sort of a love the one you're with kinda thing.

Whatever the reason, getting involved with him physically would be foolish. She'd wanted excitement over her holiday break, but having sex with a gallery owner wasn't exactly what she had in mind. In fact, sex wasn't even on the radar for the kind of excitement she'd hoped to experience, and especially not with a man she knew wasn't right for her. Though she had to admit, learning there might be a bad boy lurking beneath Dalton's stuffy outer layer definitely added to his appeal. But even if they gave in to their mutual desire, she just couldn't envision anything permanent between them.

Although the logical part of her brain told her to follow her own advice and stop what was about to happen, on some level she sensed it was only a matter of time before she and Dalton became intimate. Which led to another startling truth. Regardless of her reservations, she wasn't sure she could—or even wanted to—stop them from becoming lovers.

The best she could do was enjoy the ride while it lasted and hope that when the fires of passion cooled and their relationship ended—as it inevitably would—neither of them would get hurt.

Her decision made, she pushed all her misgivings and inner arguments from her mind. Instead, she concentrated on the present, giving herself over to the incredible sensations whipping through her.

As Dalton continued kissing her, he rolled to reverse their positions, then eased back enough so he could reach between them and slide his hand under the hem of the tee shirt he'd loaned her. She murmured her encouragement against his lips, no longer caring if this was the right decision. She'd worry about the consequences later. Because at the moment, all she could think about was how much she wanted him to touch her bare skin.

Annie heard a moan. Had something that raw, that primitive actually come from her? Distracted by Dalton's fingers skimming over her hip, trying to decide if she was capable of making such a sound was not an easy task.

Then his hand found one breast, his thumb brushing over her already peaked nipple, chasing all thoughts from her mind. Another moan filled the air around them, this one deeper, throatier, more savage than the first.

He pulled his mouth from hers and drew a shaky breath. "God, Annie," he whispered in a thick slur, "you're incredible."

Eight

Annie arched her back, pushing her pelvis against him, her fingers clutching the hair at his nape. His hand might be on her breast, but she swore she could feel the heat of his touch between her thighs, the ache there accelerating to an insistent throb.

She dropped her hand to the sleeping bag, murmuring his name over and over, rolling her head from side to side.

Dalton pushed himself up onto one arm and stared down into her flushed face. "I'm here, babe."

He gave her nipple a gentle tweak, then grabbed a fistful of her tee shirt and pulled the material up above her waist. His heart hammering in his ears, he allowed himself a moment to gaze at the triangle of golden curls he'd uncovered before he nudged her legs apart and stroked his hand up the velvet of her inner thigh.

As he inched higher, he felt her muscles tense, saw her hand curl into a fist beside her thigh, heard the cadence of her breathing change. And when he traced a finger over the folds of her sex, she gasped, her hips lifting off the floor.

"Dalton, please," she whispered.

"Easy now," he replied. "We have lots of time. No reason to hurry."

"Dammit, yes there is." She glared at him. "I need—"

"Shh, don't worry," he said, chuckling at her impatience. "I know what you need, and I'll see you get it. Just relax and enjoy."

"But—"

"No buts. Only this." He opened her with his fingers, rubbed his thumb over her clitoris, and watched her eyelids drop closed. A second stroke of his thumb rewarded him with her quick gasp, followed by another of her sexy-as-hell moans.

His gaze locked on her face, he gauged her reaction to his intimate touch, concentrating solely on learning how to please her. He'd never been selfish with any of his former lovers, always making sure they were satisfied. But the shameful truth was his own release had been his primary goal for taking those women to bed. Yet with Annie, his entire focus was on her pleasure. Bringing her to orgasm was more important than reaching his own. In fact, he realized with mind-numbing shock, his climax wasn't even necessary.

Maybe he'd studied the *Kama Sutra* too long. Why else would he suddenly be more concerned about his partner's pleasure than his own? Especially when he had a raging hard-on. Refusing to speculate on an answer, he bent to nuzzle the side of Annie's neck.

She smelled of something flowery, probably that fancy soap Daphne liked and kept in his guest bathrooms, and the underlying heady musk of female. He ran his tongue upward along the cord of her neck, to the underside of her jaw, then up to her ear.

"I wanna make you come, Annie," he murmured. "So tell me how to touch you." When she didn't respond, he pressed a quick kiss on her lips, then lifted his head. "Annie. Open your eyes."

After several seconds, her eyelids fluttered open.

He gave her an encouraging smile. "Talk to me,

babe." He stroked her moist center again, then halted his movements. "Am I rubbing the right spot?"

"I—" she gulped in a deep breath. "I can't."

"Sure you can. I know you're close, so just tell me how to take you over the edge."

She didn't speak for several long seconds. Finally, she whispered, "A little lower."

He made the adjustment, then resumed rubbing her swollen clit. "Better?"

"Uh-huh."

"Good, now what else?"

At her blank look, he said, "More pressure? Faster, slower?"

"Umm . . ." She ran her tongue over her lower lip. "Faster."

He complied. "Like this?"

"Ohmygod, yes!" Her breathing growing more ragged, she began moving her hips. Taking his cue from her, he let her set the pace, which quickly escalated.

He bent to press a brief kiss on her mouth. "Annie, you're so hot and wet," he murmured. "You're almost there, babe. Come for me."

Her eyes went wide for an instant, their color darkening to an even deeper green. She gave a sharp gasp, her body going rigid for a split second. "Oh, God. Dalton, I'm . . ." Then she screamed, her hips pumping wildly as her climax crashed over her.

Several moments later, she shuddered a final time, then went limp, her flushed face turned away from him. Dalton stared down at her, fighting and losing his battle not to grin like an idiot.

Annie's a screamer. Who would've thought?

Still grinning, he stretched out next to her, then pulled her into his arms and tucked her head under his chin.

"Hey, wait," she said, trying pull away from him, but he wouldn't release her.

"Shh, just lie still."

"But you—"

He chuckled. "There you go with those buts again." When she started to speak, he shushed her with a quick squeeze, then finally said, "Just go to sleep, babe." Reaching behind him, he grabbed a blanket and pulled it over them.

She held herself stiffly against him for a few seconds, then drew a shuddering breath and cuddled closer. Rubbing her cheek against his chest, she sighed.

Dalton lay awake long after he felt Annie's muscles go slack with sleep, thinking about the woman he held and what had just taken place. He should have felt only sexual frustration, yet he was startled to realize that wasn't an issue. Instead, he knew a quiet satisfaction, a sense of peace he wasn't sure he'd ever known. Equally surprising, he realized he didn't want whatever was between the two of them to end. And being totally honest, he sure as hell wasn't ready to ditch their budding intimate relationship. He'd never experienced anything close to what he'd shared with Annie, and he wanted the opportunity to experience it again. That and a whole lot more.

He could still taste her sweet mouth, feel his fingers glide over her slick flesh, hear her throaty moans and then that piercing scream when she came. He wanted to make her scream again. Except next time, he wouldn't deny himself his own climax.

As he'd told Annie, the *Kama Sutra* taught men to make sure they pleased the women in their lives, and that remaining celibate wasn't acceptable. Apparently, she felt the same way, unless he'd misread the protest she'd tried to make before falling asleep. And she hadn't been shocked by the graphic paintings she'd looked at, hadn't seemed more than mildly surprised by his interest in both erotic art and the ancient book. In fact, she'd seemed genuinely curious, as if she would be willing to— He frowned up at the ceiling. She would be willing to do what, exactly?

Oh shit! The answer hit him like a punch to the gut, rocking him to the core. He'd always believed his interest in the *Kama Sutra* had been strictly on an intellectual level. With sudden clarity, he realized there may have been a second reason for the book becoming a passion in his life, that his fascination with the work was more than scholarly. Had all the years he'd devoted to studying the *Kama Sutra* been for an underlying purpose—a personal one?

No doubt, his mother would take great delight in the suggestion. When she'd first found out about his interest, she'd teased him unmercifully about using what he learned to improve his sex life. And every once in a while, she still got in a dig about why his sexual drought hadn't improved, given the length of time he'd been studying the *Kama Sutra*. Although he knew her comments were meant in jest, he'd felt the need to defend himself by repeatedly denying her innuendos and calling the idea absurd, even perverted. And up until two days ago, he would have continued his denials, trying again to make her understand that he would never consider what she suggested. But then Annie Peterson had come knocking at his door.

And now he knew, with absolute certainty, that neither absurdity nor perversion had anything to do with what he wanted to have happen. He wanted to experience firsthand the *Kama Sutra's* teachings, personally explore all the sensual pleasures the book described. And he wanted to do that with only one woman. Annie.

He rubbed one of his temples, trying to ease the

sudden pounding in his head. Oh man, this self-discovery crap really sucked. Finding out he'd had an ulterior motive all these years for studying the *Kama Sutra* came as a huge shock. And as for what he wanted to do about it, that went beyond shock. He stifled a groan, wishing he'd wake up from what had to be a bad dream. *Yeah, that's it. I must be dreaming.* Squeezing his eyes closed, he pinched the bridge of his nose. *Or maybe I've lost my mind. Otherwise, there's no way this can be happening. No fucking way.*

The sound of the furnace kicking on pulled Dalton from a dream filled with tiny, fur trimmed, red velvet jackets dancing around his bed. When he opened his eyes, he couldn't figure out why he was on the floor of the living room, lying spoon fashion with Annie, her sweet little ass pressed against his crotch. Then he remembered the power outage, how he'd roused her from her bed, followed by how he'd brought her to an explosive climax. His piss hard-on jerked against her backside.

Grateful the power had been restored, he pulled his arm out from under Annie's shoulders, then eased away from her and sat up. After tucking the blanket more securely around her, he got to his feet.

While standing over the toilet, waiting for his morning erection to go down enough so he wouldn't piss in his eye, he wondered how Annie would act when she woke up. Would she look at him with the heat of passion in those gorgeous eyes, or cool indifference? He wasn't sure which he should hope for. As much as he wanted to see passion, he knew indifference would be safer for both of them.

As he dressed, more memories surfaced from the night before, specifically after Annie had fallen asleep. Analyzing what he'd discovered in the minutes before he'd finally dozed off, he knew he hadn't been dreaming, nor had he lost his mind. What he'd learned about himself was all too real. Though still shaken, he had no choice except coming to terms with a side of himself he never knew existed.

Annie set her coffee cup on the kitchen counter a little more forcefully than she intended, inwardly wincing at the loud thud. "There's something I need to say." She turned to face Dalton, hugging the blanket draped around her shoulders a little tighter.

His expression guarded, he said, "Sure. Go ahead."

"Um, okay." She took a deep breath, carefully considering her words. "It's about last night. You never had . . . That is, you . . . um . . . didn't . . . well . . . you know." She pressed her lips together before she continued babbling, unable to believe one mind-blowing orgasmic experience had turned her into a moron.

"Shoot my wad." He grinned. "Get my rocks off. Cream my—"

Her angry glare ended his list of crude slang. "All right, you made your point."

His smile disappeared. "Sorry, I couldn't resist." He cleared his throat, then took a step closer and lifted a hand to tuck a strand of hair behind her ear. "I assure you, a man never died if he didn't"—he waggled his eyebrows—"you know."

She stared at him for several seconds. Deciding he was sincere beneath his outward attempt at more humor, she managed a weak smile. "Maybe not," she whispered, shifting her gaze to his impressive chest. "Still, your unselfishness wasn't fair. What happened was—" She frowned, once again searching for the right words. "The truth is, I don't know how to describe what happened. I've never experienced anything even approaching what happened last night, and I . . . I want to give that back to you." Her voice dropping lower, she added, "Though you did set the bar pretty high, so I'm not sure that's possible."

He chuckled. "Don't sell yourself short. I have no doubt you'll clear that bar with no problem at all."

Her head snapped up. "Does that mean there's going to be a next time?"

"Oh yeah." Dalton hadn't decided yet what to do about his recent discovery about himself, but he did know with unflinching certainty that he did want a next time with Annie, in fact a lot of next times. "If you thought one little appetizer was enough for me, think again, babe, 'cause that sure ain't the case."

An hour later, Dalton took the dogs outside with him while he hauled in more firewood, preparing for another possible blackout. Annie used the time alone to do her laundry. After putting her sweatshirt and leggings in the washing machine and starting the wash cycle, she rinsed out her panties and bra in the bathroom sink. Since the only other clothes she had was her strip-o-gram costume, she'd reluctantly accepted Dalton's offer to help herself to whatever his sisters had left in the guest bedroom. She'd chosen a set of pale blue sweats, but opted to go commando rather than wear her only other set of underwear, a skimpy red push-up bra and that damn red thong.

As she wrung out her wet undies and draped them over the shower door, memories of the previous night came flooding back. Dalton's hand between her thighs, his fingers doing wonderfully wicked things to her aching flesh. Just thinking about how he'd skillfully brought her to orgasm rekindled her need for more of the same.

She scowled at her reflection in the mirror. What was with her? Had she suddenly become obsessed with sex? Not that she and Dalton had actually had sex by the go-all-the-way definition. All they'd done was some heavy foreplay, followed by his giving her one hell of an incredible orgasm. A memory that got her hot every time she thought about it, which had been pretty much every minute since she'd awakened that morning.

Though still mortified that she'd actually screamed when Dalton pushed her over the edge—something she'd never done—she wanted to experience that moment again, plus a whole lot more. She wanted the entire shooting match—hot and sweaty, full penetration, wild and wicked, breath-stealing sex—resulting in not just another earth shaking climax for her, but one for Dalton as well.

Just thinking about it caused an embarrassing gush of moisture between her thighs. She shut her eyes, uncomfortable with both the direction of her thoughts and her body's reaction, and no longer able to meet her own gaze. She groaned deep in her throat. Oh God, she *was* obsessed with sex!

Darcie Stoner made a sound of disgust, tossed down her pen, then swivelled her desk chair around so she could look out her office window. Normally, the view of the snow-capped Rockies had a calming effect on her, their spectacular beauty easing whatever lay heavy on her mind. But that day the mountains failed her.

Ever since the conversation she'd had with Daphne in her sister's apartment the previous afternoon, she had been edgy, out of sorts. And worse, she realized with a groan, she knew the reason behind her moodiness. Quinlan Jett. He filled her thoughts constantly, much to her annoyance, and totally demolished her normally excellent power of concentration.

She loved being an attorney, was right on track to achieve her professional goals, and had adamantly refused to allow anything to distract her from her work—especially a man. But Quin, damn his amazing topaz eyes, was doing exactly that. Not that he had any idea, of course, and she planned to keep it that way. Admitting the truth to herself, that she had a weakness—something she couldn't abide—was difficult enough, but make the admission to someone else? Nope, wasn't gonna happen. Not to her family—she'd already told her sister far too much—and especially not to Quin. She suspected he would take great delight in learning that bit of information about the formidable Darcie Stoner, Attorney-at-Law—the woman he called sugar puss while taking her on erotic journeys she never could have imagined.

God, how could she allow him to call her by such a cutesy nickname? But the first time he'd whispered the name, he'd just pulled her up onto her knees in the center of her bed and entered her from behind. He filled her so quickly, so completely, and inflamed her already highly aroused senses to the point that she'd been robbed of the ability to speak. Ensnared so tightly in the web of passion he'd spun around her, only sobbing gasps and pitiful moans had come out of her mouth.

Dammit, stop thinking about him!

She pushed herself out of her chair and strode across the room, her muscles protesting the quick movement. Making love with Quin was better than aerobics, but she was paying the price. He'd kept her up half the night with his bedroom gymnastics, and even a long, hot bath hadn't helped much.

How had this happened? How had she let a man she barely knew get under her skin? Even more disconcerting, had she actually fallen in love with him? Daphne thought so. Although she really didn't want to consider the possibility that her sister might be right, she could think of no other explanation for the bewildering feelings playing havoc with her emotional state.

She rubbed the back of her neck, trying to ease the kinks of tension. God, she hated not being in control.

The ringing of her phone brought her disturbing musings to a halt. Taking a deep breath, she shifted into business mode, crossed to her desk and picked up the handset.

"Darcie Stoner."

"Hey, darlin', are you free for lunch?"

She should have been annoyed at the interruption during working hours—though she certainly hadn't accomplished much work that morning—yet her pulse quickened at hearing the voice of the man who was causing her so much anxiety.

"I'm not sure," she replied. "What have you got in mind?"

A deep chuckle rumbled in her ear, sending a warm shiver up her spine. "I have lots of things in mind. But I'll save those for later. For the moment, I was thinking more along the lines of a real lunch. Food and drink with a lovely lady."

"Um . . . let me check my day planner." She already knew she had a free schedule but needed the few seconds that looking at her calendar would take to pull herself together. Debating with herself about the sanity of seeing the man who already filled most of her thoughts and all her free time, she finally decided spending time with Quin—without the distraction of sex—would give her an opportunity to learn more about him.

Maybe she'd find some serious flaw in his character. Something that would totally destroy her glowing opinion of him. Something that would reveal him as a real sleazebag. Something that would break the spell he'd cast over her and allow her to once again be in control of her life.

"Okay," she said at last, "but I'm swamped, so I can't be gone long."

"No problem. Decide where you'd like to go and I'll pick you up in, say, forty-five minutes."

"No, I'll meet you," she said, struck with the need to reassure herself that she could still call the shots in her life, even on the small things. "There's a great deli not far from my office. I walk there all the time."

"Fine, darlin', whatever you'd like to do."

After giving him the name and location of the deli, she hung up, the soft drawl of his, "I'll be waiting," echoing in her head.

Quin took a seat in the deli, choosing a small booth by the window so he could watch for Darcie. After removing his gloves he rubbed his hands together, longing for the warmer winters of southern Texas. He hadn't been thrilled about making the trip to Denver in December, but he'd had no other choice.

Besides, if he hadn't made the trip when he did, he would have missed his chance to meet Darcie. Not that he was a firm believer in destiny, but he did think fate played some part in a person's life.

The problem was, meeting Darcie couldn't have happened at a worse time. A time in his life when he wasn't sure what would happen next week, let alone next month. Even so, he couldn't turn his back on what could well be his only opportunity to experience true happiness—even if it was short term.

Darcie Stoner was a helluva woman, a real one of a kind, and he planned to spend as much time with her as possible in the coming days. Though he longed for more, a chance to turn their relationship into something permanent, he didn't delude himself into thinking that would happen. He'd already stuck around Denver longer than he'd anticipated. But at least he could take solace in knowing that when he left, he'd carry memories of what they'd shared with him, cherished memories that might well have to last a lifetime.

Nine

Dalton entered the door of his home office just as Annie pushed the Off button on his phone.

"Did you retrieve your messages?" he said, moving into the room.

"Yes," she replied, not looking up. Small furrows forming between her delicate eyebrows, she ran her fingers along the edge of his desk.

He studied her in silence, trying to decipher her mood. When they'd come face-to-face for the first time that morning, there had been none of the usual awkwardness of that dreaded initial morning-after moment. Instead, they soon were talking and laughing, comfortable with each other like they were old friends. Or lovers.

He frowned at the direction of his thoughts. He shouldn't have taken things as far as he had the night before. He really hadn't meant for their kissing to go beyond a few caresses. But as soon as his fingers slid between her thighs and he felt her moist heat, experienced her instant reaction to his intimate touch, he'd been crazy for more. And so had she.

Dammit, he knew her response had been genuine, was certain his statement that morning about continuing a physical relationship met with her approval. But now that she'd had more time to think about it, maybe the change in her mood meant she'd also changed her mind.

He had the sudden urge to cross the room, take her in his arms and kiss that full mouth, remind her of their incredible chemistry. But he didn't move. Sticking his hands in his pockets, he tried to sound casual when he said, "Something wrong?"

"Uh, no, not really. My mom called to see if I'm driving up for Christmas, and"—she lifted her gaze to meet his—"Daphne left me a couple of messages."

Relieved his speculations were wrong, the tension in his shoulders seeped away. "I told ya," he said with a laugh, "she was trying to set us up."

She frowned. "You don't know that for sure."

"Why else would she call you?"

"To see if I made the delivery."

"No way, babe," he said, shaking his head. "Customers call the company office to make sure their deliveries were made, not the delivery person."

"But Daphne knows me."

"True, but I know my sister. Daf definitely has the two of us on her radar screen. I'd bet my last dollar on it."

Her frown deepened, but she didn't respond.

"If you need to call your mom, go ahead."

"Thanks, but I'll wait until after I talk to Charlene, my boss at the messenger company. There was also a message from her on my machine. I'm sure she wants to know why I didn't check in yesterday, like I told her I would."

A knot formed in his gut. He'd forgotten the reason she might not be spending Christmas with her family. Her holiday job. The idea of her delivering a strip-o-gram to someone else— Unable to finish that thought, he eased out a deep breath, then said, "You're welcome to make as many calls as you like."

"I appreciate that."

He started to turn away, then stopped. "By the way, Charmed is number 6 on speed dial if you want to call Daf."

"Yeah, okay." She rubbed her forehead. "Maybe I will. But I need to call Charlene first."

As he moved toward the door, he said, "The snow finally stopped, so I'm going out to do some shoveling."

"I'll come out and help in a few minutes."

"No, stay in where it's warm. You don't have the clothes to be outside."

"I have thick mittens and a heavy coat and boots, so if I keep moving, I'll stay warm. Besides"—she rubbed her forehead again—"I really need some fresh air to clear my head."

His earlier fears returning, he didn't ask her to explain her last statement. He'd thought they were on the same page about what happened the night before. Once again, he wasn't so certain. The knot in his gut returned, pulling a little tighter this time. He nodded, then left her alone in his office.

He managed to take a couple of steps down the hall, then stopped and leaned a shoulder against the wall. Closing his eyes, he wondered why he cared if Annie now regretted what they'd done and wanted to call a halt to their budding physical relationship. Perhaps it would be better that way. After all, their forced togetherness would end soon. And once she left, he'd fall back into his normal routine, Annie Peterson quickly becoming a distant memory.

That's what he wanted—to get his life back on an even keel. So why then did the idea of never seeing Annie again, of never having another opportunity to kiss her, touch her, make her scream with pleasure, cause a weird sensation in his chest, a hollowness he couldn't explain? He didn't know the answer, and he sure as hell wasn't about to go poking around in his psyche to find one.

After Dalton disappeared through the door, Annie drew in a deep breath, then exhaled slowly. Though curious to find out if his suspicions about Daphne were correct, she decided to put off calling his sister. That conversation could wait for another time. At the moment, talking to Charlene was more important.

As she dialed the number, she hoped she still had a job.

"Naughty or Nice Messenger Service. Let us deliver a revealing holiday message to that special someone on your gift list."

"Hi, Charlene, it's Annie."

"Annie! Where've you been?"

"Uh, would you believe me if I said I was abducted by aliens from outer space?"

"Not on your life, and quit kidding around. We've been worried about you."

"Sorry. I know I should've called sooner, but ever since I got here, I . . . I guess I haven't been thinking too clearly."

"Here? Where's here, exactly?"

"Dalton Stoner's house. We're . . . um . . . snowed in."

"No shit?" Charlene's throaty laugh made Annie smile, giving her hope that she wouldn't get fired. "Well, that's a relief. When I didn't hear from you yesterday, I started having all kinds of god-awful pictures in my head of what might have happened to you."

"Like finding my car at the bottom of a ravine in the spring?"

"Yeah," Charlene replied in a thick voice. "I'm glad you're safe." She cleared her throat, then said, "Anyway, when you didn't check in yesterday, I had to give the Mattimore delivery to someone else."

"No problem, I understand. Listen, have you heard any road reports this morning?"

"No, sorry. Dan might have, but he's out making a delivery."

"That's okay. At least it stopped snowing up here, so the road crews should start plowing soon."

"It could still be a day or two before the roads are reopened."

"I know," Annie replied with a sigh. "So, um . . . have you got anything lined up for me?"

"Yeah, a couple."

"Great. Tell me about them." She listened to Charlene's rundown of the deliveries she'd booked, then burst into laughter. "A harem girl, huh? Sounds like fun."

Dalton pushed away from the wall. He hadn't meant to eavesdrop on Annie's conversation, but once he realized who she was talking to, he couldn't make himself move. Hearing her side of the conversation about her upcoming strip-o-gram deliveries made him crazy. Dammit, she wasn't going to strip for anyone else. Not if he had anything to say about it . . . and he sure as hell did.

Except he didn't have any right to voice his opinion about what Annie did. His scowl deepening, he stormed down the hall, not sure who to blame for his annoyance. Annie for her enthusiastic response over the deliveries her boss had lined up. Or himself for his irrational reaction to the mental image of her arriving at someone else's door wearing a skimpy harem girl costume.

* * *

Annie stepped onto the front porch and took a deep breath, filling her lungs with crisp, clean mountain air. Though the temperature was below freezing, the sky was crystal clear, the snow blinding in the late afternoon sunlight. Slipping her sunglasses on, she moved down the steps then looked around.

When she arrived two days ago, the snowstorm had prevented her from seeing anything but a few feet in front of her, and sometimes not even that far. Now everything was visible, snow-covered and sparkling in the sunshine.

Dalton's house was tucked close to the base of a rocky peak in a high mountain valley. Only enough land had been cleared for the house and a small yard, leaving many magnificent ponderosa pines and large boulders in their natural state.

She grabbed the shovel leaning against the porch railing, then headed down the path Dalton had already cleared. When she reached his side, she said, "What a beautiful setting."

He tossed aside another shovelful of snow, then straightened. "Thanks. The first time I came up here, I knew this is where I wanted to build."

"I can see why." She glanced around at the surrounding mountain peaks. "But doesn't the quiet get to you?"

He resumed shoveling. "The quiet is another reason I live up here."

She frowned. "Don't you miss the excitement of living in the city?"

"Nope."

"So you never go out to eat, or see a movie, or go to an Avalanche game?"

"It's too far to drive back to the city at night, and I can't stay in town after work because of my dogs. Once in a while I go into Denver on a weekend to have dinner with one of my sisters, but not often." He stopped working again and turned to face her. "You a hockey fan?"

She grinned. "Yeah, big time."

"Me, too. But I'd rather stay home and watch a game on TV."

"They're more fun in person. Wish I could afford to go more often."

He nodded toward the shovel she held. "You'd better start using that if you want to stay warm out here."

"That's good enough, Annie."

She turned to face Dalton from where she'd been shoveling snow for the past half hour. "Are you sure?" She looked at the sidewalk she'd cleared and the section in front of the garage he'd shoveled. "We didn't get much done."

"The rest is drifted too deep. Besides, as soon as the roads are reopened, the guy who plows my drive will head up here."

"What about behind the house?"

"I took care of that while I had the dogs out earlier. Speaking of dogs." He turned and gave a loud whistle. "Data. Worf. Time to go in."

Annie looked across the yard, seeing one, then both wire-haired dogs, their tongues lolling, bound toward them. She grinned at their obvious enjoyment. "Those guys really love the snow, don't they?"

"Yeah. Too much. They come in sopping wet or caked with balls of snow and ice, then give me a hard time when I try to dry them off."

She nodded, then trudged behind him toward the house. "Whew," she said, stopping at the bottom of the porch steps and handing him her shovel. "That's quite a workout."

He chuckled, propping both shovels against the railing. "Really gets the blood going, doesn't it?"

She started up the steps first, then turned. "Yeah, it . . ." He stood one step below her, which brought his face level with hers. When her gaze met his, the blue fire flaring to life in his eyes sent her pulse into double time. She swallowed hard, then whispered, "It sure does."

Smiling, he lifted one gloved hand to tuck an escaping curl back under the stocking cap he'd insisted she wear. "Let's go in and get warmed up."

Unable to get a word through the tightness in her throat, she bobbed her head then turned and continued up the steps.

As soon as Dalton closed the door behind them, he reached for Annie and pulled her into his arms. "Hmm," he murmured against her mouth. "Your lips are cold."

"Not for long," she replied, grabbing a handful of his jacket and hauling him closer.

He tasted and teased, loving how she opened her mouth to him, loving the way her tongue dueled with his, loving the little purring noise she made.

With a groan, he swung her around, pressed her back to the door, and deepened the kiss. Finally, he wrenched his mouth from hers, reaching for the buttons on her coat. "We need to"—he sucked in a rasping breath—"get you warm so you don't catch cold."

"Got something in mind?"

"Yeah, you're gonna take a hot shower."

She smiled up at him, her eyes sparkling with mischief. "Alone?"

"Not if you don't want to be," he replied with a chuckle.

"Here, let me do that." She pushed his hands away and began working her coat buttons free. When he just stood there watching her, she cocked an eyebrow at him. "Are you planning on taking a shower like that?"

He blinked, then looked down at himself. "Oh yeah, right." Grinning at her, he tugged off his jacket, then bent to remove his boots. "Damn."

"What?"

"I need to dry off Data and Worf."

"Need some help?"

He glanced up from where he was loosening the laces of his boots. "Thanks, but I can handle them. Get the shower going in the master bath, and I'll join you in a couple minutes."

She ran a hand over his shoulder, then started down the hall. "Don't be long."

Even though he wore a heavy flannel shirt over a thermal undershirt, he swore he could feel her fingers touching his skin. He drew a shuddering breath to temper the desire surging through him, then straightened and grabbed the towels he kept in the hall closet. "Okay, you two," he said to his dogs, "let's get this over with."

As if reading his mind, Data and Worf endured getting dried off like perfect gentlemen, not squirming and struggling as they normally did.

He reached his bedroom several minutes later, then started pulling off his clothes and giving them a toss, not caring where they landed. The bathroom door stood ajar, and he heard the shower running.

His heart hammering, he approached the door and eased it open. Expecting to find Annie already in the shower, he frowned at finding her standing in the center of the room, still dressed.

"Darn," he said, suddenly feeling ridiculous wearing only his briefs, "I thought I was gonna find a naked woman waiting for me in here."

Annie turned around, flashing a smile. "Sorry. I went to my room to get this"—she held up a large hair clip—"or I would've been."

He took a step toward her. "Let's see if we can remedy that right now." He lifted an eyebrow, waiting for a protest. When her smile widened, he reached for her sweatshirt and pulled it up and over her head. Then just as quickly, he grabbed the waistband of her sweatpants and gave them a downward tug. She braced a hand on his shoulder while he helped her step out of the pants.

As he straightened, his gaze landed on the curls between her thighs. "Jesus, Annie," he whispered, desire running thick and hot through his body, settling in his groin. "You're not wearing underwear."

"Your powers of observation truly are amazing."

His gaze snapped from her crotch to her face. Fighting not to grin at her sarcasm, he said, "Damn right they are, and I think such amazing talent deserves a reward."

"Really?" She tipped her head to one side, her lower lip caught between her teeth while those gorgeous eyes gave him a thorough once-over. "You got something in mind?"

"No, but I'm sure I'll think of—"

"I already have an idea." She smiled up at him, then stuck her fingers inside the waistband of his briefs. "How about if I"—she started pulling his underwear down in a slow, torturous motion—"offered to wash"—another slow pull and his swollen penis popped free—"your back?" She glanced down. "Or other parts."

The suggestion sent his already scorching need a few degrees hotter. Summoning every bit of self-restraint he possessed not to haul her into his arms, he pushed her hands away, then shoved his briefs to the floor and kicked them aside. "No more teasing. Get in the shower. Now."

Her eyes going wide at his sharply spoken words, she stared up at him while securing her hair atop her head with the hair clip. Apparently satisfied with whatever she'd found in his expression, her mouth twitched. "Yes, sir." She gave him a mock salute, then turned, opened the shower door and stepped inside.

Son of a bitch. He dropped his chin onto his chest and huffed out a breath. What had he done to deserve a smart, sexy-as-hell, give-as-good-as-she-gets woman like Annie Peterson? He didn't know the answer to that, and at the moment, he wasn't the least bit interested in trying to find out. He was, however, interested in finding out a lot of other things. Like the weight and feel of her breasts, the taste of her wet skin, the feel of her naked body pressed against—

"Hey, what are you doing out there?"

Startled back to the present, he looked up to find Annie staring at him through the glass door, her hands on her hips. Chuckling to himself, he moved to the door and stepped in beside her.

"Sorry," he murmured before giving her a quick kiss. "I was just thinking about what I'd like to do to you."

"Mmm, that's what I was doing, too." She ran a hand through his chest hair. "Do you think we should"—her fingers moved lower—"compare notes?"

He shook his head, bringing his hands up to her waist. "I'm guessing we're probably pretty much on the same page. So how about we just wing it for now?"

"Sure." Her fingers closed around his erection, then squeezed.

His breath caught, hands involuntarily tightening on her waist. "Easy, babe."

She immediately released him. "Did I hurt you?"

"Yeah, but in a good way."

Her mouth curved in a slow smile. "Good. Wouldn't want to hurt the merchandise before I get a chance to use it."

"Is that what you're gonna do? Use me?"

"Would that be so bad? Two consenting adults enjoying each other's company for however long we're stuck here together." She leaned forward and pressed a kiss on his chest. "Besides, I suspect you're thinking the same thing about me."

"Maybe," he replied, though the truth was, his thoughts had taken a startlingly similar path that morning. Learning they were more alike than he'd originally thought was a pleasant surprise, yet for some reason, he didn't want to admit the discovery aloud.

"Now what are you thinking?"

He slid his hands up her rib cage. "That I wanted to do this." He cradled her breasts, loving the way the creamy skin felt against his palms. He brushed his thumbs over her peaked nipples. "And this."

Her head fell back, a moan vibrating in her throat. "I'll give you about ten years to quit that."

He laughed. "I was thinking more along the lines of ten minutes, then we'll move this to my bed."

"You sure you don't have some kind of psychic power?" She lifted her head and met his gaze, her eyes sparkling with both humor and growing desire. "'Cause you're reading my mind again."

"Yeah, I'm sure." He moved his hands to her hips

and pulled her against him, his throbbing erection trapped between them.

"Must be that old saying my grandmother likes, something about"—she grabbed the hair at his nape and tugged his face closer—"great minds thinking alike."

Before he could reply, she pressed her mouth to his then pushed her tongue past his lips. Her kiss scorched a trail of red-hot lust all the way down to the soles of his feet. If not for the water pelting them, he was certain he would've gone up in flames.

He grasped her upper arms and gently pulled her away from him. "Whoa, babe," he said in a raspy whisper. "Let's slow this down."

She blinked several times. "What?"

"I said, I think we need to slow down."

"But—"

He pressed a finger to her lips. "I thought you'd stopped with the buts."

She scowled at him. "Dalton, I want us to make love. Now."

He chuckled, loving her bluntness. "Believe me, babe, I want that too. Only, our first time is not going to be in the shower."

"So we are going to make love?"

"Oh yeah."

"Today?"

He raised his right hand. "I swear. As soon as we finish in here."

"Then grab the soap, so we can get this show on the road."

He had to bite his lip to hold back a laugh. Picking up the bar of soap, he said, "Turn around so I can wash your back."

* * *

After Dalton stepped out of the shower and dried off, he wrapped Annie in a thick towel then led her into his bedroom.

He sat down on the edge of the bed, then patted the mattress beside him. Unsure how to word what he wanted to say, he finally decided to take his cue from Annie and be blunt. "There's something I need to say, something I've been thinking about all day."

She gave him a quizzical look. "Okay. What is it?"

"During all the years I've studied the *Kama Sutra*, my interest has always been strictly academic. Until last night. Now, my interest has also become personal, and I want—" He took a deep breath. "I want to explore more of the *Kama Sutra*'s teachings. With you."

Ten

Annie opened her mouth to reply, then snapped her lips closed, needing a moment to gather her thoughts. She wanted Dalton, there was no doubt about that, and she wanted excitement in her life. Though sex with a man she barely knew wasn't the excitement she had been hoping for when she and her friends made their pact. Of course, she'd never figured on meeting a man like Dalton Stoner either. So, unless she'd totally misunderstood him, she'd just been offered a way to have both.

At last, she said, "Are you asking if I want to take part in these explorations, as you called them?"

"Well, yeah. But I'd never pressure you to agree. So, if you're not comfortable with the idea, say the word and I'll drop it."

She studied him in silence for a moment longer, then said, "If I were to agree, what we do won't be hands-on research that will end up as an article in some kind of sex journal, will it?"

His jaw tightened, his eyes turning a stormy gray. "Hell, no! I would never do that. Whatever happens between us, stays between us. You have my word."

"That's what I figured." Hoping to calm his rising temper, she smiled. "I hope you understand why I had to ask." She lifted a hand and ran her fingertips over his mouth then the small cleft in his chin. "Okay then. My answer is yes."

Dalton held her gaze for a few seconds. "You're sure?"

"Absolutely." When he remained silent and un-moving, she said, "So, do we start now, or what?"

His lips curved in a lazy smile. "Mmm, so eager. I think I like that."

She edged closer. "Eager, huh?" Her lips grazed his chin. "I guess you could say I am." She nipped him with her teeth. "But I've always liked learning new things."

"Me, too. And this time, we'll learn together," he replied, getting to his feet, then pulling her up beside him and tugging on the end of the towel tucked be-tween her breasts.

As he worked to free her towel, she released the hair clip then gave her head a shake. "Look who's eager now."

His response was a quirked eyebrow and a low growl. Giving her towel another tug, he grunted with satisfaction then tossed it aside. His towel quickly landed atop hers. Giving her a gentle shove, he said, "Lie down, babe."

She followed his instruction, her gaze raking over him as he settled beside her. "Mmm, this is better," she said, shifting to her side, so they lay face to face.

He smiled, lifting a strand of her hair and curling it around his fingers. "There's something else we need to discuss before we go any further. Protection."

"Yes, of course," she replied. "I'm on the pill so birth control is covered. I haven't . . . um . . . been with any-one since my last GYN appointment, so no STDs."

"Good. Me, too. After my divorce, I got checked every six months just to make sure Maureen didn't leave me with any going away presents."

"She cheated on you?"

"Yeah. As soon as I found out, I never touched her." His mouth tightened. "The truth is, we hadn't been intimate for months before that, so there probably wasn't much chance of her passing something on to me. But I wasn't sure how long she'd been playing around, and considering the other things she was into, I couldn't take that risk. Anyway, my last check-up was a few months ago. My doctor gave me an all clear."

Annie stared at him for a moment, wanting to ask for more details about his ex-wife. But it obviously was a painful subject, not to mention, none of her business. Instead, she said, "Well then, that's settled."

Still rubbing her hair between his thumb and fingers, he nodded, his eyes changing to a deep blue, growing hot with need.

When he remained silent, she shifted restlessly. "So, what are you waiting for?"

A corner of his mouth lifted in amusement. "Actually, we've already started."

"What?" She arched her eyebrows. "But all you're doing is fiddling with my hair."

"Uh-huh. The *Kama Sutra* teaches to take things slowly, to build up the anticipation, that lovemaking should be delayed, not rushed."

"No quickies, huh?"

"Not according to Vatsyayana. So, to follow his teachings, I'm taking my time. Besides, I love your hair."

She wrinkled her nose. "This curly mess? You might not like it if you had to deal with it all the time."

A smile played across his lips. "Probably not, but I still love touching it." He lifted another curl, twirling the end with his fingers. "The ancient Hindus realized that men have always been fascinated with women's hair, and they believed that running his hands through his partner's hair could be a powerful aphrodisiac."

"Interesting. So, is it working?"

He thrust his hips forward, bumping his rock-hard penis against her thigh. "What do you think?"

"Very nice." She smiled, shifting her leg to rub his erection, making it twitch between them. "Though I'd like to think my hair isn't the only thing that caused such impressive results."

"Impressive, hmm?" A low chuckle rumbled in his chest. "Thanks, and you're right. It wasn't just your hair, babe. It's the entire deal. Your beautiful hair. Gorgeous eyes. Sexy mouth. Great legs. Sweet little ass."

"That's all physical stuff."

"Yeah, but guys are visual creatures. We get turned on by what we see."

"So you're saying my charm, wit and captivating personality have nothing to do with your wanting me?"

He chuckled again. "Of course they do. Initially my attraction to you was purely physical, but now that I've gotten to know you better, those other things play a big part in doing this." His flexed his hips again.

Delighted by his comments, a flush warmed her cheeks. Reaching up to trace his upper lip with her fingertips, she said, "I could say the same things about you, ya know. That I'm attracted and turned on by the entire deal."

He cocked an eyebrow. "Don't tell me you think I have a sweet little ass?"

She pretended to consider his question for a second, then laughed. "Okay, so maybe the adjectives aren't right. But you do have a great rear end."

"Thanks, I'm pretty attached it to myself."

"Ha, very funny," she murmured, wiggling close

enough so her lips replaced her fingers on his mouth. "Now, let's get back to the *Kama Sutra*."

"Okay." He untangled his fingers from her hair then tucked the strand over her shoulder. His hand moved lower, skimming over the tip of one breast, down her ribs, then stopped at her belly and reversed direction. "The *Kama Sutra* teaches that there's no correct order to how things should be done in an intimate relationship. Embracing, kissing and touching can be done in any combination to increase the pleasure of both partners."

Skin tingling wherever Dalton touched, she said, "The more I hear about the book, the more I appreciate the writers' wisdom on sex."

"Yeah, and I don't think their wisdom was just conjecture. I think the writers, especially Vatsyayana, had plenty of first-hand knowledge about the topic."

She shifted again, trying to ease the throbbing between her thighs. "So . . . um . . . when do we get to the section about inserting part A into part B?"

His body shook with silent laughter. "The *Kama Sutra* calls part A the *lingam,* and part B"—he slid his hand down to cup her mound—"is the *yoni.*"

"I don't give a damn what they're called. I want our parts together. Now."

While opening her folds with his fingers and deftly finding her clitoris, he pressed a lingering kiss on her mouth. When he lifted his head, he said, "I already told you, we're supposed to be exerting self-control to delay getting our parts together, because the reward will be that much better when we do."

She gave him a mutinous glare. "Yeah, but my self-control has deserted me. Now give it up, Dalton."

This time he laughed out loud. "Why don't you tell me what you really want?"

"Sarcasm won't buy you more time," she replied,

slipping her hand between them and wrapping her fingers around his engorged penis. "Come on, slick. We can drag it out next time, but right now, I can't wait."

"I think that's usually the man's line," he murmured, lazily stroking her with his fingers.

"Yeah, well . . ." A shudder rippled through her. "I can't—" She gulped in a deep breath. "I can't think when you're doing that."

"Then don't. Just feel."

She moaned deep in her throat, arching her back to press her pelvis closer to his magic fingers. "Oh God. Oh God."

"That's it, babe." He leaned closer, pulled her earlobe between his lips and suckled gently. Then as he slowly removed his mouth, he murmured, "I want to do that to another sweet spot." He flicked a finger over her clitoris. "Here. Would you like that?"

Her breath caught in her throat at his words. She fought to pull air into her lungs, barely able to hear over the blood rushing in her ears, totally unable to speak. She moaned again, pushing her hips against his insistent fingers in an escalating rhythm, desperately seeking, needing her release. Then suddenly the pressure intensified, becoming almost unbearable. With a long, low groan, her climax began.

Clutching Dalton's arm, her fingernails digging into his skin, she rode the waves of intense pleasure to their crest as a scream ripped from her throat.

Before her pulse leveled out and before she could gather her thoughts, he rolled her onto her back, shoved her legs farther apart and settled between her thighs.

As he pushed her knees toward her chest, he leaned forward until the head of his penis touched her still throbbing feminine flesh. "Insert part A," he murmured, then flexed his hips and slid inside her, "in part B."

Her throaty laugh ended with a soft gasp. The feel of him filling her to the max sent a new round of intense sensations shooting through her, shocking her with the resulting fresh jolt of need. She wrapped her legs around his hips, allowing him to sink even deeper.

"Ohmygod," she said, not recognizing her own voice. "That's incredible."

Dalton drew a shaky breath, the control he'd managed to maintain for so long quickly disintegrating. "Yeah," he managed to get out. "Perfect."

"No," she replied, lifting her hips from the mattress to get even closer. "Better than perfect."

He clenched his teeth, driven closer to the edge by the squeezing of her inner muscles. Another time he'd welcome the sensation, relishing the tightening of her slick heat around him, allowing himself to enjoy the slow burn of escalating arousal. But not now. His aching dick wasn't going to wait much longer.

Clinging to the last thread of his shredded control, he shifted and ran his tongue over her left nipple, then pulled the beaded peak into his mouth. She bucked beneath him, murmuring something he couldn't make out.

He shifted his mouth to her other breast, then started moving his hips, pushing as deep as possible then nearly withdrawing. Annie met him stroke for stroke, her breathing as ragged as his. Though he wished he could make their first time last a whole lot longer, he knew his climax was only seconds away. Picking up the speed of his thrusts, he released her nipple and sought out her mouth.

"Dalton, help me," she whispered against his lips, her fingers clutching at his shoulders. "Please. I'm so close." She wiggled her hips, trying to find the best angle for the needed friction.

"Easy, babe," he told her, shifting to support his weight on one forearm and sliding his other hand between their bodies. "I'll help you."

He'd barely touched her clitoris when she moaned his name and pushed hard against his hand. As the tremors of her second climax began, the last of his self-restraint snapped with a speed that shocked him.

With her scream of pleasure echoing in his head, he thrust hard and fast, finally allowing his body the relief it craved. Burying his face in Annie's neck, his lips pressed to her warm, silky skin, he came in one hot, throbbing spurt after another, leaving him weak, sated, and stunned.

Several minutes passed before he could summon the strength to move. Somehow he managed to roll off Annie, flopping onto his back beside her.

"Are you okay?" she said, running her fingers up his arm in a gentle caress.

He wiped a hand over his face, uncertain how to answer that. What just happened was far beyond his experience. He'd never experienced anything even approaching what he and Annie had shared. He'd never been left feeling so complete, or so confused. Damn, what the hell was happening to him?

Not wanting to explore the possible answers to that question, he answered Annie's instead. "Yeah, I think I'll live." He turned his head to meet her gaze, then winked. "So much for self-control, huh?"

She smiled. "You did get kinda wild there for a minute."

"Minute, hell. More like twenty seconds."

"You're not having performance anxiety, are you? Because you'll get no complaints from me." She gave a shaky laugh. "I've never had multiple orgasms in my life."

"Yeah?" He lifted his eyebrows. "That surprises me. Your little man in the boat is so—"

"My what?"

"Clitoris. You've never heard it called that?"

Her brow wrinkled. "No. A lot of other names, but not that one." She chuckled. "Guess it is kind of appropriate."

He grinned. "Anyway, as I started to say. You're so responsive that I figured your coming more than once was the norm for you."

"Nope."

"Then I'm glad I was the one to initiate you."

"Me, too." She returned his grin. "Either you're incredibly talented or the other men I've been with were totally incompetent."

"Well, I don't want to brag," he replied, purposely keeping his voice light. "But, it's me, of course."

Her smile disappearing, she stared at him through troubled eyes for several seconds. Finally she said, "I think so, too."

Still reeling from his own confused emotions, he had enough to deal with and didn't want to probe into the reason for her change in mood.

Annie sat staring at the rapidly falling darkness through the windows in Dalton's living room. After what had happened earlier that afternoon, he'd gone off to his office, leaving her to fill the time in whatever way she could.

She'd tried reading, but couldn't concentrate. Tried watching TV, but turned off the set a few minutes later, unable to find a program that held her interest long enough to take her mind off what had taken place in his bedroom.

Not only had she had the most memorable sexual experience of her life—one her mind insisted on replaying time after time—but in the hours since, she'd also made a disturbing discovery. She now knew she wasn't obsessed with sex; she was obsessed with Dalton Stoner. In fact, her obsession was dangerously close to changing into love.

With a groan, she dropped her head against the back of the chair. *This can't be happening.* Somehow she had to prevent her heart from getting involved. Because falling for the man would be a huge mistake. Dalton was all wrong for her. He led a boring life, a real house plant who preferred staying cooped up at home rather than enjoying an active social life. He liked the quiet seclusion of the mountains rather than the pulsing excitement of a big city.

She sighed, realizing that to be fair she had to acknowledge his good points. He was intelligent, fun to be around, and his love for his dogs told her he had a kind, gentle heart. Then there was his fascination with erotic art and the *Kama Sutra.* Though that revelation had come as a total surprise, she had to admit his unusual interests definitely fell on the positive side of the equation. Plus the man was an incredible lover. Or maybe his skill was a direct result of their unique chemistry, something only the two of them could create.

She squeezed her eyes closed. *Oh, God, what a mess. All I wanted was a little excitement in my life and look what happens? I end up in a sexual relationship with a man who's the opposite of what I'm looking for. And worse, I may be falling in love with him.*

Not wanting to continue thinking about how her decision to spice things up could turn around and bite her in the ass, she shifted her thoughts to other topics. When the roads might reopen. Her family and whether she'd see them on Christmas. Her job with the messenger service and the deliveries Charlene had booked for her. Her friends' holiday jobs, and whether they'd succeeded in finding the excitement the three of them had made a pact to experience over their Christmas break. Even if they had, she doubted it came even close to what she'd stumbled onto with Dalton.

She bit back a groan. No matter what she tried to think about, her mind persisted in sneaking that man back into her thoughts.

The ringing of Dalton's phone pulled him from musings about Annie. For the past several hours he'd tried to get some work done, but he couldn't concentrate for shit, his mind constantly bombarded with memories of Annie. The scent of her heated skin. The sexy sounds she made. The look on her face when he'd slid inside her. The way her body tightened just before her climax began. Damn, he was hard just thinking about her.

He waited for the tug of desire to cool before answering the phone after the fourth ring. "Stoner."

"Well, damn, you are there. I was beginning to think your assistant musta been pulling my leg about you being snowed in."

Dalton leaned back in his chair, grinning at hearing the voice of Jackson Kidd. "Jack, you sorry son of a bitch, how the hell are you?"

"Tired of this latest tour of showings, but otherwise I can't complain."

"Rough schedule, huh?"

"Yeah, but it's winding down. Only a couple more stops. Then the finale in LA on January second."

"LA, huh? Any chance you can work in stopping at Denver on your way to the West Coast?"

"Man, you must've read my mind," Jackson replied with a laugh. "That's the reason I called, to ask if I could hide out with you for a day, maybe two if I can swing it."

"You know you don't have to ask," Dalton replied. "Though your choice of words has me wondering if you're running from something. Or maybe someone."

Jackson laughed again. "Nothing that dramatic. I just need a break from all the PR bullshit, and thought I could combine some down time with a visit to an old friend."

"You're welcome here any time, you know that."

"Yeah, but I wasn't sure you'd want another houseguest so soon."

"You know about Annie?"

"Not by name. Your assistant mentioned you had a houseguest because of the snowstorm. But I didn't know your guest was female." He paused, then said, "So tell me, is she a hot chick?"

Dalton scowled, his temper doing a slow burn. "What the hell kind of question is that?"

"Whoa, man, what's with you? I ask a simple question and you snap at me like I asked if you're sleep—" Jackson's pause ended with a low chuckle. "Shit. That's it, isn't it? You're gettin' in her pants. I can't believe you're finally using your pecker for something besides taking a piss."

"Jesus, Jack." He sighed. "Now you sound like my mother."

"Dolly Stoner would actually use the word pecker around her son?"

Dalton's annoyance fled at the shock he heard in his friend's voice. "You don't know the half of it. I'm sure my mother knows more euphemisms for penis than I'll ever know, so pecker's pretty mild for her."

"No kidding. Well, that's better than growing up in a house where your parents wouldn't say shit if they had a mouthful."

"I don't know. There were plenty of times when I wished my parents, especially Mom, were more like the parents of my friends."

"I guess everyone has something about their childhood they wish had been different. Now, to get back to what started this conversation, what's the deal with Annie?"

Dalton sighed, knowing there was no point in denying anything. From the first time they met, Jackson had been able to read him with incredible accuracy. And if his friend sensed he was holding something back, Jack would keep badgering him until he finally coughed up the truth. Figuring he might as well get it over with, he said, "She came up here to make a delivery last Saturday, got caught in the snowstorm, and has been here since. And before you ask again, yeah, we've made love."

A moment of silence followed his statement, then Jackson said, "Uh-oh."

"What does that mean?"

"Don't you realize what you just said?"

"Yeah, you asked about Annie, and I told you."

"You said love, man. You said you and Annie made love."

"Yeah, so?"

Jackson didn't respond for several seconds. "Listen, it's none of my business, so forget I said anything. Now, about my visit. I'm gonna try to rearrange my schedule so I can get to Denver on the thirtieth, but it might not be until the thirty-first. And I'll probably have to fly out on the first. The gallery owner in LA is trying to line up some charity dinner thing that night." He exhaled heavily. "I wish I could stay longer, but looks like that's the best I can do. I'll get back to you once I finalize my plans."

Dalton blinked, forcing his thoughts away from Annie. "Uh . . . sure. No problem. And a short visit is better than none. So, let me know when you're arriving and I'll pick you up at the airport."

"Thanks, but I was figuring on renting a car. I'll drop by the gallery as soon as I get in. I have a new sculpture I just might let you keep for a while."

"Great. Can't wait to see it. Your other pieces have been one of High Country's most popular attractions." He paused for a moment, then added, "Listen, is there any chance I can talk you into doing an appearance while you're here?"

"If anyone else asked, I'd tell 'em to fuck off. But since it's you, I'd be happy to . . . provided you keep it small and brief."

"You got it. Short guest list and no more than a couple hours. Since you're not sure you can get here on the thirtieth, how about New Year's Eve, say from six to eight? The people I'll invite will have plans for later, but they won't pass up the opportunity to put in an appearance. Everyone will be obligated to leave early and you won't be committed to a long, boring evening of pressing flesh and making nice to the guests."

He grunted. "I should have you planning all my appearances."

After Dalton covered the rest of the details for his friend's mini-showing at the gallery, he sat back in his chair, mulling over their conversation.

What had Jackson been hinting at after finding out he and Annie had made lo— Dammit, so that was it! Now that he thought about what he'd said, he did wonder at his choice of words to describe his relationship with Annie. And since Jack had picked up on it immediately, obviously his friend wondered as well.

As the one person who knew more about the hell of his first marriage than anyone else, Jack should also know that his getting involved in a serious relationship was the last thing he wanted to do.

Even though he knew all of that to be true, Dalton couldn't stop thinking about why he hadn't said he was screwing Annie, or something equally crude. He hadn't been talking to his sisters or another female where he felt the need to clean up his response. So what other reason could there be? The answer that popped into his head wasn't one he wanted to hear. Falling in love with Annie Peterson wasn't acceptable.

But acceptable or not, the uncomfortable niggling in the back of his mind told him he might've already started to fall.

Eleven

"Eight ball. Corner pocket," Annie said, nodding toward the pool table's far left corner.

Dalton watched her line up the shot, then stroke the cue just as he'd taught her, sending the eight ball into the pocket she'd called. She was getting much too good at this, he mused. She'd already beaten him on their two previous games, so that last shot made it a clean sweep. Of course, his own game had been hampered by his lack of concentration. After his conversation with Jackson Kidd and the resulting examination of his emotional state, he'd been zoning out with more frequency than he wanted to admit.

All through supper and while they'd cleaned up the kitchen, Annie filled his thoughts no matter how hard he tried to keep her out. And even when they played pool, he hadn't been able to keep thoughts of her at bay. Playing pool had always been his escape from the demands in his life, a great way to relax, clear his head, and not have to think about anything other than sinking his next shot. He'd always been able to do just that, tuning out everything else while he played. But not tonight.

He started toward the cue rack. "That's enough for tonight."

"Don't like getting your ass whipped by a woman, huh?"

He heard the laughter in her voice but could manage only a weak smile in response.

As she helped him cover the table, she said, "I was only teasing. I know I didn't really win those games fair and square."

"Are you accusing me of purposely playing like shit so you could win?"

"Of course not. I know you wouldn't do that." She gave him a thoughtful glance. "I've watched you play enough to tell you were really off your game tonight."

He shrugged. "Everyone's entitled to an off night."

She stared at him a moment longer, then finally nodded. "Well, next time I'm sure you'll get even by kicking my ass."

For reasons that totally eluded him, having her mention her perfect tush sent a wave of lust rushing over him, his blood pooling hot and heavy in his groin. "Dammit to hell."

Her brow wrinkled with concern, she took a step closer. "What is it?"

When he didn't answer, she moved even closer. "Dalton, what's wrong?"

Irritated by his lack of control, he grabbed her hand and placed it over the fly of his jeans. "That's what's wrong. You're driving me crazy. Looking at your ass every time you bend over to make a shot. Remembering the touch of your skin when we were in the shower, the taste of your mouth, the way you scream when you—"

"Shh," she whispered, the fingers of her other hand pressed to his lips. "I understand. I can't stop thinking about it either." As she removed her fingers from his mouth, she leaned closer then rose onto her toes and gave him a quick kiss. "I have an idea."

"What?"

"I was looking at one of your books on the *Kama*

Sutra earlier, and I thought we should try a few things."

His dick flexed beneath her hand. "Yeah?"

"Yeah. Are you—" She gave a throaty laugh that kicked his pulse rate even higher. "I was going to ask if you're ready, but"—she squeezed his erection—"it's obvious you are. So I'll rephrase. Do you want to try them?"

He bit back the urge to shout, "Hot damn, do I ever!" Instead, he cleared his throat then flashed a crooked smile. "Does a bear shit in the woods?"

Annie laughed again, a warm bewitching sound he realized, with a jolt of surprise, he'd never tire of hearing.

"I'm pretty sure that was a yes," she said, nipping his chin with her teeth. As she eased away from him, her hand remained on his fly. "I hope you mean now, because I'd sure hate to waste"—she gave him another squeeze—"this."

This time he laughed. "You're a real smart-mouth, you know that?"

"Probably, but I'm also"—she looked at him through partially lowered lashes—"horny." She dropped her voice to a silky whisper and added, "Real horny."

"Jesus, Annie." His mouth went bone dry, his heart pounding even harder. "More talk like that and I may do what I've thought about doing since the first time we played pool and I had to endure the torture of watching you bend over to line up your shots."

"Really?" Her eyebrows arched, she glanced at the pool table. "Hmm, I wonder what . . ." She brought her gaze back to meet his, her eyes wide and glittering, lips curved in a big smile. "Playing pool in the buff?"

A burst of choked laughter erupted from his throat. "Not exactly, but that isn't a half-bad idea." He lifted a hand to brush several soft curls off her cheek. "We'll have to try that sometime."

"As long as you wouldn't be concerned about winning, 'cause I'm pretty sure naked pool would be very distracting."

"Oh, I'd win all right. One way or another."

Her lips twitched. "Yeah, I see your point. We'd both be winners."

A low chuckle vibrating in his chest, he bent and took her mouth in a slow, gentle kiss that quickly escalated into a hot, wild melding of their lips.

When he lifted his head, he heard the harshness of their mingled breathing, noted the flush of her cheeks and the throbbing of her pulse at the base of her throat.

"I think we should move this to my bedroom."

She started at the sound of his voice. Then after a moment, her eyelids fluttered open, allowing him to see the heat of desire smoldering in those gorgeous green eyes. Her tongue slid over her lower lip, her breasts rose with a deep breath, then she whispered, "Yes."

As they headed for Dalton's bedroom, Annie struggled to pull herself together, trying to keep her desire for the man walking beside her from bubbling over.

She'd never considered herself a cold fish when it came to sex, but she also never thought of herself as, nor had any of the men she'd been with given any indication they thought of her as, an extremely passionate woman. Yet, since meeting Dalton she'd discovered desires she hadn't known she possessed, and reacted in ways she never could've imagined. With only the slightest provocation from him, something as simple as a look or a touch, her blood immediately hummed with need and her body ached with intense arousal, a reaction she found almost as frightening as it was exciting.

That strange mix of emotions made her uneasy. She'd already acknowledged her growing feelings for Dalton. Just as she'd also acknowledged there could be no future for the two of them. So getting more deeply involved was a really bad idea—especially if she ended up falling in love with him. But in spite of all her inner warnings and the possible consequences of her actions, she couldn't make herself stop what was about to happen.

Drawing a steadying breath, she followed him into the bedroom, stopping at the foot of the bed.

"What's this?" He picked up a book lying on his nightstand. After reading the title, he smiled. "Is this the book you were talking about?"

"Uh-huh." She moved to stand beside him, then lifted her chin and met his amused gaze. "I brought it in here earlier."

"Planning ahead, I see."

Though the heat of a blush crept across her cheeks, she didn't look away from him. "I'm a teacher, remember, so it's in my nature to develop a lesson plan."

"So you're going to be teaching this class we're about to have?"

She gave him a gentle punch to the arm. "No, silly. My plan is for us to learn together."

"Hmm"—he leaned closer—"I like the sound of that." His lips brushed over hers in a soft kiss. "So what's today's lesson?"

For a moment she thought her heart might leap from her chest. Exhaling slowly, she took the book from him and flipped to the page she'd marked. "This." She held the opened book toward him.

"Side-by-side clasping position," he read aloud, then lifted his gaze to meet hers. Blue-gray eyes smoky with desire, his nostrils flared. "Excellent choice." He lowered his face to hers again. "For starters," he whispered, then ran his tongue over her lower lip.

For starters. Oh God! Her earlier inner warnings forgotten, she gulped in a deep breath, her fingers curling into her palms to keep herself from reaching for him and ripping off his clothes. Combating the lust-filled haze his words had spawned took all her concentration.

When the fog cleared enough for her to speak, she said, "What a sweet-talker you are. Knowing just the right thing to say to get my engine going."

"Oh yeah?" A smile played over his lips. "Can I look under the hood?"

She chuckled, giving his arm a playful swat. "Now, who's a smart-mouth?"

"Guilty," he replied, placing the book on the nightstand then reaching for her. "Time to start our lesson, babe."

"Yes," was all she could get out through the tightness in her throat.

She reached for the hem of her sweatshirt. "Are we . . . um . . . starting now?"

He chuckled. "Is that desperation I hear in your voice?"

She released her sweatshirt, shooting him an annoyed glare. "Don't you wish." She folded her arms across her chest. "I just wanted to"—she huffed out a breath—"oh, all right. So I'm desperate, what's the big deal?"

He pulled his shirt out of his jeans, then paused when he started to free the buttons. "Need some help, babe?"

"No . . . uh . . . I can do it."

This time when she grabbed the hem of her sweatshirt her hands shook, her blood humming with anticipation.

Neither spoke while they tugged and shoved at their clothes, though a few grunts and muttered curses accompanied their efforts. When the final piece had been tossed aside, she turned to face him.

"Mmm, that's better." Her gaze raked down his body in a quick, appreciative glance. "Yum."

He grinned, tracing a finger over her collar bone, then lowering his hand to cup one breast. "You're pretty yummy yourself," he murmured, brushing his thumb over her nipple.

"Enough chit-chat," she said, gritting her teeth against the pleasure dancing over her skin. There'd be plenty of time for more of his exquisite ministrations soon enough. "Let's move on to the good stuff."

"There's that impatience again." He shook his head, choking back a laugh. "You've really got to learn to—" He landed on the bed with a soft grunt, then blinked with surprise. "Hey, no need to get pushy. If you wanted me to lie down, you should have said so."

"What I want, slick, is for you to stop talking and kiss me."

His lips quirked in a fleeting smile, then he reached up to hook a hand behind her neck. As he pulled her down atop him, he said, "You got it, babe. One kiss coming up."

And wow, what a kiss it was, sending her senses spiraling out of control.

She lay sprawled across his chest, her tongue dueling with his, her fingers kneading his shoulders and upper arms. Shifting the position, she wedged a hand between them, wanting to touch more of him. Her fingers pushed through the thick mat of his chest hair, moved over his ribs and flat stomach, then stopped on the warm, taut skin of his hipbone. "I want you, Dalton."

A low hum rumbled in his throat. "And you'll have me, Annie. Soon."

"Promise? Because I—"

"Shh, we're not supposed to rush, remember?" He brought her wandering hand up to his mouth and kissed her fingertips. "One of the things I've learned from the *Kama Sutra* is that couples today don't take enough time on the preliminaries. Lovemaking isn't just the sex act itself. It's about the intimacy of touching and kissing, and using those things to become better attuned to each other. To increase the anticipation and the ultimate pleasure for both of them."

She sighed. "That sounds great. In theory. But in reality, it sucks."

The bed shook with his silent laughter. "Once again, impatience rears its ugly head."

"And once again, your attempt at humor is really lame."

Laughing aloud this time, he rolled them so they lay on their sides facing each other. "Never claimed to be a comedian, babe," he said, stroking his palm up one thigh and over her hip. Splaying his hand on her bottom, he pulled her closer. "But, tell me something, does this"—he flexed his hips forward, bringing his hard erection flush against her belly—"feel lame to you?"

"Smart ass." She gave his shoulder a gentle nip with her teeth, then immediately soothed the spot with a swipe of her tongue. His penis twitched between their bodies. "Does that mean you like having me bite you?"

"Actually, I was thinking about what I'd rather have you do with your tongue."

She levered her upper body away from him so she

could see into his eyes. "Yeah? I've got some ideas of my own about that. Should we compare notes?"

"No way." Dalton grinned up at her, then winked. "I'd rather be surprised."

Her head fell back, her chuckle quickly changing to a full-fledged laugh. The sexy, throaty sound wrapped around his heart and squeezed, momentarily halting his ability to breathe. Refusing to speculate on the possible meaning behind his unsettling reaction, he forced himself to concentrate on the moment.

"Back to our lesson," he murmured, bending to kiss the side of her neck. His mouth still pressed against her skin, he inhaled deeply, filling his head and lungs with the scent of warm, aroused female. Slightly woozy, he ran his palm up her spine, reveling in the smoothness of her skin and the silkiness of her hair tickling the back of his hand.

She groaned, arching toward him.

With slow, thorough precision, he explored the dips and curves of her body. Shoulders, back, bottom and thigh—everywhere he could reach without changing their positions—memorizing the shape and texture of each place he touched. She grew restless under his tactile assault, her breathing becoming more labored.

When he finally slid his hand between her legs, he heard her sob his name, her hips rocking against his probing fingers.

"Easy, babe. Just relax and let me touch you here."

She stopped moving, though not all of the tenseness left her body.

He brushed the curls of her pubic hair several times, then slipped lower and found her hot and wet. His blood roaring in his ears, he pushed a finger inside her. He heard a groan but wasn't certain which of them had made the sound. As he began stroking her, her inner muscles clenched around his finger, her hips quickly catching the rhythm.

Immediately, he stopped. "Uh-uh." He kissed the underside of her jaw. "Not yet."

"Dalton." His name came out as a plea. "You're torturing me."

"It'll be worth it," he murmured. "Promise." Not allowing her to reply, he took her mouth in a blistering kiss, his tongue mimicking the resuming movements of his finger in her heated core.

Apparently unwilling to be the only one suffering, she began some exploring of her own. Her hand moved up his arm, her fingers curled around his biceps for a moment before continuing onto his shoulder then began a slow descent down the length of his back, making his skin tingle in the wake of her touch. She gave his ass a quick squeeze, then trailed her fingers down the side of his hip. Abruptly, her hand slid over his thigh and between his legs. When she cupped his balls, he jerked in surprise. How she'd managed to maneuver around his arm and insinuate her hand between them without his being the wiser he hadn't a clue. But she sure as hell was there now.

He yanked his mouth from hers, struggling to catch his breath. "Jesus, Annie, watch those sneak attacks. Grabbing a man like that when your tongue is in his mouth is a good way to get yourself bit."

She stared at him with wide eyes, her lower lip caught between her teeth. Instead of being contrite at her boldness, she laughed, damn the little tease.

He glared at her, then before he realized what was happening, his shock switched to amusement and his own laughter joined hers. He couldn't remember ever having so much fun during the preliminaries to sex. Of course, he'd never known anyone like Annie either— a direct correlation he had no trouble recognizing.

And he was smart enough to realize there was more between them than great sex. She intrigued him like no woman ever had, challenged him at every turn, made him laugh—even at what seemed to be the most unlikely of times—and most disturbing, had him thinking about things he had no business considering.

As he'd reminded himself a few hours earlier, loving her was not an option. Her apparent propensity to seek excitement made her exactly the type of woman he didn't want in his life. He'd just have to work harder at keeping that thought in the forefront of this mind.

Of course, she knew nothing of the battle raging inside him, and he had no plans to tell her. As he repeatedly had to tell himself, she was a temporary fixture in his life. Like the old saying about ships passing in the night, they would have their brief time together, then each would continue on their own path.

A pang of regret tried to take hold in his chest, but he resolutely pushed it away. Determined to forget all of that and concentrate totally on the moment, he lowered his head and nuzzled the side of her neck.

"While you're down there, babe"—he shifted his hips slightly away from her—"how 'bout giving the one-eyed monster a little attention?"

She went still for a moment, then gave a hoot of laughter. "Sure," she said in a choked voice. Releasing his balls, she curled her fingers around the base of his penis, then began moving her hand up and down in a slow stroking motion. "Like this?"

"Tighter." When she immediately gripped him more firmly, he clenched his teeth. The pressure and rhythm of her hot little hand were perfect, intensifying his need, sending him closer to the edge. Fighting against the staggering urge to let her get him off, he drew a shuddering breath. "Enough."

Thankfully, she must've heard the desperation in his voice, because her hand stilled, her grip relaxing.

He needed a minute to get himself back in control, then he said, "We . . . uh . . . kinda got off-track. We're supposed to be trying the side-by-side clasping position."

"That's your fault." Narrowing those beautiful eyes, she pulled her mouth into a frown. "You distracted me with wanting your one-eyed monster to get—"

"Okay, my bad. Now, are you ready to get back to our original plan?"

"Sure."

More slowly than he would've liked, she removed her hand, the final brush of her fingers over the head of his dick causing an involuntary thrusting of his hips.

"Oops, sorry," she said.

He searched her face, looking for a sign to confirm that her actions were accidental. Was that humor he saw lurking in those amazing green eyes? Had she purposely taunted him with that last touch? He suspected she had, but couldn't be certain, so he decided not to pursue the issue.

Shifting slightly, he guided his penis between her legs, probing for entrance. She was slick and hot, so ready for him.

As he pushed into her, she tried to spread her legs, to take more of him inside.

"No, babe. Stay still. This position doesn't allow more than minimal penetration. The full body contact is meant to create strong feelings of intimacy between the couple. And kissing and caressing each other's face is supposed to intensify those sensations."

"Damn," she muttered, "Bad choice."

He chuckled. "Not at all. Remember, the *Kama Sutra* teaches to draw out lovemaking, to delay full penetration as long as possible."

Her breath came out in a huff. "Yeah, yeah. I got

that." She lifted a hand to the nape of his neck and pulled his head down to hers. "Now hush up and kiss me," she whispered against his mouth.

The beginnings of another chuckle ended with his groan. Returning her ardor with his own blistering lust, he deepened the kiss. As his lips and tongue worked their magic on her mouth, his hands cupped her bottom, his hips moving in a series of shallow thrusts.

She moaned. "Mmm, this is better than I thought it would be," she murmured between kisses.

He felt a shudder ripple through her. "Yeah," was the only answer he could make. Though he longed to push her onto her back, spread her legs wide and shove into her as far as he could, the friction created by their current position really was extremely stimulating.

The *Kama Sutra* had it right: the feeling of intimacy was incredible, his senses aroused, his body aching with anticipation.

She abruptly pulled her mouth from his. "Dalton." Her voice was breathless, strained. "I need to come."

His own desire spiked at her words, but he held it in check. "Go for it, babe."

"I don't think I can." She wiggled her hips. "Not like this."

"Yes, you can," he whispered, tightening his hold on her bottom, keeping her pressed against him. "Just imagine I'm touching you. My fingers rubbing your clit, making it swell even more."

She closed her eyes, let her head fall back. A low moan vibrated in her throat.

"You're thinking about it, aren't you? How good it feels when I touch you. How much you want to come."

She moaned again, her fingers digging into his upper arms.

He kissed the underside of her jaw, then ran the tip of his tongue up the side of her neck. "Tell me, Annie."

Twelve

Annie gulped in a deep breath. "I can't do this."

"Yes you can," Dalton replied. "Let your mind take over, babe. Concentrate on thinking about me touching you." He waited several seconds, then added, "You are, aren't you?"

She bobbed her head.

"Good girl," he whispered, pressing a kiss to her neck, then her jaw, and finally her ear. "Now I want you to think about me doing this"—he pulled her earlobe into his mouth and gently suckled—"between your legs."

She gasped, her hips bucking hard against him.

He laughed softly, flicking the flesh of her earlobe with his tongue. "Yeah, I know. Thinking about going down on you is taking me pretty close to the edge, too." His lips tugged on her earlobe again. "I can't wait to make you come that way."

"Oh God, oh God," she sobbed. Her breathing ragged, fingernails digging into his arm and head falling back, she started moving against him faster, more fiercely.

"That's it, babe. Now imagine me tasting you, licking you."

She gasped again, her fingers biting deeper into his arm.

"Imagine me working your clit with my tongue. Sucking the hard nub. Taking you over the—"

She screamed his name, arching hard against him, her body convulsing with the spasms of her climax.

When she finally stilled, he pressed his face into her hair. "Annie, you're unbelievable," he murmured, somehow tamping down the urge to reach his own release.

Her head jerked back and forth. "Uh-uh," she said, her voice husky and breathless. "You. You're the one who's unbelievable."

He lifted his head, then brushed several curls off her damp face. "Thanks, but you're just being modest. You're the one who got her gun off so eas—"

She pressed her fingers to his lips. "Dalton, I've never, ever climaxed without . . . um . . . physical stimulation." She released a long sigh. "I can't believe you actually talked me into orgasm."

He chuckled. "I've always heard the brain is a really powerful sex organ. Guess we just proved that theory right, huh?"

Annie stared into his eyes for moment, then said, "Yeah, we did." She started to say something else, decided this wasn't the time and swallowed the words.

Instead she wiggled her hips, sending post-orgasmic shockwaves of sensation zinging through her. "Can we get back to our lesson, or have we totally blown that out of the water?"

"Actually, I think we've completed the lesson. Now we know the *Kama Sutra* was right about this position being stimulating. And it definitely does increase the anticipation. But it's time to switch to a new one."

He rolled onto his back, pulling her with him so she lay on top of him. "How about this?"

"Nope," she replied, shifting until she sat astride his hips, the change allowing his erection to slide fully inside her. She shifted again, pushing him even deeper. "Mmm, that's better." She tightened her inner muscles, giving him a firm squeeze. "Don't you agree?"

"Jesus, Annie." His hips lifted of their own accord. "You could drive a man crazy doing that."

"Not crazy," she whispered, smiling down at him. "I want to drive you to come."

His breath whooshed out of him with a half-laugh. "Believe me, it's not going to take much."

As her smile broadened, she flexed her inner muscles again.

"Devil," he murmured through clenched teeth. Gripping her waist, he dug his heels into the bed, then began thrusting into her.

She matched the rhythm he set, bracing her hands on the bed, her gaze locked on his face. As he strained toward his climax, she watched his jaw tighten, his nostrils flare, his eyes go cloudy before his eyelids drifted shut.

True to his claim. He didn't need much to bring him to the brink of orgasm. A few more thrusts and he sailed over with a deep guttural groan.

The beat of the music throbbed in his living room, the volume cranked up high. Dalton looked over at Annie, wondering how the hell he'd let her talk him into this. He'd never done much dancing, especially the line-dancing she liked, and the idea of having her witness his first attempt wasn't a pleasant thought. God, what if he stunk? He'd tried to make excuses, yet somehow, she'd managed to sweet-talk him into agreeing to join her morning dancing-for-exercise gig.

His gaze raking over her face, he wondered how she could look so rested. After a night spent making love four—no wait, make that five times—she was wide awake, brimming with energy, and he could barely keep his eyes open, was barely able to walk upright. Stifling a yawn, he tried to pay attention to what she was telling him.

"The steps are easy. Watch me." Her feet moved in what looked to be a fairly simple pattern.

After repeating the steps several times, she stopped, then tossed a bright smile in his direction. "Okay, you try."

Not seeing a way out of this, he took another fortifying gulp of coffee, then set down his cup. "Don't you dare laugh," he said, pointing a finger at her.

Her eyes went wide in a "who, me?" look, then she motioned for him to begin.

Surprisingly, the steps proved to be as easy as she'd claimed. He faltered a couple of times, but nothing serious enough to make him look like a total dufus. At least he hoped not.

"I don't know what you were worried about," she said, moving to the entertainment center. "You're great. Natural sense of rhythm. Very light on your feet."

"Yeah, right," he muttered under his breath, but he couldn't stop the sudden burst of warmth her praise created.

"Let me start the song over and we'll do it together."

He grinned at her back. "We'll do it together all right," he said, then when she swung around to face him, her eyebrows pulled together in a frown, he added, "Oh, you meant dance?"

She lunged toward him, giving his arm a gentle punch. "Is sex all you think about?"

"I never used to," he replied, immediately chastising himself for not coming up with a clever retort. Before he blurted out more truths, revealing things he had no business sharing, he clamped his mouth shut.

Annie stared up at him, wondering what had brought about the odd expression on his face. "Is something wrong?"

"No. Are we gonna dance, or not?"

She blinked at the curtness of his words. Swallowing the urge to press the issue, she nodded. "Sure."

The music did its usual magic, pulling her into the joy of dancing. Though her muscles initially protested, sore from the vigorous workout she'd received during the course of the night, the tightness quickly faded. Who would've thought sex could be such great exercise? Or such a great motivator. She couldn't remember ever getting so little sleep yet waking up feeling so energized.

If this was what being in love felt like— No, she warned herself, don't go there! This is about sex, nothing deeper. But even as she thought the words, tried to convince herself they were true, she already knew they weren't.

Determined to get her thoughts away from such dangerous ground, she forced herself to concentrate solely on the music. "I'm gonna do a new step," she said. "Watch me, then you try it."

A moment later, she watched Dalton imitate what she'd demonstrated, feeling her pulse spike at the rotating movement of his hips. *Oh God, why did I have to pick that move!*

"What do you think, teacher?" he said. "Am I doing it right?"

"I'd say you've got it down pat," a voice said from the doorway.

Annie gasped, and Dalton stumbled to a halt, then they turned in unison to face the hall.

A woman, probably in her mid fifties by Annie's estimation, stood in the doorway. Her dark hair, heavily sprinkled with silver, was cut in a short, classic style that flattered her oval face, and her eyes appeared to be blue, though Annie couldn't be sure of their color from so far away. She wore a red parka over a pair of jeans, and large gold hoops swung from her ears.

"Mom!" Dalton said. "What are you doing here?"

The woman smiled, her gaze skipping over Annie before returning to her son. "As I recall, you invited me."

He groaned, wiping a hand over his face. "Uh . . . yeah, I did." His eyes went wide. "Damn, I was supposed to pick you up at the airport."

"No, you weren't." A husky chuckle accompanied the woman's statement. "I told you I was going to rent a car this time, remember?"

"Oh, right. Obviously the roads have been reopened, but how'd you get in the driveway?"

"The roads still need some work, but yes, they're open. As for your drive, the man who does your plowing was just leaving when I pulled in. I had no idea how bad it was up here."

"I should've called you, but I . . . um . . . totally forgot you were coming."

She smiled, her gaze flickering briefly to Annie. "Yes, I imagine you did. But don't worry about it. I would've come anyway."

"Nothing will stop Dolly Stoner, right?" he said, returning her smile.

"Damn straight."

He chuckled, then remembering he hadn't heard his dogs, he said, "Where're Data and Worf?" He glanced around the room, then craned his neck to look into the hall. "I didn't hear them bark when you came in."

"I didn't realize you were home, so I came through the garage. They barked a couple of times, but I suppose you had the music turned up too loud to hear them. Anyway, once they saw it was me, they were too busy sniffing my pockets to bark."

"What'd you bring 'em this time?"

"Just a couple of biscuits from that gourmet pet store down the street from me."

"I should have known," he said with a shake of his head.

"Well, until you or one of your sisters gives me grandbabies, I have to settle for spoiling your dogs."

He sighed. "Don't start, Mom."

"I'm not starting anything," she replied, "Just stating the facts." She took a step into the room, glanced briefly in Annie's direction then back to him, eyebrows arched in question.

"Oh, yeah. Sorry. Mom," he said, taking Annie's arm and pulling her forward, "this is Annie Peterson." He looked down at Annie. "This is my mother, Dolly Stoner."

Annie took the woman's extended hand, seeing now that her eyes were blue-gray, though a shade or two paler than her son's. "Nice to meet you, Mrs. Stoner."

"Call me Dolly. Or D.J. And it's nice to meet you as well." She angled her chin toward Dalton. "So what were you teaching my son?"

After she explained about dancing for exercise, Dolly said, "Great idea. In fact, I should try it. It's hard finding a way to squeeze in some exercise when I'm on a tour. But I could dance in my hotel room."

"On tour?"

"A book signing tour," Dalton said. "Mom's a writer."

"Writer?" Her brow furrowed, then just as quickly cleared. "You're D.J. Stoner?"

"That's me," Dolly replied with a smile. "You've read one of my books?"

"Several actually. They're great. I bought your latest

a couple of weeks ago but haven't had a chance to start it. I planned on reading it over break."

"Annie's a high school teacher," Dalton told his mother.

Dolly nodded, her lips pursed thoughtfully.

"I . . . uh . . . suppose," Annie said, "you're wondering what I'm doing here?"

The older woman waved her hand in a gesture of dismissal. "That's none of my business, dear. Dalton's a grown man. He doesn't tell me all his secrets." She winked. "Just like I don't tell him all of mine."

"Yeah, well, you tell me more than I want to know," he grumbled.

A smile teased his mother's mouth, her eyes twinkling with mischief, but she remained silent.

Annie looked back and forth between mother and son, waiting for one of them to elaborate on their strange exchange. When neither seemed inclined to say more, she turned back to Dolly. "Well, to set the record straight. I came here to make a delivery on Saturday, but the storm hit on my way up from the city."

"Ah, that's your car I saw sticking out of a snowbank down the driveway. Oh, that reminds me. Dalton, the man who plows your drive said to tell you he needs to come back with a different truck to get the car pulled out of the snow. And he might not get to it until tomorrow." When he nodded, she turned back to Annie. "So, you've been snowbound here with Dalton since Saturday?"

"Yes, ma'am."

"I see. Well, I hope my son has done a good job of keeping you entertained."

"No complaints from me," Annie replied, flashing a wide-eyed innocent glance in his direction. "I couldn't ask for a more accommodating host."

Dalton narrowed his eyes, wondering what was

going on inside that beautiful head of hers. Finally, he said, "Entertaining Annie hasn't been a problem. We watch TV. Take the dogs out to play in the snow. And we shoot pool. I taught Annie to play. She's damn good."

"Really?" His mother smiled at Annie. "You must be good, or he wouldn't say that."

Annie returned the smile. "I can't take all the credit. Your son's a wonderful teacher." She turned her head enough to give him a wink without his mother seeing. "His lessons have been enlightening. Real thorough and very satisfying."

A long pause followed Annie's words, then finally Dolly said, "Are we still talking about pool, because it sure sounds like something a lot more . . . personal."

He blinked, stunned by the heat of a blush working its way up his neck and cheeks. He hadn't been this embarrassed since he was thirteen and his father caught him with an adult magazine. Not that adult magazines were forbidden in their house, but he'd still been mortified when his father found him in the bathroom with a lush centerfold looking at him while he— He shoved that memory aside, cleared his throat, then tried for an easy smile. "Annie's just having some fun with you, Mom. She's a real kidder."

He turned to Annie, silently daring her to disagree. She met his gaze, chin lifted, amusement dancing in her green eyes. *Dammit, she's enjoying this.* Sending her a knock-it-off glare, a warning he hoped she'd heed, he exhaled heavily, then said to his mother, "I'll get your bags out of the car. The coffee's fresh, so help yourself."

By the time Dalton returned from putting his mother's luggage in the second spare bedroom, he found her sitting with Annie at the table in his kitchen. The two women were talking like old friends.

He watched them from the doorway for a moment, surprised and at the same time, uncomfortable at how easily they had adapted to the other's presence. Though glad they hadn't taken an instant dislike to each other, forcing him to act as referee, he wasn't entirely happy with their apparent immediate bonding either.

His mother needed to know that Annie wouldn't be around much longer. Now that the roads had been reopened, as soon as her car got dug out, she'd be on her way. And he'd never see her again.

He took a step back, as if something or someone had landed a solid fist to his gut. He didn't doubt for a minute that Annie was totally wrong for him. So why then did the thought of her disappearing from his life make him feel as though he'd been sucker punched?

His mother's voice saved him from digging deeper for a possible reason to explain the odd sensation.

"Dalton." She smiled at him, waving a hand toward the coffeemaker. "Pour yourself a cup and join us."

He'd just finished filling his cup when his mother said, "Annie was telling me about her holiday job. Doesn't that sound like fun?"

He cursed silently, then turned to face the table. "I suppose," he said over the rim of his cup, eyeing Annie, "for some people."

His mother's brow furrowed at his response, but rather than ask for an explanation, she shifted her attention back to Annie. "Well, I think it sounds like so much fun that I may have a character deliver strip-o-grams in one of my books. Of course, that means doing some research."

Dalton nearly spit out a mouthful of coffee. Remembering other "research" she'd done for her writing, he swallowed carefully, then said, "Jesus,

Mom. You're not seriously considering working for a company that delivers strip-o-grams, are you?"

"I'll have you know, I could do it," she replied, shaking a finger at him. "And I'd be damn good." She dropped her hand to the table, then sighed. "I doubt they'd want a woman my age. But if I were a little younger, you bet your ass I'd apply."

He groaned inwardly. *God save me from adventurous women, especially my own mother!*

"There's no need though," Dolly continued, "not when I have a personal contact in the business." She looked at Annie. "That is, if you wouldn't mind answering some questions when I get to that point."

Annie laughed. "Of course not. I'll give you my number."

His mother smiled. "Thanks, dear." She started to take another sip of coffee, then changed her mind and pushed her cup to the center of the table. "I don't need more caffeine. I need a nap. Early flights are a real bear, especially when you're up as late as I was." She chuckled. "Buzz didn't want to go home. Guess he had to get enough nookie to hold him over until I get back. Anyway, after he left, I got only a couple hours sleep before the alarm went off." She put a hand over her mouth to cover a yawn. "So if you two don't mind, I think I'll lie down for a little while."

"Sleep as long as you want," he replied.

Shoving her chair away from the table, she got to her feet then moved to stand in front of him. "We'll catch up later. Okay, sweetheart?"

"Sure, Mom."

She gave him a quick kiss, smiled at Annie, then left the kitchen.

* * *

After Dolly's departure, Annie sat back in her chair, dazed by what had just happened. "Your mom is an amazing woman."

"Yeah, tell me about it."

Annie bit her lip to hold in a laugh. "I take it you're not thrilled about being D.J. Stoner's son."

"Listen, my mother loves writing, she works damn hard and I'm really proud of her success."

"Of course you are." She studied him in silence for a moment, then added, "So why do I get the feeling there's a *but* in your statement?"

He sighed, rubbing a hand over his face. "I'm really happy Mom's doing something she loves, but I wish she'd picked another genre."

"Erotic fiction is a little too . . . what? Over-the-top, maybe?"

"Yeah, I guess that's one way of putting it."

"I can understand why you'd feel that way. But I seriously doubt she chose to write erotic fiction just to make her son squirm with embarrassment."

The corners of his mouth lifted in a weak smile. "No, probably not."

"Even though I just met her, my impression is, given her personality, I suspect writing anything else would be stifling for her."

"Maybe you're right," he said after a moment. "She's always been passionate and vivacious, and as you heard for yourself, a real ballsy woman. So I guess writing anything less flamboyant would be going against her nature."

"Being true to yourself in life is important for everyone, but maybe that's even more important for a writer."

He stared at her for several seconds. "Painters and sculptors have told me the same thing about their artwork, but I never stopped to think that writing is also an art form." He shook his head. "You're absolutely right: Mom would never be happy writing anything else."

He set his cup on the counter, then moved toward the table. "I think you deserve a reward."

"For what?"

"Giving me a new perspective on why my mother writes what she does."

She laughed. "No big deal. I just made a couple of observations."

"Observations I should've been able to make."

"Not necessarily," she replied. "Family members are too close to the situation, too emotionally involved, and don't always see the obvious. Yet what the family can't see can be immediately apparent to a stranger."

"You're hardly a stranger."

"To you," she replied, giving him a cocky smile. "But I just met your mom. I really like her, by the way. And listening and watching the two of you interact told me a lot about—"

He grasped her arms and hauled her to her feet.

"Hey, what are you—"

His mouth pressed to hers halted further talk.

When he finally ended the kiss, out of breath, pulse racing, his dick throbbing painfully, he dropped his forehead against hers. "I need a shower," he murmured. "Care to join me?"

"Don't tease, Dalton."

"Who said I was teasing?" He flexed his hips forward, letting her feel his erection.

She pushed against his chest, then moved away from him. "Have you forgotten your mom's here?"

"Hardly. But she's probably already asleep."

"She's still in the same house."

"Yeah, so what's that got to do with—" He chuckled. "You think Mom would be upset if she knew her thirty-one-year-old son was playing hide the weenie with you in the shower?"

"This isn't funny," she replied, a withering glare accompanying her words.

"Never said it was, babe." He started toward her, but she took another step back, so he stopped his approach. "She's sleeping, so she won't know what we're doing. And even if she does find out, she wouldn't be upset, I promise you."

She crossed her arms over her chest but didn't respond.

"Mom is always telling me I should be using my equipment before it shrivels up and falls off. So if she somehow finds out that's what I've been doing with you, believe me, she'd be thrilled."

Annie stared up at him, mulling over what he'd told her. "Your mother really said that to you?"

"Oh, yeah," he said with a laugh. "The old use it or lose it line is one of her favorites. Among others."

She suddenly burst out laughing.

"What's so funny?"

"I was just trying to picture my mother saying something like that to one of my brothers." She shook her head. "If she even brought up the topic of their sex lives, Ryan and Joey would probably die of embarrassment on the spot. I mean, they got the facts-of-life talk, like I did, but beyond that, the subject wasn't openly discussed."

"Well, as we've already established, Dolly Stoner is an amazing woman."

She nodded, thinking that Dolly Stoner's son was pretty amazing, too. The problem was, she didn't want to think of him as amazing. She wanted him to be the dull, boring man she'd expected before they met. If he were, maybe she wouldn't be falling for the guy.

Yeah, right, and maybe—

"Annie, are you okay?"

Thirteen

"What?" Annie blinked several times, bringing Dalton's face back into focus. He stared at her through narrowed eyes, his eyebrows knitted in a frown and mouth pinched with concern. She forced herself to smile. "Yeah, I'm . . . fine. I was just . . . thinking."

"But not about us taking a shower together."

She shook her head.

"Is it my mother?"

"No. I told you, I like her."

"What then?"

"Dalton, it's not important."

He continued staring at her for several more seconds, then his features relaxed and he nodded. "Okay, the shower thing is out. So, how about tonight?"

This time she didn't have to struggle to smile. "You're incorrigible."

"Probably." He tapped a finger on her nose. "But it's all your fault."

Her eyes went wide. "Just how is it my fault?"

"By agreeing to explore the *Kama Sutra* teachings with me"—he moved across the room to stand in front of her, then ran his fingertips down the side of her face—"you've turned me into an insatiable sex junkie."

She swallowed. "Yeah, well, I could say the same thing about me."

Dalton grinned at her response. "Good. Then I'll slip into your room tonight after Mom—" The dull flush working its way up Annie's face snagged his attention. "Did I say something wrong?"

She fiddled with the fabric of her sweatshirt. "Um . . . I think I should come to your room."

"If you want," he replied with a shrug. "Though I don't see what difference it makes."

"Your room is farther away from your mother's."

"Yeah, so what—" The reason behind her statement clicked into place. "Ah, I get it." He stared at her for several seconds, waiting for her to confirm his suspicion. When she didn't, he said, "If we're in my room there's less chance of any . . . um . . . noise carrying to Mom's room. That is what you're concerned about, isn't it?"

Her face turning even redder, she nodded.

"Well, you do get pretty loud." When his comment drew a fierce scowl, he bent to give her a quick kiss. "Sorry, I couldn't resist," he murmured against her mouth.

He straightened and offered her a smile, which only made her scowl deepen. "Hey, don't be upset, babe. I love the sounds you make, especially you screaming like a banshee when you come."

"Dalton, I'm serious," she said, giving him a frosty glare. "I'll try not to scream, but I"—she exhaled heavily—"I'm not sure I can." The iciness left her eyes, replaced by sadness. "I'd be so embarrassed if your mom heard me."

"She's a real sound sleeper, so you're worrying for nothing." He brushed another kiss over her lips. "Tell you what I'll do, though. How about if I stash a clean pair of socks under my pillow? That way, if you get too loud, one of us can stuff a sock in your mouth to stifle your scream."

A growl rumbling in her throat, she brought her hands up to his chest and gave him a shove. "Dammit, stop making fun of me."

"That's not what I—" The firming of her lips and the anger swirling in her eyes halted his denial. He ran a hand through his hair, then sighed. "Look, Annie. I really wasn't making fun of you. I just thought a little humor would ease your concerns."

When she didn't look convinced, he said, "I meant what I said a minute ago: I love your screams and I don't give a rat's ass who hears them. But I swear I really do understand how you feel, so if you want to forget about coming to my room tonight, I'll accept your decision."

Annie's heart clenched hard in her chest. She turned her back to him, hoping he hadn't seen the sudden moisture in her eyes. He'd just confirmed her earlier conclusion about being an amazing man. How else would he understand her so well? Or always know the right thing to say? She inhaled a shuddering breath, wondering how she'd let herself get involved with this man. But it was too late for self-condemnation. Way too late.

She needed a minute to compose herself. After blinking away the last of the threatening tears, she took another deep breath, then swung around to face him again. Meeting his gaze, she said, "I don't want to forget about it."

His chest rose and fell with a sigh, then he smiled. "Thank God, because staying away from you tonight would've been damn tough."

"Well," she replied, returning his smile, "now you don't have to."

Dalton entered the living room carrying a beer for himself and a glass of wine—a Rhine he kept on hand because he knew it was one of his mother's favorites. After handing her the glass, he settled on the opposite end of the couch. Annie had excused herself to make some phone calls, so he and his mother were alone in the room.

"So," he said, scooting over to make room for Data and Worf, "how's everything in Virginia?"

"Perfect. Just got a new three-book contract, so I can't complain."

He nodded. "And how's Buzz?"

She chuckled. "You don't have to ask about him. I know you think I should be seeing someone closer to my own age."

"True," he replied with a shrug. "But I asked because I wanna make sure he's treating you right."

"Absolutely." She flashed a big smile. "Buzz is exactly what I need right now. So please try to be happy for me."

He took a long swallow of beer, then said. "Okay, as long as you don't tell me about your sex life."

"I'll try to restrain myself," she replied, laughter in her voice. She sipped from her glass, eyeing him over the rim. "Speaking of happiness. You look happier than I've seen you in a long time."

"That right?"

"Mmm." She took another sip of wine. "My guess is Annie's the reason."

Dalton carefully swallowed a mouthful of beer. "Why would you think that?"

"Observing people is part of being a writer. I saw how you two light up when you're in the same room. The not-so-subtle glances when you thought I wasn't looking. The stolen touches."

"Listen, Mom, don't get any ideas about Annie and me. She's here only because she was foolish enough to head into the foothills during one helluva snowstorm, and as soon as her car gets dug out, she'll be outa here for good."

"That sounds so permanent." When he didn't respond to her statement, she said, "Are you saying you're not planning to see her again after she leaves?"

He huffed out a breath. "Yeah, that's what I'm saying."

"I don't understand. Annie and you are so well suited, so I thought—"

"No way, Mom," he replied with a snort. "Annie is too much like Maureen."

"That's ridiculous."

"No, it's not. Annie is an excitement freak, always looking for a new thrill." A muscle jerked in his jaw. "There's no way I'll go through the hell Maureen put me through again."

"Is Annie into drugs? Parties? Men?"

He blinked. "You knew what Maureen was doing?"

"Not everything. But I met some people who knew her, and what they told me turned my stomach." Before he could respond to her startling revelation, she continued, "Why are you so sure Annie's an excitement freak?"

"For God's sake, look at her job!"

"Hmm, well I guess some people would call teaching high school math something of a thrill."

"Cute, Mom," he replied, scowling in her direction. "You know I'm talking about her job with the delivery service."

She studied him in silence for a moment, then finally said, "So, you assume, because of the job she took over Christmas break, that means she'll turn into another Maureen?"

"And you're saying there's no chance of that happening?"

"There's always a chance. But you have to admit,

believing she'll go from delivering strip-o-grams to a drug user who sleeps with anything that has a penis is a pretty big stretch."

When his response was another scowl, she said, "If their personalities were more alike, maybe I could buy into your theory. But they're not. Annie's warm, outgoing, and caring. Maureen was demanding, moody, and colder than the balls on a brass monkey."

He stared at her for a moment, shaken by her words. Finally, he said, "If you felt that way about Maureen, why didn't you say something?"

"Oh, baby," she said with a sad smile. "Believe me, I wanted to. But I knew you had to make your own way in life and didn't want what you'd surely view as interference from your mother. And there was the possibility, in spite of my feelings toward Maureen, that the two of you could've been happy." She sighed. "When I found out what she was mixed up in, my heart broke for you. And remaining quiet while she trampled all over your marriage vows was the hardest thing I've ever done. But there was a limit to my silence. I had just about reached the point where, if you hadn't found out the truth, I would've spoken up. Thankfully, you tossed her out, so I didn't have to."

He was silent for a long time, then finally he said, "Do Daf and Darcie know?"

"About Maureen? Lord, no. I wasn't sure either of them would keep quiet, so I never said anything."

A corner of his mouth lifted in a half smile. "Thanks. You probably saved me from one of Daf's tongue-lashings. And if she'd lit into Maureen"—he chuckled— "I'd hate to think what kind of cat fight that could've turned into."

"When it comes to family, Daphne does have a vicious protective streak."

"Remember the time she got into a fight with that

kid down the street? The one who was always pick-ing on Darcie?"

"Oh, God," she replied with a laugh, "Todd Richards. I'd forgotten about him. I tried talking to his mother, but she just shrugged and said boys will be boys. Daphne didn't quite see it that way."

"She had a helluva right cross. Caught him square on the nose. I was two houses away, and I heard his yowl of pain. He had the darkest pair of shiners I've ever seen."

"Then his pain-in-the-ass of a mother had the nerve to storm over to our house and demand I pun-ish Daphne."

"Punish Daphne for what?" Annie said, entering the room.

"Punching a neighbor kid in the nose," he replied. "Mom and I were just reminiscing."

"Do you see each other very often?" Annie said, taking a seat on the other couch. Immediately, his dogs rose from where they'd been lying next to him and joined her.

"A couple of times a year, though I wish it were more often," his mother replied. "But we all have re-ally busy lives, plus me living on the East Coast doesn't help."

"I've told you, Mom, move to Denver."

"Maybe some day I will." She shifted her attention to Annie. "I can't wait for you to meet Dalton's sisters."

He stiffened. Sisters! Damn, even after his mother's arrival, he'd forgotten Daphne and Darcie would be showing up at his house sometime the following day.

"Actually," Annie said, "I've—"

"Have you talked to either of them since you got here?" he said to his mother, ignoring Annie's look of surprise at being cut off.

His mother nodded. "Daphne sounded great. Really

excited about coming here. But Darcie was . . . I don't know what, exactly. Quiet, almost withdrawn, as if her mind was a million miles away."

"Maybe she's working on a big case," he said. "You know how involved she gets in her work."

"I asked her and she said she wasn't. Anyway, they plan on driving up late tomorrow afternoon."

"Great," he muttered, trying to dredge up a smile, though not at all certain he'd succeeded. "The more, the merrier."

His mother frowned slightly, then turned her attention to Annie. "So, what did you start to say before my son so rudely cut you off?"

"I was just going to say that I've met Daphne. I love going into Charmed."

"Oh, so do I. She always finds such delightful merchandise, don't you think?"

Before Annie could reply, Dalton said, "Mom, Daphne's the one who hired Annie."

"Hired . . ." His mother's eyes suddenly widened. "Oh, I see. Through the messenger service."

Annie nodded. "Dalton thinks Daphne was trying to set us up, but I told him he's wrong."

"I thought your sisters finally gave up on matchmaking."

"So did I," he replied with a sigh, his gaze finding and locking on Annie's. "Until last Saturday."

In the ensuing silence, Dolly Stoner covertly watched her son and Annie. From the way the two were looking at each other, the air practically crackling with sexual tension, she wondered if they had any idea she was still in the room. Probably not, she decided, lifting her wine glass to hide a smile.

She knew how frustrated Dalton had been when his sisters repeatedly threw women at him, and although she tried to avoid taking sides in her children's squabbles, she had to agree with her son. Daphne and Darcie had been out of line. But now, having watched Annie and Dalton together all afternoon, she had to admit that if Daphne really had resurrected her role of matchmaker, she must've had a damn good reason for risking her brother's anger.

As she'd told Dalton, being a writer made her a keen observer of people, and unless she had totally misread the signs, her son was interested in Annie—probably on several levels—an interest she was certain Annie returned.

In fact, based on the sizzling intimate looks they exchanged, they'd already acted on that attraction. That thought brought her wine glass back up to her lips to hide another smile. Dalton might think Annie wasn't suited to him, but she knew differently. The problem would be getting her son to realize he'd be making a big mistake if he carried out his plan to not see Annie again once she left his house.

She didn't like people telling her how to live her life, so she had no intention of attempting to meddle in Dalton's. Still, there had to be some way to encourage his relationship with Annie—nothing too obvious, of course—just a gentle nudge here and there. After that, she'd have to hope nature would take its own course.

Quin Jett watched Darcie get dressed from where he lay stretched out on the bed in his hotel room. He'd managed to get her to take a longer-than-usual lunch, and rather than waste the time eating, they'd opted to spend the full hour and a half in his room.

As she slipped on the jacket of another of her signature power suits, his chest tightened painfully, a lump forming in his throat. Swallowing hard, he

squeezed his eyes shut. Damn. This wasn't supposed
to happen. He wasn't supposed to fall for a woman,
especially not one who—

"Quin, are you all right?"

He took a deep breath, then let his eyelids drift
open. "Right as rain, sugar puss," he said, pleased his
voice carried the light-hearted tone he wanted. "Just
trying to recover from that spectacular finish to our
lunch."

She smiled at him, her beautiful eyes crinkling at
the corners. "Take a nap, darlin', you deserve it."

"Maybe I will." As she stepped into one of her low-
heeled pumps, he said, "How about dinner?"

After working her other foot into the second shoe,
she looked over at him. "Will we actually get to eat?"

He chuckled. "Sure, if you want."

The beginnings of another smile quickly faded. "Oh
damn. I almost forgot. I have to leave work early. That's
why I shouldn't have taken a lunch hour at all"—her
eyebrows arched—"let alone an hour and a half. I'm
picking up my sister at four, then we're heading to our
brother's place. Our mother got into town yesterday,
so we're all spending a couple of days together." She
glanced at her watch with a frown. "In fact, I told Mom
I'd call her an hour ago." Her frown deepened. "God,
if she asks why I didn't, I don't know what I'll tell her.
She can always tell when I'm lying. Anyway, I'm sorry
about tonight."

"Hey, no problem. Family's important. Especially at
Christmas."

"I know, but what about you? I hate leaving you to
spend the holiday alone."

"Won't be the first time."

Darcie stared at him thoughtfully, realizing again
how little she knew about the man. He hadn't told
her much about himself, and she'd respected his

right to privacy and hadn't pressed for more than he offered. Now she wished she had. Tamping down the urge to ask him to explain his statement, she said, "Are you sure, because I probably could change—"

"No. You aren't going to change your plans. Don't worry that pretty head about me. I'll be fine. Besides, not seeing each other for a while could be a good thing. You know, letting the anticipation build and all that." He grinned. "Just think how much better the next time will be."

"Right," she said, summoning a smile. "I'll be back in town Saturday, so how about us doing something that night?"

"You mean something besides jumpin' each others' bones?"

This time her smile came easily. "Yeah, besides that."

He stared up at her for a few seconds, an unreadable expression on his face. "Call me when you get back," he finally said, "and we'll make plans for the evening."

She nodded, then moved to the side of the bed and bent to kiss him. When he slipped a hand under the hem of her skirt and started to slide up her thigh, she pulled her mouth from his and took a step back.

"Uh-uh," she said, shaking her finger at him, "Don't be naughty. I really have to go."

His lips curved in a lazy smile, his topaz eyes sparkling with a mix of amusement and rekindled arousal. "But you liked it when I was naughty a few minutes ago."

She shook her head. "You are such a bad boy."

"Yeah, but you love it."

Other words of love pushed up from her chest, clogging her throat. She swallowed hard, knowing this wasn't the time to declare feelings she hadn't completely acknowledged or accepted. Hoping her expression revealed none of the thoughts going through her mind, she bent for another quick kiss, this time making sure she stayed just beyond the reach of his wandering hands.

As she straightened, she said, "I'll talk to you Saturday."

"Merry Christmas, Darcie."

She blinked, shocked to realize she was close to tears. God, she was such a basket case. Clearing her throat, she whispered, "Merry Christmas, Quin. I'll miss you."

His chest rose and fell with a sigh. "Me, too."

Unable to say more without revealing the emotions bubbling so close to the surface, she smiled, then picked up her coat, slipped the strap of her purse over her shoulder and turned to leave.

As she left his room, she heard him say, "Bye, Darcie. I—" The click of the door closing cut off the rest of his words.

She wondered what he'd said, then immediately pushed all speculation aside. The only thing she should be thinking about was the pile of work waiting on her desk, and now she had an hour and a half less time to get it done. Making her way to where she'd parked her car, she suddenly burst into laughter. She sure wasn't sorry she'd let Quin talk her into a nooner. Woo-ee, what a way to spend a lunch hour! Three orgasms should've left her drained, but she felt invigorated, like she could take on the world and win.

Quin stared at the ceiling of his hotel room long after Darcie had left. What the hell had he done? Telling her he'd see her Saturday night. He should get up right now, pack his bags and hit the road before the trail he'd been following got any colder. But no, like the lovesick idiot he was, he'd hang around another couple of days just so he could spend more time with a woman like none he'd ever known—a woman he could see himself with for the rest of his life. Except that wasn't possible.

Not now, and in all likelihood, not ever.

Although staying in town any longer wasn't doing either of them any favors and only prolonged the inevitable, he dreaded the idea of leaving. Because when he did, Darcie would then be in his past.

Just the thought of never seeing her again left him feeling like a giant hole had been bored into his chest. Pressing a hand over the imagined wound to ease the throbbing ache, he squeezed his eyes closed and released a weary sigh.

Jesus, what a goddamn mess! He had no business mooning over a woman, not when he should be using all of his energies to figure out how to save his own sorry-ass neck.

Unfortunately, his heart wasn't listening.

Fourteen

"So what do you think of my son?"

Annie stopped reading and looked over at where Dolly Stoner sat across the living room. Dalton's mother was curled in an easy chair, legs tucked under her, a spiral notebook resting on one of the chair's arms.

All morning, Annie had been on edge, afraid the woman would say or do something to indicate she knew what Dalton and Annie had done the night before. Even though they'd stayed in his bedroom, at the opposite end of the house, Annie couldn't help worrying that Dolly had some sort of sixth sense when it came to her son. Much to her relief, the morning passed without incident and she'd begun to breathe easier.

But now Dolly had asked what she thought of her son, and she couldn't help wondering if there was an ulterior motive for posing the question.

Annie finally said, "Umm, I think he's a really nice man."

Dolly clipped her ballpoint pen onto the notebook, then smiled. "Very diplomatic."

Annie resisted the urge to squirm under the woman's intense gaze.

"Mrs. Stoner, I don't know what you're—"

"Dolly, please, and I just wondered what you really

think of Dalton." Her smile widened. "He's got a great ass, don't you think?"

Annie blinked, her voice coming out as a squeak when she said, "I beg your pardon?"

"Oh, damn," Dolly said, "I've shocked you. I suppose most mothers don't comment on their sons' rear ends." She laughed. "At least, I didn't say how well he's endowed, right? And for the record, I have no idea about the size of his . . . package . . . shall we say. But then, that's something you could tell me, isn't it?"

Before Annie could form a reply, Dolly said, "Don't worry, dear, I don't intend to lecture you about your relationship with my son. Ever since his divorce, I've been telling him he needed to get some mud for his turtle, but he kept telling me not to worry about his sex life—actually his nonexistent sex life. Anyway, I was beginning to think he'd turned into a monk." She flashed another beaming smile in Annie's direction. "I'm thrilled to know he's not."

Annie closed her gaping mouth, certain this had to be the strangest conversation she'd ever had, especially considering it was with the mother of the man she'd spent the last few days with, the man responsible for the greatest sex of her life. Yet, for some odd reason, she found Dolly's outrageous candor and her bold and brassy personality totally refreshing.

She cleared her throat, then said, "I agree about his great ass, and as for the other, no comment."

Dolly burst out laughing. "Diplomacy again. Very clever." She wiped her eyes, then said, "I like you, Annie, and you'll be so good for my son."

Annie shifted uneasily. "Mrs. Sto—Dolly, I like Dalton, a lot, but I don't . . . we're not . . ." She drew a deep breath, exhaled slowly. "This won't become permanent."

"Really? May I ask why?"

"I love the excitement of living in the city, and he wants the quiet of living in the middle of nowhere."

"Hmm, I always enjoy coming here. Soaking up the beauty and peacefulness recharges my batteries. Makes heading back to civilization much easier to deal with."

Annie considered her words for a moment, then shook her head. "Maybe that works for you. But I lived the dull, out-in-the-boonies life once, and I won't go back to it."

Dolly stared at her for several uncomfortable seconds, then said, "If where you'd live is the only thing standing in the way of a future for you and Dalton, I'd say you were damned lucky."

"That's not the only thing. He owns a museum and art gallery."

"Yes, and a really fine one. So how is that a problem?"

"His life is boring."

"And your life is full of fun and games, is that it?"

The heat of a blush crept up Annie's neck. "No, not exactly, but I'd like it to be more exciting."

"You and Dalton haven't done anything exciting these past few days?"

Her blush spread to her cheeks. "Yes, only that's dif—"

"But you still think there can't be a future for the two of you?"

Annie nodded.

Dolly sighed. "Let me tell you something, dear. Most of us don't know ourselves as well as we think we do. It takes falling in love to discover who we really are." She unclipped her pen from the notebook, flipped to a new page, then started writing.

Darcie merged onto the freeway, finally starting to relax after rushing through a mountain of paperwork then taking the time to wish everyone in the law office a Merry Christmas, which made her late picking up Daphne. She expected to get a lecture, but her sister hadn't even commented; in fact, she'd barely spoken at all, but just tossed her bags into the trunk then slid into the passenger seat.

"So," Darcie said, after several more minutes went by, "what's new with you?"

Daphne shrugged, idly twisting the ring she wore on her right hand. "Not much. Business has been great. Hiring Lynn was the best thing I could've done. She's a wonder."

"She must be for you to leave Charmed in her hands so you could take off early today and not go in tomorrow."

"Yeah," Daphne replied, running her left forefinger back and forth over the setting of her ring.

Darcie could see the ring appeared to be sterling silver, the stone a deep rose color. "Is that new?"

Daphne lifted her gaze to meet hers. "What? Oh, this—" she raised her right hand. "I just got in a jewelry shipment. Some really spectacular pieces." She looked at the ring, drawing in a deep breath. "I don't normally try on any of the rings, but as soon as I saw this one, something made me take it out of the box and slip it on my finger."

"It looks beautiful. I don't think I've ever seen a stone like that."

"It's rhodochrosite, a rose red mineral made mostly of manganese carbonate."

"Whatever, but the color is lovely. I'll have to take a closer look when we get to Dalton's."

Daphne nodded, worry lines forming between her eyebrows, her lips pursed in a frown.

"Daf, what is it?"

Her sister shrugged. "Nothing, really. It's just that"—

her head came up, her gaze once again meeting Darcie's then instantly skipping away—"rhodochrosite is used by crystal healers. They say it contains the strongest power in the universe, a pulsating electric energy that emits the power of love. That's why it's called the love finder. Wearing a stone made of rhodochrosite is supposed to attract that person's twin soul."

Darcie cast a quick glance at her sister. "Do you believe that?"

When Daphne nodded, she said, "And that bothers you?"

Her sister shifted in her seat, then huffed out a breath. "Yeah, because I don't want to find love, and I'm definitely not looking for my twin soul."

Darcie contemplated her next words, then took a deep breath and plunged in. "I haven't brought up this subject in months because you refused to talk about it, but I think it's time we did. It's been more than a year since Lar—"

"Don't!" Daphne said in a sharp voice. "Don't you dare say his name."

"All right, I won't. Look, Daf, I know that bastard hurt you. His taking advantage of your psychic abilities for his own gain makes him lower than slime. But not all men are like that."

"No, the rest just think I'm a freak."

"Dammit, Daf! You don't believe that, so don't even say it. You have a gift."

"Yeah, well, sometimes it feels more like a curse."

"Bet you don't feel that way when you pull out your crystal ball and snoop into someone's life."

Her sister's lips curved into a reluctant smile. "Touché."

"Listen, Daphne, the point I'm trying to make is, maybe it's time you gave the rest of the male population a chance to prove they aren't out to use you."

Daphne sobered and gave her head a fierce shake. "I'm not ready, Darcie." Daphne turned toward her, eyes wide and pleading. "Please, tell me you understand."

"What I'll tell you is, I think you've been hiding in your den licking your wounds long enough, but"— she sighed—"yeah, I do understand." She indicated the ring that had started their conversation. "So, if wearing that bothers you so much, take it off. Problem solved."

Daphne snorted. "I tried, but—" She touched the stone with a fingertip, her face scrunched in a scowl. "It's as if the ring has become a part of me. When I took it off, I felt . . . weird. Like I was incomplete. Empty."

Darcie waited for her sister to continue, but when Daphne remained silent, she said, "Well, then, I guess your only choice is to wear it."

"Yeah. That's what I decided." After touching the ring one final time, she tucked her right hand into her coat pocket. "Enough about me. How's Quin? Things still hot and heavy between you two?"

"He's fine, and our sex life is none of your business."

"Come on, Darcie, ever since we were in high school, we've always shared everything about the men we dated."

Darcie chuckled. "You just want a vicarious sexual thrill."

"What's wrong with that? I'm not getting any, so is it so terrible that I want to enjoy your sex life?"

That remark earned a laugh. "Sorry, big sister, but I'm not talking."

Daphne stared at her for several seconds, then said, "My God, you really are in love."

She pressed her lips together, tightening her grip on the steering wheel. "Yeah. I never thought it was possible to fall so fast, but"—she swallowed the sudden lump in her throat—"I'm head over heels."

"You should've invited him to come with us. Dalton wouldn't care, and Mom would be thrilled that one of the Stoner sisters has a man in her life."

"I thought about it, especially since he'll be alone for Christmas." She shrugged. "I decided it's too soon for the meet-the-family phase."

"I suppose you're right. But you know Mom is going to grill each of us about finding a man and settling down."

"I'm hoping she'll be so ecstatic about Dalton and Annie that we won't be in her crosshairs."

"That's assuming there *is* a Dalton and Annie." Darcie gave a soft gasp, then sent a sharp glance in her sister's direction. "You didn't do another reading, did you?"

"Nope. Just the one." She waited until Darcie had turned her car into their brother's driveway before she added, "I'll decide about doing a second one after I see the two of them together."

"You think Annie is still at his house?"

"Looks that way," she replied, pointing through the windshield to a spot farther up the driveway, where the rear end of a car poked out of a snowbank. "That's her SUV."

"I can't wait to meet her."

"You'll love her." Daphne flashed a grin, her eyes sparkling. "This could turn out to be a really fun Christmas."

Annie laughed at the antics of Worf and Data. Both dogs ran as fast as the deep snow allowed, chasing after another snowball she'd lobbed across Dalton's backyard. She'd learned by accident that the dogs loved fetching snowballs and had spent the past half hour indulging their fun to expend some of their energy.

Worf was the first to reach the spot where the latest snowball landed, then rooted around in the snow. Several seconds later, he raised his snow-covered head, what was left of the snowball clamped gingerly between his jaws.

"Good boy, Worf," Annie called to the dog. "Bring it here."

Worf bounded back to her and obediently dropped his prize at her feet.

When she bent over to give Worf a congratulatory pat, Data pushed his nose between her hand and his brother. "Okay, I'll pet you, too. I won't be able to do this much longer." She swallowed a sudden surge of emotion. "I'm really gonna miss you guys."

From the long looks the pair gave her, they must've understood. "Now, don't you go getting all sad-eyed on me, or you'll make me cry."

Before she'd come outside, Dalton told her Jim, the guy who plowed his drive, would be arriving within an hour, which meant her time as his houseguest would soon end. And as soon as her car had been dug out, she planned to give a quick thank-you to Dalton and then make a speedy exit.

She gave each dog a final pat, then turned toward the house. "Come on. Time to get you two dried off."

As she approached the back door, she heard a car door slam. Wondering if Jim had already arrived, she hurried Data and Worf into the mud room, pulled off her gloves then grabbed the towels Dalton kept there for drying the dogs.

* * *

"Yoo-hoo," Daphne called, pushing the front door inward and stepping into the foyer. "Anybody home?"

As Darcie followed her inside, their mother and then Dalton entered the hallway.

"There they are," Dolly said, rushing to envelop both her and her sister in a group hug. "I'm so glad you're here."

"We are, too, Mom," Darcie replied.

Dalton stepped forward to shut the door, then added his hugs of welcome. When he released Darcie, he said, "How were the roads?"

"Fine. Still snow-covered in a few places, but nothing I couldn't handle."

"There's not much you can't handle, sis," he replied with a smile. "Now I suppose I'll have to make a dozen trips to unload the car."

Daphne gave him a playful punch on the arm. "We didn't bring that much." She grinned. "Six trips ought to do it."

He shook his head. "Women," he said, but he was smiling.

As he moved away from her, she followed. And when he reached for the closet door, she grabbed his arm. "Wait," she said in a low voice. "Where's Annie?"

"She took the dogs outside."

"She likes dogs? Great. I thought so, but I wasn't—"

"Cut the crap, Daf. I'm on to your little scheme."

"What scheme?"

His jaw tightened. "Don't play dumb."

"I never play dumb," she snapped, then looked over her shoulder to make sure Darcie and their mother wouldn't overhear. "Dalton, look, I'm sorry if you didn't enjoy Annie's performance. I know she was nervous, but I thought once she—"

"I'm not talking about her goddamn striptease act, which I never got to see, by the way, so you should ask for a refund. I meant, I know the real reason she came here." A muscle flexed in his jaw. "You promised me you'd stop horning in on my social life, stop shoving women at me, but you just couldn't keep your word, could you?"

She sighed. "All right, fine. Don't get yourself all worked up, big brother. I made that promise and I kept it for a long time. But then Annie walked into my store. As soon as I met her, I knew she was perfect for you."

He snorted. "Well, you were wrong."

Daphne stared up at him for several seconds, trying to see past his simmering anger. "Are you saying you don't like her?"

"That's not . . ." He scowled. "Listen, whether I like Annie or not is immaterial. The point is, regardless of what you think, she is not perfect for me. So do both of us a favor and stay out of my life." With those words, he snatched open the closet, jerked a jacket off a hanger then headed for the front door.

Daphne silently watched him slip outside. She knew he'd be upset when he found out she'd broken her promise about fixing him up, but she still had to wonder at the reason behind his display of temper. When the answer came, she chuckled. *Well, well, brother dear, looks like I was right, after all. You're just too damned stubborn to admit it. Unless, of course, you haven't figured that out yet.*

The sound of a third voice added to those of her sister and mother pulled Daphne from her musings. Turning, she saw her mother introducing Darcie to Annie.

As she approached the group, Annie turned. When their gazes met, Annie's eyes narrowed and her mouth firmed. *Uh-oh, looks like I've gotta do some more damage control.* Pasting a smile on her face, she said, "Hi, Annie. Has Dalton been showing you a good time?"

The sudden bloom of a blush on Annie's cheeks told she'd been right to arrange for Annie to meet her brother—even if the man was too stubborn to see it—but she schooled her features not to reveal the triumph swirling inside her.

"Dalton has been great." Annie glanced at the other two women. "If you don't mind, I'd like to speak privately with Daphne for a minute."

"Not at all," Dolly replied. Grabbing Darcie's arm, she gave her a gentle tug. "Come on, honey, let's get a glass of wine and you can fill me in on what's going on in your life."

After the two disappeared down the hall, Annie said, "Why didn't you tell me about your brother?"

"Tell you what?"

"That his gallery specializes in erotic art, or about his fascination with the *Kama Sutra?*"

She tipped her head to one side. "I don't understand. Are those a problem for you?"

"Yes. No. I don't know." Annie blew out a puff of air. "I wanted some excitement, but I didn't—" Her eyes closed for a moment, then she exhaled a long sigh. "Never mind, it doesn't matter now anyway."

She stepped closer and touched Annie's arm. "Are you okay?"

Annie nodded. "Just tired. I plan to sleep the clock around when I get home. Which reminds me, I need to finish packing." She flashed a wan smile. "Not that I have much to pack."

"You're leaving?" At Annie's nod, she said, "But you and my brother were getting along so good."

"Did Dalton tell you that?"

"Um . . . not exactly. I just got the impression the two of you were—"

"You don't have to make up something. Dalton told me."

"Told you what?"

"That you're psychic."

She blinked with surprise, then pulled her eyebrows together in a scowl. "He knows I don't like him telling people about me."

"Actually, he made a comment," Annie said, "and I guessed the rest. But why don't you like people to know? I think being psychic is wicked cool, as my students would say."

"Then you're in the minority," she said with a laugh. "Of the few people I've told, nearly every one of them looked at me like I'd suddenly grown a third eye, then either changed the subject or made up some half-baked excuse to leave."

"Then they're pretty narrow-minded."

"Probably," she said with a shrug.

"So, does what you said about Dalton and me getting along so well mean you did one of the readings he told me about?"

"And he claims women are bigger blabbermouths." She shook her head. "Anyway, to answer your question, yes, I did one reading. But I swear I didn't do it to be a snoop. I couldn't reach you Saturday night, and I was getting worried, so I decided to find out what happened."

Annie smiled. "It's okay, Daphne. I'm not angry."

"Thank goodness, because Dalton will be furious if he finds out." She gave Annie's arm a gentle squeeze. "Please don't tell him. He's already p o'd at me for throwing another woman at him, so he sure doesn't need another reason."

"So he was right about you setting us up?"

As she removed her hand, she studied Annie's face. Finding no censure in the woman's expression, she said, "Yes, and I won't apologize for it. I told Dalton this and I'll tell you the same thing. As soon as I met you, I thought you were perfect for him. Though it nearly killed me, I held off doing anything because I'd promised to butt out of his love life. But I was so sure I was right about the two of you, regardless of my brother's reaction, which I knew could get really ugly." She smiled. "Anyway, I also knew I'd eventually break my word, but my biggest problem was figuring out a way for you to meet him. I'd pretty much exhausted my bag of tricks. Then you told me about your job with the messenger service, and voila, there was my solution."

"Great. My decision to work over Christmas break makes me partly to blame for my own downfall."

"Yes, I guess it does." Her smile faded. "But why did you say downfall? You and Dalton didn't get along?"

"We got along fine," Annie replied, another blush spreading up her neck and onto her cheeks, "but believe me, we're not right for each other."

"So you don't plan to see him again?"

"I haven't—" The front door opening saved Annie from having to answer the question.

Dalton stumbled through the door, a suitcase under each arm and clutching several overstuffed shopping bags, brightly wrapped Christmas presents sticking out the top. One bag started to slip from his grasp.

"Here," Annie said, taking a step toward him, "let me help you."

With a quick, if not particularly deft juggling act, he managed to get his fingers back around the handles of the shopping bag. "Thanks, but I've got it. Just close the door."

As Annie slipped past him, Daphne watched in fascination as her brother's gaze locked onto Annie. His eyes went kind of smokey, the harshness of his features changing to another kind of tension—raw and primitive.

She bit her lip to hold in a shout of glee, shifting her attention to Annie. Not surprisingly, she saw a reciprocal flare of desire ignite in her eyes and her blush deepen. Sexual awareness throbbed in the air surrounding the couple, generating enough heat to melt the polar ice cap.

Daphne mentally snorted. And these fools say they aren't perfect for each other! Just goes to show how blind some people are to the truth. Maybe Annie's leaving was a good thing. With a little distance between them, maybe they'd realize they were meant to be together.

In the meantime, she decided, heading for the kitchen, she needed to talk to her mother and sister. If her stubborn brother didn't come to his senses soon, they'd have to figure out something to help him along. Surely, between the three Stoner women, they could come up with a way to give him a needed metaphoric crack over the head with a two-by-four.

Love was all too rare these days, and she had no intention of letting it slip away from her brother and Annie. And perhaps Darcie would be the next Stoner to be taken off the market. She smiled, happy for both her siblings.

The ring finger on her right hand suddenly tingled with an odd surge of warmth, almost like an electrical charge just below the skin. Twisting the ring with her thumb, she wondered at the sensation.

Before she could further contemplate the odd feeling, the phone rang. She heard Darcie answer the call, then shout, "Dalton, it's for you. It's Jackson Kidd."

Daphne stumbled to a halt in the kitchen doorway,

heart pounding, the tingling in her finger intensifying.

"Daphne," her mother said, rushing toward her, "what is it? You look like you've seen a ghost."

She tried for a smile, though she couldn't be certain her lips had actually moved. "Mom, you know better than to say things like that to a psychic."

Dolly took her arm and steered her toward one of the chairs. "Stop teasing, honey. You didn't see the look on your face." She urged her to sit. "What happened just now?"

"I . . . I'm"—she drew a shuddering breath, more shaken than she wanted to admit—"I'm not sure." She inhaled deeply, needing a moment for her muddled senses to settle. "Maybe it's the burrito I had for breakfast."

"Daphne Marie," her mother replied with a laugh, the worry lines between her eyes smoothing. "When are you going to learn to eat a real breakfast?"

This time, she found smiling a little easier. "Probably never, but I will try to do better."

"Well, I hope you really mean it this time, honey." She bent and pressed a kiss to her forehead. "How about a glass of wine? That'll put some color back in your cheeks."

She nodded, then looked down at the ring on her still-tingling finger.

In spite of what she'd told her mother, the burrito she'd eaten that morning had nothing to do with what had just happened. Though she didn't know the why, she did know the cause. Two words.

Jackson Kidd.

Fifteen

Annie hadn't been gone twenty minutes when Dolly cornered Dalton in his office.

She stopped in front of his desk, arms folded across her chest. "I can't believe you just let Annie walk out of here."

He sat back in his chair with a sigh. "Mom, don't start on me again. We've been over this already. Annie had every right to leave. She probably couldn't wait to get home. Can't say as I blame her for wanting to get back to her own clothes, her own bed." Bed. He swallowed a groan. He had to stop combining Annie and bed in the same thought.

"I don't either," his mother replied, "but you could've at least asked to see her again."

"Has it ever occurred to you that I don't need you, Daphne or Darcie trying to run my life?"

Her lips thinned. "Dalton, don't be obtuse. Of course, I know you don't need any of us running your life. And believe me, I wouldn't be saying anything now if I didn't think you were making a huge mistake."

Certain he'd be sorry for asking, he said, "And just what is this huge mistake?"

"Honey, Annie's the best thing that's ever happened to you." When he opened his mouth to protest, she silenced him with one of her patented

don't-you-dare looks. "I saw the two of you together
enough to know what you have is rare. You enjoy
each other's company, you make each other laugh."
She gave him a long, considering look before adding,
"And you probably set the sheets on fire."

"Mom!" he practically shouted, the burning of his
face telling him he'd undoubtedly turned beet red.

"You don't have to answer that; your blush con-
firms it. My point is, relationships like that are few
and far between. Dalton, if you let Annie slip away
from you, not only will you be making a huge mistake, you'll also be sorry for the rest of your life."

"I appreciate the advice," he replied, trying to keep
his voice calm, "but what I'd appreciate more is your
not bringing up Annie again."

She uncrossed her arms, then smoothed the fabric
of her blouse. "You're certainly your father's son.
Stubborn to the core."

"Mom, I mean it."

"Yes, dear, I know you do." She exhaled with a sigh.
"All right, how about this? If I promise not to mention her again, I'd like your promise that you'll think
about what I said. Do we have a deal?"

He stared up at her, wanting to refuse. But the
truth was, even if he did say no, he doubted he'd be
able to stop thinking about the advice she'd given
him. Because he sure as hell wouldn't be able to stop
thinking about Annie. Certainly not in the next few
days or weeks. And maybe not ever.

He rubbed a hand over his face, suddenly bone-
tired. "Okay, it's a deal."

The flickering flames cast a soft yellow-orange glow
over Dalton's living room, the fire's occasional
crackle the only sound filling the late-night silence.

Daphne and her brother were alone in the room, their sister and mother having retired an hour ago.

Daphne stared into the fireplace, one hand idly stroking Data's head. The silence stretched on, her brother apparently as caught up in his thoughts as she was with hers.

In her peripheral vision, she saw him turn his head toward her.

"You're awfully quiet tonight," he said. "In fact, you haven't said much since you got here. Are you all right?"

She nodded absently. "Yeah, fine." Suddenly making up her mind to ask the question burning the back of her tongue all evening, she said, "Who's Jackson Kidd?" Even saying the name sent a weird tingle through her body.

Dalton settled deeper in his chair. "An artist, a sculptor actually, who's done some of the most spectacular bronze nudes I've ever seen. There's a display of his work at the gallery. You don't remember?"

"Guess not," she said, searching for a memory but coming up empty. "At least I don't remember seeing his name."

"He doesn't like his name prominently displayed, so the placards by his sculptures are pretty small."

"An artist who doesn't have a big ego," she said with a laugh. "Now there's a concept."

He flashed a smile in her direction. "It's true. He wants his work to speak for itself, to draw people's attention on its own merit, not simply because it's a Jackson Kidd."

She thought about that for a moment, then said, "You must be friends if he called you at home."

"Yeah, we are. We met while I was in college and he was just beginning to establish himself as an up-and-coming artist. We really clicked and have stayed in touch over the years, not that Maureen approved of my being friends with a bohemian nobody."

She huffed out a breath. "Who cares what that first-class bitch thought."

"Gee, Daf," Dalton said with a laugh, "why don't you tell me what you really think of her? Anyway, I haven't seen Jack in a couple years, so I'm looking forward to seeing him next week."

Her heart rate picked up. "Next week?"

"He's winding up a PR tour, has a free day between stops and thought he'd come for a visit. He'll be getting in around noon on New Year's Eve. Which reminds me, I'm hosting a small party at the gallery for him that evening. I'd really like you, Darcie and Mom to come."

Her heart beat even faster. "I don't know if—"

"It'll be early and will only last a couple of hours, so it won't interfere with anybody's plans for later that evening."

She looked down at her ring, the firelight reflecting in the stone, making it appear to be alive. A mixture of anticipation and apprehension fluttered in her belly, frightening her with its intensity. She desperately wanted to tell Dalton she couldn't go to the party, but that would be the coward's way out. And if there was one thing she wasn't, it was a coward. Meeting her brother's gaze, she said, "Sure, I'll be there."

"Great. I'll ask Darcie and Mom in the morning."

"Will Mom still be here? She mentioned something about driving down to the Springs for a couple days to visit friends."

"She is, but that's early next week. She'll be back on Wednesday, and her flight home isn't until the third."

She nodded. "So what about Annie? Have you already asked her?"

Dalton's low groan drifted to her. "Don't you start, too."

"Start what? I just asked a simple question."

"Get real. Nothing's simple to the Stoner women! I don't need you pushing Annie at me. Or telling me she's the best thing that's ever happened to me. That I'd be an idiot to let her get away. Mom's already covered that territory."

Her eyebrows lifted. "Mom said those things?"

"Oh yeah."

"Hmm," she said, her lips twitching, "and I thought I was the only psychic in this family."

"Whatever it is, it's damn annoying."

"Doesn't have to be. You could just admit we're right and call Annie."

"You'd love that, wouldn't you? Me crawling on my belly, admitting my mother and sisters know what's best for me." He snorted. "Ain't gonna happen."

"Dalton, that's not what we want. All we want, all we've ever wanted is for you to be happy."

"And you think Annie is the woman to do that. The one who can light up my life with just her presence. Fill my days with unbridled joy and happiness."

"I'll ignore your sarcasm and just say, Annie most definitely is the right woman for you."

Dalton snorted again, then fell silent. He didn't want to talk about Annie. He didn't even want to think about her. But as he'd already realized, damned if he could stop.

A wet nose on his hand pulled Dalton from a light doze. "Hey, boy," he murmured, giving Worf—or was it Data, he couldn't tell in the pre-dawn light—a lazy pat. "Did my tossing and turning wake you up?"

He smiled at the dog's soft whimper. "Sorry 'bout

that," he said around a yawn. Christ, he'd barely slept, and when he finally had managed to drift off, his restless sleep had been filled with dreams of Annie.

Certain there was no point in staying in bed any longer, he flipped back the covers then turned and sat up on the edge of the mattress, glancing at the digital readout of the clock on his nightstand. 5:30. He groaned, remembering another morning he'd gotten up at the same time and what he'd found in his living room. Annie dancing for exercise, looking adorable with her sleep-mussed hair, wearing his tee shirt, and wiggling that cute little ass of hers.

He squeezed his eyes closed, as if that would banish the memory from his brain. *Man, you've got it bad.*

Several minutes passed before he finally wiped his hands over his face, then pushed himself to his feet and grabbed a set of sweats. Coffee. That's what he needed.

While the coffee brewed, he caught himself continually checking the clock, wondering if she— *Nope, don't go there! She might not even be home, so there's no point in wondering anything.*

Before he realized what he'd decided to do, he poured a cup of coffee, then reached for the phonebook.

Annie pulled off the headphones then grabbed the ringing phone. It's a wonder she'd heard it ring at all, since she had the volume cranked up on her CD player. But a song had just ended, allowing other sounds in her apartment to reach her.

She dragged in a deep breath. "Hello."

"Annie?"

The sexy timbre of the male voice made her already racing heart pound even harder. "Dalton, hi."

"Did I interrupt your dancing?"

"Yeah, but it's fine."

"After I dialed your number, I was afraid you might still be in bed." He cleared his throat. "Um, I can call later if you want to get back to your dancing."

"No, I was about to quit anyway. And it's a good thing you called now. If you'd waited, you would've missed me."

"Missed you? Oh, right. Those other deliveries your boss lined up for you."

"No, actually. I spoke to my boss last night and asked her if I could change my schedule. As soon as I shower and pack, I'm heading up to my folks."

"When are you coming back?"

"I'm not sure. Either Christmas night or the next morning."

"Good, then you'll be home before the weekend. Do you have plans for Saturday night?"

"Um . . . no. Why?"

"Since you've never seen my museum and gallery, I was thinking I could give you a tour, then take you out for dinner."

She smiled. "How could I possibly turn down the chance for a private tour, and by the owner, no less?"

His chuckle sent a burst of warmth over her already overheated body. "I guarantee, you won't be sorry."

"Oh, I'm sure of that," she said with a laugh.

After agreeing on a time for him to pick her up on Saturday, he told her to have a safe trip, then they wished each other a Merry Christmas before saying good-bye. She pushed the Off button to end the call, her smile fading as she thought about seeing Dalton again.

Bad idea, she told herself. She should've come up with an excuse not to see him. But idiot that she was, she'd let her heart jump right in and do the talking.

Dropping the phone on an end table, she headed for the bathroom.

As she turned on the shower to let the water get hot, she considered calling Charlene to see if she could still make a delivery today. That would get her mind off Dalton, and she'd still have plenty of time to drive up to Wyoming. Except what reason would she give Charlene for suddenly changing her mind? Last night, she'd asked the woman to have someone else make her deliveries because she had so many things to catch up on. Charlene had agreed, but something in her voice made Annie wonder if she had bought the story.

At the time, making up an excuse had seemed easier than admitting the truth. That she was having serious second thoughts about delivering strip-o-grams. The job had seemed so exciting, just exactly what she needed to spice up her boring life, before she met Dalton. And now . . . well, now, she couldn't imagine taking her clothes off in front of anyone other than him.

She frowned at her reflection in the bathroom mirror. *You wanted some excitement in your life, so don't you dare chicken out now.*

In theory, the advice she gave herself was sound. But in reality, following it would be a different game entirely.

Normally, Dalton enjoyed Christmas with his sisters and mother, but this year he found himself constantly on guard that one of them would start in again about Annie. To their credit, and his relief, none of them broached the subject. And although he tried not to let her monopolize his thoughts, he repeatedly found himself waiting for her to enter a room, listening for the sound of her voice. Even his dogs wandered around the house, searching in vain for their new friend.

He scrubbed a hand over his jaw, then heaved a deep sigh.

"You okay?"

"Fine," he replied, pulling his gaze away from the fireplace and sending Darcie a weak smile. "Just thinking."

She nodded, moving to stand next to him. "I can tell you've got a lot on your mind. You zoned out on us a few times today."

"Sorry."

"No problem. I've been kinda spacey today myself."

"Working too many hours, counselor?"

"No more than usual."

He stared at his youngest sister for several seconds, noting her pinched mouth, the dark circles under her eyes. "I hate to say this, but you look beat. I know making partner is important to you, but I think you're pushing yourself too hard."

"I haven't been sleeping well, but it's not because of my caseload."

"You know I've never stuck my nose in your personal life, or Daf's either, and we both know why. But that doesn't mean I don't care what happens to you. So if there's something on your mind and you need to talk, I want you to know I'm here for you. Any time."

"Thanks. That means a lot," she said, her voice wobbly. "But I need to work this out on my own."

"I understand." He turned her toward him, then pulled her into his arms for a hug. "But the offer stands."

She sagged against him, looping her arms loosely around his waist and dropping her head onto his shoulder. After a few seconds, she whispered, "I think I might be in love."

He blinked, totally caught off guard by both her statement and the despair he heard in her voice. Since high school, the whole focus of Darcie's life had been her career. She seldom dated, claiming she didn't have the time. So finding out she'd met someone, and perhaps fallen in love, momentarily stunned him.

"Maybe it's my imagination, sis, but you don't sound happy about the possibility."

"I'm not sure I am. Sometimes I feel like I'm about to burst with happiness, then others I'm convinced I've lost my mind. The only thing I know for sure is, I'm confused and scared."

"Confused, maybe. But Darcie Stoner, the formidable attorney who brings her courtroom opponents to their knees with just a look or a few choice words, scared? No way, I don't believe it."

"It's true, Dalton. I'm scared to death of what I feel for a man I barely know. It's so consuming, so overwhelming, that"—she drew a shuddering breath—"I don't know how to handle it."

"Have you talked to Mom or Daf?"

"Daphne. A little."

He hugged her tighter. "Wish I had something wise to tell you, but my mind is pretty muddled right now, too."

"Because of Annie?"

He exhaled heavily. "Yeah."

She took a step back, then looked up into his face. "You care about her, don't you?"

"A lot more than I should," he replied in a low voice.

"Are you saying you're in love?"

An excellent question. One he'd asked himself a dozen times over the past several days, yet he still didn't have a definitive answer. "I'm not sure," he said, choosing his words carefully. "Maybe it's love, but I'm not ready to tack a label on what I feel for her."

Darcie smiled up at him. "She seems really nice, so I hope it works out for the two of you."

"I doubt it will, but thanks." He gave her a gentle chuck under her chin. "Same goes for me. I hope this guy is the real deal for you."

"Thanks, me, too. But I"—her smile faded—"I've got this really ominous feeling, and I just can't shake it."

His heart aching for his sister, he tried to lighten the mood by saying, "Are you telling me you've developed psychic power?"

She blinked several times, then chuckled. "Perish the thought. Having one psychic in this family is more than enough, don't you think?"

As Dalton drove his Blazer out of the parking lot behind Annie's apartment building, he glanced at her and said, "Did you have a good Christmas?"

"Yeah, I did."

"You weren't totally bored being isolated . . . let's see, how did you put it . . . out in the middle of nowhere?"

"You're a regular comedian, aren't you?" Before he could respond, she said, "I also told you I could handle a couple of days on my folks' ranch, and I did." She turned to look out the passenger window, watching but not really seeing the other vehicles on Denver's crowded streets.

The two days she'd spent in Wyoming had been wonderful. Of course she'd expected to enjoy seeing her family again. But this visit had been different. For the first time, she'd actually found the isolation of the ranch appealing—a reaction that disturbed her as much as it surprised her. She'd even given serious consideration to staying longer—something she'd never done. Seems meeting Dalton was having more of an effect on her than she thought.

"Almost there," he said, his voice pulling her back to the present.

She glanced around, stunned to find they'd driven across town to Capitol Hill, one of the oldest sections of Denver, and she hadn't realized the passage of time.

He parked on the street in front of a three-story mansion made of reddish-colored stone, then got out and came around to open the passenger door.

"I haven't been to Capitol Hill in years," she said, stepping out of the Blazer. "I'd forgotten how beautiful the old mansions are here."

"That's one of the reasons I chose this part of the city. These old homes have so much character. A lot more than any new, modern building would have."

"Well," she said, looking up at the impressive house, "I'm glad you saved this old beauty."

He smiled. "Yeah, me, too. I looked at several other mansions in this area, but the turret and ruby sandstone of this one really appealed to me. And after going inside and finding most of the interior had already been restored by the previous owner, I knew this would become my museum and gallery."

His hand resting on her lower back, he escorted her to the front steps and up onto the curved porch. With the shortness of the winter days, the interior lights had already been turned on, sending a soft glow through the windows.

"Closing time isn't for another few minutes," he told her, opening the front door and stepping aside to allow her to enter first. "Then we'll have the place to ourselves."

The idea of being alone with him started a wild fluttering in her chest that quickly slid down to her belly. She nodded and smiled, afraid to meet his gaze or trust her voice for fear of giving away her reaction to his statement.

When he led her across the large entry with a vaulted ceiling to the doorway of what would have been the living room when it was a single-family home, her breath caught. "Oh, my God!" She moved into the room, then did a slow pirouette, taking in every detail. The beveled glass windows. The gold textured wallpaper. The gleaming golden oak woodwork and fireplace mantel. The patterned plaster of the high ceiling.

Most of the furnishings had been removed to make room for easels and various sized display cases and pedestals, but what remained were all period pieces. Annie wasn't an expert on antique furniture, but if the settee and chairs weren't authentic, they had to be first-class reproductions.

She turned back to face him. "Dalton, this is gorgeous."

"Thanks," he replied, his expression clearly revealing his pleasure at her praise. "This side of the main floor is the museum portion of the place. In this room are paintings and sculptures that represent the earliest known examples of erotic art. And in what was originally the dining room"—he nodded toward a wide arched doorway—"is a small library, filled with books on the history and evolution of erotic art, covering everything from ancient times up to the present."

After Annie had explored both rooms, he led her to what was originally the parlor.

"In here," he said, "is where we set up displays that are changed every month or two. Right now, we're featuring the paintings of a new artist I discovered last summer. He does beautiful work."

"Mmm, I agree," Annie replied, wandering around the room, stopping to study each painting. "Are these based on the *Kama Sutra*?"

He shook his head. "The artist's inspiration was the *Ananga-Ranga*. Same cultural heritage as the *Kama Sutra* but written fourteen centuries later."

"Based on these paintings, it must've been written for the same purpose."

"As a love manual? Yeah, but the author of the *Ananga-Ranga* was writing for husbands, not lovers."

She arched an eyebrow. "Ah, the roots of male chauvinism, perhaps?"

"That's how society had evolved from Vatsyayana's time."

"Yeah, downhill. Glad I didn't live back then."

He smiled. "My mother and sisters feel the same way."

"So what's upstairs?"

"The gallery. Come on, I'll show you."

The second floor was just as lovely as the first, each room housing a collection of artwork. Paintings of all sizes hung on the walls, and sculptures in several mediums sat on pedestals or were arranged on tables of various heights.

Annie moved from room to room, admiring the beauty of each piece and applauding the talent of the artists who created such fabulous artworks. But in addition to her appreciation, she had another reaction to looking at paintings and sculptures of couples in every imaginable sexual position. A reaction she hadn't expected.

She was getting turned on.

For a moment, she couldn't breathe. She was an adult, for God's sake, not some teenager with raging hormones who gets aroused at even the slightest provocation. Yet there was no denying, she definitely was getting hot. A reaction no doubt greatly influenced by the man standing nearby—a man she'd been naked with, a man with whom she'd done some of the things she now saw painted on canvas or cast in bronze. And what they hadn't done, thanks to the visual stimuli before her, her mind's eye now saw them doing in vivid detail.

Her pulse quickened, the earlier fluttering in her belly intensifying before sliding even lower and turning into a throbbing ache between her thighs, and her panties grew moist. Swallowing a groan, she took a slow, deep breath, then glanced over at Dalton.

Could he be reacting the same way? No, that was ridiculous. Erotic art was his business, so getting sexually aroused by his work would be like her getting turned on by a math textbook or a stack of final exams. Still, he did look slightly flushed. And was it her imagination, or was there a new tenseness in his face?

Just then, he turned, their gazes met, and she knew.

She moved closer to him. "Is there some place private where we can go?"

He blinked. "Uh, my office."

"Let's go." She grabbed his hand.

"But you haven't seen the rest of the displays."

"Later," she replied, trying to tug him toward the door, but he wasn't cooperating.

"Annie, what—"

"Okay, I'll spell it out for you. I want you. You want me. So"—she gave him another tug—"let's go to your office."

"Now?"

"Yeah, now."

"But—"

"Uh-uh, no buts. That's what you're always telling me, so right back at ya." When he didn't look convinced, she leaned close and pressed her mouth to his in a brief kiss. "Come on, Dalton, you know you want to."

Sixteen

Dalton sucked in a deep breath, filling his lungs with a combination of Annie's shampoo, a subtle hint of her perfume, and aroused woman.

Her proposition to go to his office, along with her intoxicating scent, swelled his dick—already sporting half a boner from watching her reaction to the pieces in his museum and art gallery—to a full throbbing erection. Damn, he was in real trouble now.

"Dalton, you're stalling."

"What?" He gave his head a shake, hoping to clear the fog from his brain. "No, I'm just—" He pinched the bridge of his nose. "Actually, I don't know what I'm doing."

She stared up at him, those gorgeous green eyes ablaze with simmering desire. "Then, maybe you need a little nudge."

Before he could respond, she had flattened herself against him, arms wrapped around his neck, her lips seeking his.

A low groan rumbling in his throat, he clutched her tighter against him, shoving his tongue into her mouth, tasting, teasing, taking them both deeper into the depths of need.

She sucked on his tongue, pressing her hardened nipples into his chest, rubbing her mound against the ridge of his penis. Still kissing him, she eased away from him enough to get one hand between them. When she gripped him through his slacks, he nearly came right then. Jesus, he hadn't been this horny since he was a sex-crazed teenager bent on screwing everything with boobs. He hadn't had much success back then, but that didn't mean he hadn't thought about sex. He had. A lot. And right now, getting Annie's panties off and burying himself deep inside her was all he could think about.

He jerked his mouth from hers. "Let's go to my office," he said in a strangled whisper.

She laughed softly. "I knew I'd bring you around to my way of thinking."

"You damn near did more than that," he grumbled, grasping her arms and spinning her around to face the door.

"Oh yeah?" she said, smiling at him over her shoulder. "You're in a bad way, huh?"

"Paybacks are hell." He curved his lips in a lecherous grin. "And you, babe, are gonna pay."

Her chin came up. "Pretty big talk there, mister."

"That's not all that's big," he replied, leading her into the hallway.

"I noticed." Eyes flashing more green fire, she flicked a glance at his crotch. "Unless you've got a salami stuffed in your shorts."

He couldn't hold back a laugh. "You groped me, remember. And a salami doesn't twitch when it's squeezed, so you know you wrapped your fingers around the genuine article."

Before she could respond, he grasped her elbow with one hand and practically ran down the hall to his office.

Once inside the room, he used his foot to slam the door shut, then turned the lock before pulling Annie into his arms.

After giving her a kiss that left him dizzy, he buried his face in her hair. "I want you," he whispered. "I need you."

He heard her draw an unsteady breath. "Me, too," she said, her hands fumbling to unbuckle his belt. When she accomplished the task, she unfastened the hook on the waistband of his slacks, then found the tab of his zipper.

As she lowered the zipper, the backs of her fingers grazed his erection, eliciting his sharp gasp. "Easy, babe. I'm already gritting my teeth here."

She dropped her hand, leaving the fly of his slacks gaping open. "Okay, my turn."

With quick, efficient movements, she toed off her shoes, removed her socks, then shoved down her wool slacks. Her panties quickly followed suit. Grumbling under her breath, she worked to pull her feet out of the garments caught around her ankles. Then with a triumphant cry, she freed her second foot and kicked the clothes aside.

She met his gaze, wearing just her sweater and a siren's smile. When she reached for the open fly of his slacks, he caught her hand before she could do more than brush her fingertips over the head of his dick.

"Hadn't better," he said, his voice rough with his growing need.

Her lips puckered in a pout. "I want to touch you."

"Uh-uh, not yet."

She stared at him for a few seconds, then announced, "I want to do it like that one sculpture."

"Uh, babe, you're gonna have to be more specific. There must be close to twenty sculptures here."

"The one in that last room we were in. The bronze, sitting on the center of the round display table."

He nodded. "Ah, that one. You have a good eye for

quality artwork. That sculpture's going up for auction next week. Should go for a high six figures."

"Really? Well, recognizing quality work had nothing to do with it. I just know I'm horny, and that position looked . . . mmm . . . interesting."

"Interesting, huh?" he replied with a chuckle, realizing she was making him view the pieces in his gallery under a whole new light. And surprisingly, he was enjoying the process. "You could be right."

"Only one way to find out."

"True."

He glanced around, then bent to scoop her into his arms. His office wasn't a particularly good place for what was about to happen, but at the moment he really didn't give a damn. He just wanted to bury himself in Annie's heat as quickly as possible.

Crossing to the far side of the room, he came to a halt beside a grouping of low tables and straight-backed chairs. He held meetings here with his staff, artists or customers, but never for the purpose of hot and heavy sex. His dick swelled a little more at the thought.

He set Annie on her feet long enough to dispense with his slacks and briefs, then he took a seat on one of the chairs, pulling her down so she sat sideways across his thighs.

She stared at him, her eyes dilated, glowing with desire. When her tongue slid over her bottom lip, he bit back a groan.

"Annie," he whispered, pushing his hands through her hair to cup the back of her head, then brought her face closer to his. He took her mouth in a fierce kiss, telling her with his lips and tongue how much he wanted her, letting her feel the heat of the need raging through him like wildfire.

She whimpered, wiggling her bottom, each movement bumping against his erection.

He untangled one hand from her hair, then slid his fingers down her belly to the triangle of springy curls. When he found her clitoris, she gasped and her hips jerked in reaction. He started stroking her, soft little brushes with the tip of a finger, and soon she was rocking against him.

Her head fell back, another whimper vibrating in her throat. "God, Dalton, that's so good."

He dipped his head and nuzzled the side of her neck. "It's gonna get better," he said, running his tongue over her warm skin.

Moving his hands to her waist, he turned her so she sat with her back to him, then spread her legs so they were draped over his thighs, her feet just touching the floor.

"Did I get the position right?"

"Yeah, except—" He heard her swallow then draw an unsteady breath. "Except for one thing."

"Really? Are you sure, because I thought—" He grunted, the sudden jab of her elbow against his ribs taking him by surprise. "Hey, take it easy, babe. There's no need for violence."

"You're stalling again, slick."

"And you are the most impatient wom—" He twisted his upper body just in time to miss a second jab by that wicked elbow. "Okay, that's it." He grabbed her hips and lifted her off his thighs.

"No!" she practically yelled, planting her feet more firmly on the floor to keep her balance. "Dalton, wait. I'm sor—"

"Shh," he whispered, chuckling at the panic in her voice. "Relax. I've got what you want right here." He reached between them to grasp his penis, then brushed the tip against her wet flesh. "Take it, babe."

Her breath catching on a sob, she braced her hands on his knees then lowered herself, inch by torturous inch until she'd taken all of him into her heated center.

"Sweet heaven," he muttered through gritted teeth.

"Yeah," she replied, wiggling her hips and forcing him even deeper.

After a moment, Dalton said, "This is your show. I can't move much like this, so you're in control."

Annie nodded, exhaled slowly, then began rocking her pelvis, forward and backward. Groaning with frustration, she abruptly stopped.

"I can't move very much either," she said. "Maybe this wasn't such a good position after all."

"I disagree. What you were doing felt damn good to me," he replied, sliding his hands under her sweater to cup her breasts. He pressed a kiss to the side of her neck while giving her nipples a gentle pinch through the fabric of her bra. "Tell me what you need to make it better for you."

She did more experimental rocking, then said, "I need you to touch me." She grabbed his right wrist and pulled his hand out from under her sweater. "Now." She directed his fingers to between her spread thighs.

At the first stroke of his fingers on her clitoris, she moaned his name, then began her rocking movement again.

"You're so hot and wet," he murmured against her ear. "Touching your swollen clit like this, knowing I'm going to make you scream when you come, makes my dick even harder." He flexed upward as much as he could to prove his point.

"Oh God." Her hips rocked faster, the knowing glide of his finger bringing her closer and closer.

"Annie." His tongue flicked her earlobe. "My sweet Annie."

"Dalton, don't stop. Please . . . don't stop."

"Never, babe," he whispered, the roughness of his voice telling her he was nearing his own release.

As he continued to work his magic, she curled her hands into fists, barely registering the sharp bite of her fingernails digging into her palms. Squeezing her eyes closed, she teetered on the threshold of relief, desperate to ease the throbbing ache of need clawing at her.

Then suddenly she was there, shoved over the edge with the power and strength of an armored tank. The first spasm made her gasp.

"Yes. Yes." Arching against his hand, her body quaking with more spasms, she screamed.

Over the roar in her head, she heard Dalton's guttural groan, felt the pulsing of his climax deep inside her. Finally, he exhaled a long sigh, moving his hand up to her belly where he traced patterns on her skin with his fingertips.

Annie couldn't think, could barely hear over the wild pounding of her heart, and moving for the moment was impossible. All she could do was feel, and what she felt was scaring the wits out of her. Not physically—though knowing she could experience amazing physical pleasure like what they'd just shared still shocked her—it was what she felt emotionally that frightened her. There was no longer any doubt in her mind. She had fallen in love with Dalton Stoner.

Perhaps that was why making love this time had been more intense, more satisfying. But realizing she'd done something incredibly stupid and fallen in love with him didn't mean she planned to speak her feelings aloud. The fact remained that, regardless if she loved him or not, they weren't right for each other, so telling him how she felt would serve no purpose.

Making sure the words didn't slip out while she was most vulnerable—like while they were making love—would be tricky. But somehow she would have to find the inner strength to make sure she kept her lips sealed.

Dalton shifted beneath her, bringing her back to the present.

"There's a bathroom over there," he said, pointing to a door to their left.

She nodded, then eased off his lap. Not looking at him, she retrieved her clothes from the floor and went into the bathroom.

Dalton knew something was different after they'd taken turns cleaning up in his bathroom. Annie seemed more subdued, almost reluctant to meet his gaze. Before he could figure out the puzzle, she asked to see the rest of his gallery.

After touring the displays in the remaining rooms, she stopped in front of the stairs to the third floor, where a rope, with a Private sign, had been strung across the staircase.

"Private, huh?" Her eyebrows lifted, a smile teasing her mouth. "So what's up there? Your secret lair?"

"Uh . . . no," he replied, glad to see her emerge from her somber mood. "We use one of the rooms for storage. Most of the others are empty."

"Can I see?"

He shrugged. "Sure."

As they started up the stairs, she said, "Do you plan to expand your gallery up here some day?"

"We have plenty of room on the first two floors.

Luckily, pieces sell quickly enough that I don't antic-ipate needing additional space."

They reached the landing at the top of the stairs, then Annie went ahead of him, the heels of her shoes clicking on the wood floor. "I love these old houses," she said, moving through the rooms. "So much char-acter and—" She gasped. "The turret room! Oh my God, it's great."

He smiled, watching her explore the small room built in the rounded turret.

"This is the perfect spot for a bathtub," she said, running her hand along the oak woodwork sur-rounding the room's single window. "And what a view." She spun around to look at him. "These rooms would make a great apartment. Have you considered the possibility?"

"Can't say I have," he replied. "But it wouldn't work. There's no private entrance, and I can't very well have tenants traipsing through the gallery to get up here."

"I hadn't thought of that." She sighed. "Too bad, though, 'cause I still think it would make a great apartment." After giving the turret room one last glance, she moved past him to check out the remain-ing rooms.

Daphne took a seat at the small table, still debating with herself over whether she was doing the right thing. She disliked doing a crystal ball reading for herself—she preferred not to know what the future held—and if it weren't for the rhodochrosite ring and how it was affecting her, she wouldn't be consid-ering the drastic step of doing a self reading now. But she had to know.

Because crystals absorb the energy of others, she

would do the reading with a second ball, one she kept just for her personal use. She made an adjustment to the crystal's position on the table, then breathed in and out three times, trying to relax and clear her head.

When she'd calmed herself as much as she could, she gazed into the center of the crystal ball, letting her mind drift. For a long time there was nothing in the murky glass, then suddenly a man's face appeared. Trying not to panic, she studied his image. She'd never seen him before, she was certain of that. There was no way she could forget such penetrating dark eyes, the sensual arch of his eyebrows, the shaggy hair, neatly trimmed beard, or the arrogant smirk on his lips. She narrowed her eyes. *Conceited beast.*

His mouth curved in a smile, as if he'd heard her less-than-complimentary thought, then his face wavered, faded and finally disappeared. Almost immediately the image of a key took his place.

She furrowed her brow at the sudden change, but continued to stare into the crystal's center, waiting for something more to appear. When the key remained unchanged for several minutes, she knew the energy had faded and her reading had come to an end. Releasing a deep sigh, she pushed her chair away from the table then picked up the crystal.

As she rinsed the ball under cold water, she tried to come up with possible explanations for what the crystal had revealed to her. Sometimes there was no mistaking the meaning of the images that appeared during a reading. Other times what she saw made no sense at face value but was symbolic of something else. The problem was, figuring out the hidden meaning wasn't always simple.

Seeing a man's face told her she would meet him some time in the future—probably fairly soon. Maybe he'd come into Charmed, or she'd see him in a grocery store or at a gas station. The key, however, was more complicated.

A key could mean any one of a number of things was going to happen. New doors were about to open for her, or she would be moving. It could also symbolize the key to her success, or the key to her heart.

She turned off the faucet, flattening her lips in a scowl. No. Absolutely not! The key was not to her heart. That lock was permanently closed. So the key in her reading had to be a symbol for something else.

After drying the crystal ball and wrapping it in its special silk scarf, she tucked it back in the top drawer of her dresser. As she closed the drawer, she wished tucking away her reading and any possible meanings could be done as easily.

The Avalanche forward had a breakaway. He skated across the blue line, then wound up and unleashed a blistering wrist shot, sending the puck over the opposing goaltender's shoulder and into the net. The goal light came on, a siren blared, and thousands of rabid Avs fans went wild. Dalton watched Annie jump to her feet, clapping her hands and screaming at the top of her lungs. When she noticed he was still in his seat, she grabbed his arm and hauled him up beside her.

He grinned, her enthusiasm contagious, then curled his lips and gave a shrill whistle. He hadn't been to a hockey game in years, and he had to admit, she was right. Sitting in the stands definitely was a lot more fun than watching a game on TV. Though he didn't care much for crowds, he found the vibrant excitement of the packed arena energizing.

While the fans' energy and sitting five rows from

the action probably played a large part in his enjoyment, the major reason was Annie. Not only did he enjoy her company, but he discovered he also enjoyed watching her animated reactions to what was happening on the ice. Her eyes glittering and cheeks flushed with excitement, she cupped her hands around her mouth to boo the referee after a bad penalty call, or whooped with joy when the Avalanche goalie made a spectacular save, or yelled at an opposing defenseman, calling him a colorful, inventive name when his cheap cross-check sent an Avs player headfirst into the boards.

Whatever she did, Dalton was utterly fascinated, and amazingly, he spent as much time watching her as he did the players on the ice. When the final buzzer sounded, he was sorry to see the game end.

As they filed out of the arena and headed for Dalton's Blazer, his arm slung casually around her shoulders, he said, "As much as you love hockey, you should have a season ticket."

"I'd love to," Annie replied, giving him a wistful smile. "But the price is too steep for me."

He removed his arm, pulled his keys from his pocket and pushed the Unlock button on the remote. "What about your Christmas job?" he said, opening the passenger door. "Couldn't you put what you make toward a season ticket?"

She frowned. "My Christmas— Oh, right, with the messenger service." She moved past him and got into the Blazer.

He continued to hold the door open for several seconds, as if he expected her to say more. When she didn't, he said, "Look, I'm sorry I said anything. You probably have plans for the money and don't need me telling you how to handle your finances."

She wanted to tell him the truth, that taking the job with the Naughty or Nice Messenger Service had nothing to do with money. But she couldn't bring herself to speak the words. Instead, she said, "No need to be sorry." She forced herself to smile. "You didn't do anything wrong."

He leaned into the Blazer and pressed his lips to hers in a quick kiss, then he closed her door and walked around to the driver's side. As he slid onto his bucket seat, he said, "Want to go somewhere for a drink? Or coffee?"

"No, thanks," she replied. "I'm too wired to sit in a bar or a coffeehouse."

"You got something else in mind?"

"Weeelll, actually, I do. I think we should go back to my apartment."

He glanced over at her, his eyebrows arched. "Yeah, and . . ."

"How about we just see what comes up?"

He choked back a laugh. "I can guarantee you, I already know what that's gonna be."

"Okay, smart ass," she replied, giving his arm a punch. "So, I made a bad choice in words."

"But not a bad choice in after-hockey activities." As he started the Blazer, he flashed a grin in her direction. "You picked out another position you want to try, am I right?"

She gave him an innocent smile. "I'm not saying any more."

He shook his head. "You are such a tease."

"Uh-uh, I don't tease when it comes to sex and what I want to do to you, or with you."

"Jesus, Annie, we're not even out of the parking lot and you're already making me hard."

She chuckled, then reached over and patted his knee. "Take it easy, big guy. It's only twenty minutes to my place."

"Twenty minutes," he said, exhaling with a huff. "Seems like forever to my throbbing dick."

This time she laughed, then quickly sobered. "Poor baby." She slid her hand up his thigh. "How about if I . . . you know . . . take the edge off for you?" Her fingertips grazed the hard ridge of his erection through his jeans.

"What are you suggesting?"

"Oh, come on. You aren't that much of a prude, are you?"

He stared at her long and hard, then grabbed her hand and removed it from his crotch. "You are *not* giving me a blow job right here in front of God and everybody."

She looked around the nearly deserted parking lot. "There are only a few cars left, and they're not even close to us. Besides, the possibility of getting caught just adds to the excitement, don't ya think?"

His mouth opened, but only a low moan came out.

"Let me, Dalton," she said, reaching for him again. "No one will see us." She found the tab of his zipper and started pulling it down. "It will be so exciting."

Seventeen

Dalton opened his mouth again, this time prepared to tell Annie no. He wanted nothing to do with participating in any scheme that fed her need for excitement. Unfortunately, she took his silence as agreement. And then as soon as she put her mouth on him, his dick took over for his brain, and he lost all will to protest.

Before he realized what he was doing, his fingers pushed through her hair to cup the back of her head, holding her in place, guiding her to the rhythm that gave him the most pleasure.

And then, Christ, then he'd shot his wad with a shout so loud it's a wonder the entire town of Denver hadn't heard him.

His breathing ragged, he let his head drop back against the headrest, mortified at what had happened, yet at the same time, not sorry. He squeezed his eyes closed. God, he was pathetic.

Over the roar of his pulse pounding in his ears, he heard Annie say, "Better now?"

He had to take several deep breaths before he could get any words through his tight throat. "I . . . um . . ." He sighed. "Yeah."

"But hopefully not done for the night." When she started to tuck his now-flaccid penis back through the opening of his briefs, he pushed her hands away and took care of the task himself.

As he zipped his jeans, his earlier annoyance returned. "You want me to return the favor and give you more of an excitement fix?"

"Is that what you think, that I offered to . . . to . . . service you out of some twisted need for a thrill?"

The dashboard lights weren't bright enough for him to see her expression, but the iciness of her response left no doubt that he'd pissed her off. At the moment, he didn't care, and he'd be damned if he'd retract his words.

He shrugged. "I just asked a question."

Long seconds passed, the only sound the low rumble of the Blazer's idling engine. Then finally she moved, shifting as much as the bucket seat allowed so she faced him.

"Dalton, what's going on? I can understand if you're upset or embarrassed about what just happened, but I don't think that's it. The bitterness in your voice comes from something else, doesn't it?"

He clenched his jaw, debating whether to tell her. Finally, he leaned forward and turned off the engine. "Yeah," he said, sitting back and wrapping his hands around the steering wheel. "It's about Maureen. She was always looking for something more exciting, too." He clenched his hands tighter. "She put me through hell, and I can't— No, I won't go through that again."

Empathy for the pain Dalton had suffered welled up inside Annie. She swallowed hard, then said, "You want to tell me about it?"

He didn't respond for so long that she thought he wasn't going to answer. Then she saw his chest rise and fall, heard him exhale a deep breath.

"I was such an idiot," he said in a low voice. "I thought she loved me, but turned out the only person she's capable of loving is herself. Things were rocky between us at first, but I figured we both needed time to adjust. To get used to being married. But things didn't improve."

"Did you try to talk to her?"

"Yeah, for all the good it did. Her response was always the same. Our marriage wasn't giving her what she needed." He huffed out a breath. "What she needed was to have our marriage be one big social event. Hanging out at parties, spending the weekend in the Bahamas, flying to Europe whenever the mood struck. I told her we couldn't afford to take off any time she wanted, that I had to work. I knew she was disappointed." He sighed. "I just didn't realize how much. When she started going out a couple nights a week, I thought she just needed more time to adjust, so I cut her some slack. But as the months passed, she went out more and more, staying out longer and longer."

Annie sat quietly, listening as he continued talking, pouring out the whole story of his failed marriage. He told her how Maureen's evenings out changed to all-nighters, soon stretching into being gone entire weekends. And then one weekend she didn't come home. In spite of being furious with her, he'd also been worried and tried without success to track her down. Unfortunately, her new circle of friends were people he'd never met, and he didn't even know their names, so he had no real leads on who to call or where to look. Then when she strolled in two days later like nothing had happened, he'd had enough.

"You confronted her?" she said.

"Oh yeah. At first she just sat there. But I guess she finally must've realized I was really pissed, because she started talking, trying to defend herself." He snorted. "That was a real eye-opening conversation.

She told me again that our marriage wasn't what she thought it would be. Besides hating everything I enjoy, she said she needed excitement, new thrills, which I wasn't providing. Then she said being married to me was boring. No, actually, her exact words were, 'Dalton, you're the most boring man I've ever known.'"

Annie's breath caught. How could a woman say something so nasty to her husband? Maybe he hadn't led an exciting life then—still didn't from what Annie knew about him—but that didn't excuse such a cruel comment. "A lot of nerve she had," she muttered, then in a louder voice, added, "How'd you react?"

"Shocked mostly, I guess. But I was also relieved that she'd finally decided to open up. And for the first time in our marriage—probably the first time since we met—I was certain she was being totally honest with me."

"Hell of a time to start with the honesty."

His low chuckle drifted to her, followed by another heavy sigh. "She . . . um . . . also said since her need for excitement wasn't being filled at home, she went looking for it elsewhere."

"That's when you found out about her cheating on you?"

He nodded. "I thought I'd prepared myself for her answer, but I was wrong. She matter-of-factly told me booze, drugs and partying naturally led to sex, and it was no big deal. I don't know why I pressed the issue, but I asked her point blank if she was admitting she'd slept with another man." He paused for a moment, seeming to gather his thoughts. Then in a low voice, he said, "She shrugged and told me not to get upset because none of the men meant anything to her."

"None of them!" Annie couldn't keep the outrage out of her voice. "Did she really expect you to accept her statement as if a woman playing around on her husband with multiple partners is no big deal?"

"I don't know what she expected. Maybe she wanted to hurt me for not being the kind of husband she wanted. But once the initial shock wore off, I realized I no longer cared."

He laughed, a brittle sound that held no amusement. "Helluva note when a man doesn't give a damn if his wife spends all her time with her jet-setting friends, going to parties with an unlimited supply of booze and every sort of drug, and screwing any man she thinks is more exciting than her husband."

"Is that when you split up?"

"Yes. Seeing the real Maureen for the first time that night, I knew I had to make a decision about my future. I was sick of lying to my family and friends about where she went, and worse, sick of lying to myself that our marriage had a chance. I forced myself to face some cold, hard truths after our talk that night. One was whatever love I felt for her had died months before. And another was even if I wanted to stay married, I could never be the husband she wanted, and she sure as hell wasn't what I wanted in a wife. As soon as I got to my office the next morning, I called my lawyer and had him start divorce proceedings. I moved to Denver as soon as it was final."

Annie didn't say anything, waiting to see if he would continue. When he remained silent, she thought about everything he'd told her. In particular, one thing he'd said nagged at her. His remark about looking for excitement. Then she remembered him telling her something similar once before—at his house on the day they met. All at once it clicked into place, and her eyes widened in shock. *Oh my God!*

She must've made some sort of sound, because he reached over and placed his hand atop hers. "Are you all right?"

"You . . . you think I'm like her, don't you?"

"What?"

"A minute ago you said Maureen was always looking for something more exciting, too. Unless you're seeing another woman, it's pretty clear you were referring to me." She lifted her chin. "I'm the 'too,' aren't I?"

He removed his hand from hers but didn't answer.

"I can't believe this," she whispered. "You actually think I'm like her."

His voice was flat when he replied, "Aren't you?"

She didn't respond. She couldn't, not when the censure lacing those two words formed a lump the size of a hockey puck in her throat. Summoning all the inner strength she could, she pulled herself together enough to say, "It's getting late. We'd better go."

She knew he was staring at her, but she refused to meet his gaze.

"Annie, I—"

"Don't say any more. Please." She turned to face the windshield then reached for her seatbelt. "Just take me home."

Several seconds passed, then he sighed. "Sure."

On the drive back to her apartment, Dalton kept hoping she would say something to break the uneasiness that had settled between them. But she stared straight ahead, not saying a word.

Twenty minutes later, he brought the Blazer to a stop in the parking lot behind her building. Glancing over at her, he said, "I take it you've changed your mind about wanting me to come in."

She started at his voice, then flicked a quick glance in his direction. "Yeah, I . . . I think that would be best."

He nodded, wishing he could read her mind. "The reception for Jackson Kidd is day after tomorrow. Have you changed your mind about going?"

The lighting in the parking lot provided enough light for him to see the corners of her mouth curve down and her eyebrows pull together in a frown. After a moment, her expression cleared. "No, I'll go with you."

Dalton eased out the breath he hadn't realized he'd been holding. "Good. Five-thirty still okay?" When she nodded, he put the Blazer in Park then started to open his door. "I'll walk you to your—"

"That's not necessary," she said, opening her door and getting out. "I'll be fine."

"Annie?"

She turned back to meet his gaze.

"I . . . never mind. Good-night."

She held his gaze a moment longer, then she nodded, closed the Blazer door and hurried up the walk.

He watched as she entered the security code then opened the door and slipped inside. "Damn," he muttered. For a few minutes, he just sat there staring at the apartment building, wondering if she would have second thoughts about going to Jackson's reception.

Maybe it would be best if she did. Maybe it would be better to end things now before he got more deeply involved. *Knock off with the maybes, Stoner. You're already involved up to your goddamn eyeballs.*

Releasing a heavy sigh, he put the Blazer in gear and drove out of the parking lot. For once, he wished he didn't live so far from Denver, wished he had a place in the city where he could stay on nights when he didn't want to make the long drive to his house in the foothills.

But at least the ride ahead of him would provide plenty of time to figure out what he should do. After what had just happened with Annie, he definitely needed to do something. Unfortunately, he didn't know where he should start.

He let his mind drift back to the first time he'd seen Annie. Damn, she'd been something. All that wild curly hair, her delicate nose and cheeks pink from the cold, lips painted bright red, those gorgeous green eyes. And that sexy outfit she'd been wearing. His heart slamming hard against his ribs, his groin tightened at the memory. Too bad the power had gone out when it did; he would've enjoyed watching her stripping routine. He frowned. Except that she'd been sent there by Daphne, so that probably would've thrown a damper on his reaction.

Other memories of the time he'd spent with Annie ran through his mind, potent reminders of how much he enjoyed being around her. Watching her play with his dogs, hearing her laugh, making love to her. Careful now, he warned himself, don't make this about sex. In this instance, great sex wasn't reason enough to continue a relationship. Not when there were bigger obstacles to overcome—provided he decided he even wanted to try overcoming them.

Daphne thought Annie was right for him, and his mother agreed, totally dismissing his comment that Annie and Maureen were too much alike. But his family kept forgetting one important factor: This was his life, dammit, and all that mattered was what he believed and what he wanted. Which meant he had to figure out if what he believed was something he could live with, or if it was a deal breaker.

By the time he pulled into his driveway, he still hadn't made a decision. One minute he'd been sure he had to end it with Annie, that he just couldn't risk another emotional trouncing like the one Maureen had given him. Then in the next minute, he'd been close to agreeing with his mother about being a fool if he let Annie go, making him want to consider giving the relationship a chance. He'd vacillated back and forth so many times, he felt dizzy.

After bringing the Blazer to a stop inside the garage, he turned off the engine, then just sat there. How had one sexy-as-hell, hardheaded high school math teacher with a thirst for excitement managed to tip his life so far out of kilter?

The sharp barks of Data and Worf from inside the house pulled him from his musings. With a deep sigh, he pushed the remote to close the garage door, then got out of the Blazer. The reception for Jackson wasn't until Thursday evening, so maybe sometime over the next two days, he'd be struck over the head by a brilliant stick and he'd have the answer he needed to his dilemma. Twisting his lips in a wry smile at the absurd thought, he went into his house.

Annie lay staring at the ceiling of her bedroom as she'd been doing for the past hour, replaying yet again the conversation she'd had with Dalton after the hockey game.

She scowled into the darkness. Damn the man! How could he compare her to his ex-wife—a woman who was a snob, a liar, and worse, thought sleeping around on her husband was no big deal? Had he been so blinded by the behavior of one woman—as

reprehensible as it was—that he actually thought she
and Maureen were alike?

She gave a very unladylike snort, then rolled over
and punched her pillow. *Dalton Stoner, you wouldn't
know the truth if it bit you on the ass.* She sighed. *So, now
what do I do?*

Though she'd originally believed there could be
no future for the two of them, that belief had sprung
a leak somewhere over the past few days, a leak that
was getting bigger by the minute.

Okay, she decided, time to redo the mental com-
parison chart she'd made while still at Dalton's
house, then she'd rethink their relationship.

On the plus side, they both loved dogs. He was fun
to be with, and he made her laugh. They enjoyed
some of the same activities—playing pool, watching
hockey games, and she was quickly becoming a fan of
Star Trek: The Next Generation. Then there was the incredible, beyond-her-wildest-dreams sex. And of
course, she loved him beyond reason.

As for the negative side, she loved city life and he
didn't, although she had to admit, she was beginning
to view the isolation of living in the country under a
whole new light. And he seemed to enjoy the time
they spent together in Denver. She frowned. Okay,
maybe that wasn't as big a deal as she'd once thought.

So what else? Ah, there was his occupation. Owning
a museum and art gallery made him a real—no wait,
scratch that. His interest in erotic art and the *Kama
Sutra* definitely cancelled out the boring, stuffy museum owner she'd once assumed him to be. His taste
in art brought to mind their physical relationship. It
was pretty evident that he desired her, but beyond
wanting her sexually, she had no idea what, if anything
else, he felt for her. And then there was his asinine notion that she belonged in the same category as his

ex-wife. Just thinking that he had such a low opinion of her threatened to stir another round of her temper. Determined to remain calm, she took a deep breath, then finished her mental calculations.

Obviously, the pluses far outweighed the negatives—some of the latter were iffy at best anyway—yet she had no idea how to interpret the results. Did such one-sidedness really mean she and Dalton should take a chance on a permanent relationship? She didn't need long to decide she hoped the answer was yes, because she definitely wanted to try. And her first order of business would be setting the record straight on his ridiculous belief that she was some kind of Maureen clone.

She considered calling him in the morning, but dismissed the idea. She'd rather talk to him in person, which meant dropping by his gallery was a possibility. But she hated to do that since he might be too busy for a private conversation, and she definitely didn't want them to be interrupted. So the best option would be to wait until she saw him Thursday night. Then after the reception, she'd have a little chat with Dalton Stoner.

Quin Jett looked at his watch, wishing he'd followed his instincts and gotten the hell out of town before Christmas. But like a fool, he'd stuck around because he wanted to see Darcie again. And then he'd stayed a little longer, and now here it was New Year's Eve and he was still in Denver.

He checked the time again, knowing he couldn't put off making the phone call any longer. Darcie was supposed to arrive in less than an hour to pick him up for the reception at her brother's art gallery. He hated to do this, but he really had no other choice.

He never should have agreed to go with her in the first place. He knew better. But in a moment of weakness, he'd seen the hope shining in her dark blue eyes and he hadn't been able to refuse her invitation. As soon as he said he'd go, he knew he'd made the wrong decision. But the joy on her face, the brightness of her smile had squeezed his heart, making him fall more deeply in love with her, and he hadn't been able to force himself to take back the words.

He'd planned to call her the next day and tell her he wouldn't be able to go after all. But he'd come up with one excuse after another to put off calling that day, as well as the following two. Apparently, he'd turned into a coward where Darcie was concerned, unable to fabricate even a simple little story to get himself off the hook as her escort. Not a pleasant discovery for a man who had always prided himself on his ability to do whatever needed to be done without a twinge of conscience.

With time running out, there were no more excuses. He had to make the call. Now. His only hope was that he'd timed it right, and he'd get her voice mail because he didn't want to have to talk to her. Another cowardly act, he knew. But if he had to speak to her, he wasn't sure he could bear to hear the disappointment in her voice. Then he might cave and actually stay.

Heaving a weary sigh, he picked up the phone and dialed her number.

A few seconds later, he replaced the phone's handset, relieved he'd been able to leave a message. Would Darcie hear the very real regret in his voice, or would she be so hurt and angry that she wouldn't notice? Well, it didn't much matter now.

He turned to look around his hotel room a final time. Memories flooded him. Darcie on the bed, her mouth swollen from his kisses, eyes dreamy with spent passion. Darcie in the shower with him, running her hands over his shoulders and chest, and then lower.

He shook his head, chasing the unwanted images from his mind. But he knew the reprieve was only temporary. Wanted or not, those memories—along with many more—were not gone for good. They were permanently etched in his brain and his heart, and he'd carry them with him until he drew his last breath.

Calling on his years of self-discipline, he picked up his suitcase, then left the room without a backward glance.

Daphne studied the newest sculpture in Dalton's gallery, her heart thudding heavily in her chest. She'd been to High Country countless times, but none of the pieces she'd seen in the gallery affected her the way this one did.

Prior to her brother's opening his gallery, she had some knowledge of art, having dabbled with painting while in high school and taken several classes in college. So when Dalton announced his plans to open High Country, she'd been thrilled, though finding out he planned to showcase erotic art had taken her by surprise. But after listening to him go on and on about the artists and their work, she knew he'd found his passion in life. And as a result, she'd developed a better appreciation of art.

And seeing the latest addition to the gallery increased her appreciation even more, plus it did something else as well. Just looking at the piece left her breathless, her skin too warm, her pulse too fast.

Cast in bronze, the sculpture was of a nude couple,

the man sitting on a bench, the woman draped across his lap in a half-reclining position. Her arms were wrapped loosely around his neck, her head tipped back, long hair tumbling down in a cascade of waves. The man stared into the woman's face, his left arm supporting her arched back, his right hand tucked between her slightly opened thighs.

For a full minute, she stared at where his hand disappeared, her body clenching with need, wanting to be touched in such a way. Taking a steadying breath, she forced her gaze away from that spot and studied the rest of the sculpture.

The artist's skill was phenomenal, the detailing spectacular—the couple's features, their musculature and bone structure, everything about them was perfect—better than any she had ever seen. But what truly held her captive was the raw emotion reflected in those bronze faces. The intense concentration on the man's and the absolute carnal bliss on the woman's left no doubt as to what magic the man's hidden fingers were performing.

The throbbing ache between her own thighs intensified. Shocked by her reaction, she bit back a groan. Her senses overwhelmed, she took a step back, then another. Needing to get away from the sculpture before she went up in a ball of flames, she turned to leave and ran smack-dab into someone.

"Careful there," a male voice said, his hands grasping her upper arms to steady her. "I've got ya."

She slowly lifted her gaze from the muscles of his chest, clearing defined beneath his black knit shirt, to the shaggy hair brushing his wide shoulders, his neatly trimmed beard, and dark, penetrating eyes.

"You!" she said, wrenching out of his grasp. "What are you doing here?"

Eighteen

Jackson Kidd threw back his head and laughed at the woman glaring at him through steel-gray eyes. He'd watched her as she studied his latest sculpture, the one he'd brought to show Dalton.

Though he could see only the woman's profile from where he'd stood in the doorway, her full lips, up-turned nose and thick wavy hair had totally captivated him. And more intriguing was her reaction. If he wasn't mistaken, she had responded physically to the sculpture. Even from ten feet away, he'd seen the way her body tensed, noticed the quickening of her breathing and the flush of color spreading up her neck and cheeks.

Such a responsive woman undoubtedly possessed a fiery nature, one he would love to explore.

Now, looking into her eyes, he realized something more about the dark-haired beauty. Though she might have been ablaze with passion just a moment ago, she'd undergone a change and now exuded the cool calm of an ice queen. But the fire was still there, he felt certain, smoldering just below the surface. Rather than being put off by the sudden transformation, he was fascinated, more determined than ever to get to know her, to unearth more of her inner fire.

Offering her a smile, he answered her question. "I

believe, as the guest of honor, I have every right to be here."

"Guest of—" Surprise registered on her face, then she scowled. "Don't tell me you're Jackson Kidd?"

His smile widened. "Okay, I won't tell you."

"Good lord," she murmured, swaying slightly on her feet. "I suppose that's yours?" she said, waving in the direction of the sculpture behind them. "I didn't see a card with the artist's name."

"You suppose right," he replied. "And as for the card, I just brought the piece here this afternoon, so Dalton hasn't had a chance to have one professionally printed. Until he does"—he held up a small, cream-colored card, slightly wrinkled from having it in his hand when he grabbed her arm—"I did this temporary one." He handed it to her.

She turned the card over and read aloud what he'd written. "Untitled bronze sculpture. Jackson Kidd. Not for sale." Handing the card back to him, she said, "You don't have a name for the sculpture?"

"That's the weird part," he said, casting a thoughtful glance at the sculpture. "Up until a minute ago, I didn't. But then out of the blue, the perfect name came to me. Bliss."

She swayed again, a low moan vibrating in her throat.

His gaze snapping back to her, he took a step forward. "Are you all right?"

"I can't believe this is happening," she murmured, holding up a hand to keep him from touching her.

He frowned. "What?"

"That I'd see you again so soon."

"You're saying we've already met." He gave his head a fierce shake. "Not possible. There's no way I wouldn't remember you."

"Of course we haven't met. I . . . saw you once before,

when I—" She exhaled with a sigh. "Never mind. You wouldn't understand."

"Try me."

She stared up at him, emotions he couldn't name swirling in her eyes, then she shook her head. "I don't think so."

He held her stare for several more seconds, hoping she'd change her mind. When she remained silent, he said, "I watched you, a moment ago, while you were looking at my sculpture. Do you like it?"

She turned to look at the newly named sculpture. "Um . . . it's . . . like nothing I've ever seen."

He lifted an eyebrow. "Well, thanks, I think."

"What I meant was, it truly is spectacular." She glanced up at him, her forehead furrowed. "I had the strangest sensation when I was looking at it earlier. It was almost as if I could feel their emotions."

Her comment catching him off guard, he needed a moment to recover. Then he said, "That's the best compliment anyone has ever given me."

"Well deserved. Too bad it's not for sale, though. I might've considered buying it." Shifting her gaze to the doorway, she said, "I should get back to the others. Dalton probably wonders what happened to me."

His heart thudded hard. *Damn, please don't let this woman be involved with Dalton.* Then he remembered he'd already met Annie. Still, maybe his friend had been holding out on him about the women in his life. He cleared his throat, trying to tamp down the panic swirling in his gut. "How well do you know Dalton?"

She gave him a quizzical look. "Pretty well, I'd say."

"Have you known him long?"

She blinked, then laughed, the musical sound doing odd things to his insides. "All my life."

He narrowed his gaze, studying her more carefully.

"You're one of his sisters. I should have noticed the resemblance sooner."

"He told you about his family?"

"Of course. We've shared a lot over the years, swapping stories about our lives, our families. I talked about my brother and sister, and he talked about his sisters." He paused for a moment, then added, "So which one are you? The attorney or the psychic store owner?"

When she opened her mouth to respond, he said, "No, wait. Let me guess."

She tipped her head to one side, amusement dancing in her eyes.

"Not the attorney," he said after a full minute had passed. "You have too much earthy passion to make the law your life's work. No, you're definitely the owner of Charmed."

"Okay, Mr. Smarty Pants, you're right. I'm Daphne and I own Charmed. But let me tell you something." She shook a finger at him. "Darcie has plenty of passion about being an attorney. She's so passionate, in fact, it's almost nauseating. But she's still damn good at what she does."

He chuckled. "I love it when a woman defends her younger sister." He placed his right hand on his chest. "Be still, my heart."

Just that quick, the amusement left her eyes, replaced by simmering fury. "You're a . . . a . . ."

"Can't think of what to call me, sweetheart? Well, here, let me help you out. There's always stud-muffin, or hunk-alicious, or how about—"

"I think insufferable, conceited jackass about covers it." Her mouth thinned. "And I'm not your sweetheart."

"Not yet," he replied with a grin. "But something tells me you will be."

She sniffed. "Not bloody likely." With that, she moved past him and headed toward the hall.

He watched her leave the room—actually march was a more accurate description, her back stiff as a board, shoulders squared, head high. Unable to make himself move, he stared after her for several seconds, grinning like an idiot.

Daphne Stoner was quite a woman, and he was thoroughly captivated by the hotheaded beauty.

Daphne immediately sought out her brother. He was standing with their mother, Annie and an elderly gentleman she recognized as a patron of the gallery. She waited until the man moved away before turning on Dalton.

"How can you be friends with a man like him?"

He blinked. "Edward Keaton? He's a fine man, and he's been a longtime supporter of—"

"No, not him. I'm talking about Jackson Kidd. He's the most annoying, egocentric man I've ever met."

"Really?" Dolly Stoner said. "Dalton introduced us to him a few minutes ago, and I thought he was very polite, an extremely personable young man. Didn't you think so, Annie?"

Annie nodded. "Definitely."

When Daphne snorted at their statements, Dolly said, "What did he do to get you in such a snit?"

"I'm not in a snit, Mom," she replied, though she knew that wasn't true. She couldn't imagine how spending five minutes with a man she didn't even know could make her react like a spoiled brat, but whatever the reason, she did know the cause. That damn Jackson Kidd.

"Okay," Dolly said, casting a quick glance in Dalton's direction. "Then tell us what happened."

"I was looking at his latest sculpture when he came into the room."

Dalton nodded. "He went in there to—"

She waved a dismissive hand at her brother. "Yes, I know. He showed me the card." She lowered her voice to add, "And how could you tell him I'm psychic? You know I don't like you telling people about me."

Before Dalton could form a reply, Annie stepped closer. "Daphne, did he do something to you?"

She frowned. "No, not physically."

"Daf," Dalton said, "you're not making any sense."

Before she figured out how to word her response, someone else spoke.

"Dalton," Jackson said, joining their group, "you didn't tell me what a delight Daphne is."

"Uh . . . no," Dalton said, looking back and forth between his sister and his friend, "I guess I didn't."

Daphne totally ignored Jackson, scowled at her brother, then said, "I see someone I need to speak to. So if you'll excuse me."

As she walked away, Dalton noticed Jackson's gaze following her across the room.

"What's going on, Jack?" Dalton said in a low voice. "Daf came out here all stirred up and claims you're the cause."

"Yeah? Well, meeting her left me kinda stirred up, too."

"Maybe you'd better explain that."

His friend shrugged. "I was immediately attracted to her, but I guess she took exception to some things I said. We sparred verbally. She called me some names." He grinned. "But I think it was all a cover."

"A cover?" Dalton chuckled. "I hate to break this to you, old buddy, but not all women are gonna throw themselves at your feet." At his friend's scowl, he said,

"I've heard stories about your legion of female fans. Anyway, if my sister acted like she took an instant dislike to you, maybe she really did."

"First of all," Jackson replied, "about ninety-nine percent of what you've heard about women throwing themselves at me is false. And second, I realize I could be wrong about Daphne. Maybe she wasn't trying to cover her real reaction." He looked over to where she stood talking to several other guests. "But I don't think so."

"All of my children are stubborn, Mr. Kidd," Dolly said, arching a brow at Dalton. "They come by it honest, though, since their father was the most stubborn man I've ever known. But of the three kids, Daphne is probably the most headstrong. Once she makes up her mind about something, you'll have a devil of a time changing it."

"Call me Jackson, and I've never avoided a challenge or hard work."

"I believe you," Dolly replied. "But let me give you some advice. If you're planning on spending much time around Daphne, I suggest you wear a protective cup."

"Mom!" Dalton said, glancing around to make sure no one else had heard her comment.

Annie's initial shocked expression changed to a smile, and Jackson roared with laughter.

"Well, it's true, dear," Dolly said. "You know how Daphne can be when she's in denial. And I'd hate for Jackson to get hurt"—her eyebrows lifted—"especially there."

Jackson wiped his eyes, then said, "Are you saying that you agree with me? That her fit of temper was to cover up her attraction to me?"

Dolly shrugged. "Can't say for sure. But that's how

she usually reacts when she's uncomfortable with something."

"Thanks. I appreciate your insight"—he winked—"and the advice."

"Good luck, man," Dalton said, giving his friend a slap on the back. "'Cause you're gonna need it."

Daphne tried to concentrate on what the man with the ridiculous comb-over was saying, but her mind persisted in wandering to another man—the one who had her insides in such an uproar. Jackson Kidd was so infuriating. But he was also so charming, so smooth, so— God, admit it, he was the sexiest man she'd ever seen. And meeting him had rocked her down to her toes.

Not just because she'd seen his face in her crystal ball. There was more to her reaction than that, more she didn't want to analyze. Maybe later she'd be able to think rationally and figure out what had happened and why, but right now she was too raw, too unsettled.

She glanced toward the gallery's entry room, contemplating slipping out early. Dalton would be upset, but he'd— She blinked, realizing Darcie had just come through the door. Excusing herself, she rushed to greet her sister.

"You're late," she said in a low voice, then looked around. "And you're alone? I thought Quin was coming with you."

Darcie nodded. "He . . . um . . . cancelled at the last minute."

"That's too bad," Daphne replied carefully, not certain how her sister was handling the situation. "We were looking forward to meeting him."

Darcie nodded again but didn't speak.

"We'll meet him another time."

A quick flash of emotion crossed Darcie's face, something close to pain that she quickly masked. "Yeah," she finally said, her voice cracking.

Daphne stepped closer. "Are you all right, sis?"

"I'm fine." Looking around the gallery, she said, "Have you met Jackson Kidd?"

Daphne frowned. "Unfortunately."

Her sister's gaze jerked back to hers. "What does that mean?"

"Nothing. If you'd like to meet him, he's over there with Dalton, Mom and Annie."

Darcie started in that direction, then stopped when Daphne didn't move. "You coming?"

"Go ahead. I'm not up for another round with him just yet."

Darcie gave her a quizzical look but thankfully didn't ask her to explain. When her sister headed across the room, Daphne breathed a sigh of relief.

After Dalton introduced Darcie to Jackson, she said to her brother, "I just had the weirdest conversation with Daphne."

"About Jack. Right?" he replied.

"Yes, how did you know?"

When everyone in the group burst out laughing, she frowned. "What did I miss?"

Dolly stepped forward. "Come with me to get some champagne and I'll fill you in."

A minute later, she sipped from her champagne while listening to her mother tell how Daphne had spouted off about Jackson Kidd.

When her mother finished, she said, "What do you think that means?"

"Haven't the foggiest," her mother replied. "Has

she ever reacted that strongly to someone she just met?"

"Not that I remember. Maybe it has to do with her being psychic. Extrasensory perception, or something."

"Could be. Your grandmother was that way, too, picking up on things the rest of the family wasn't aware of."

"What was your impression of Jackson?"

"Really nice man. And handsome as sin." Her mother smiled over the rim of her champagne flute. "His version of what happened with Daphne is about a hundred and eighty degrees different than the one she told us. He as much as said he's interested in her."

"Oh, boy," Darcie said with a groan. "I pity him."

Her mother chuckled. "We all do. I told him to be careful, but I got the impression he can't be scared off easily." After taking another sip of champagne, she said, "He thinks Daphne's reaction to him was a cover for what she really felt, and ya know, the more I think about it, I'm inclined to believe he may be right."

Darcie pursed her lips thoughtfully, considering what her mother had said. Finally, she nodded. "I agree. Daf hasn't expressed such a strong opinion—either good or bad—about a man since she dumped that piece of crap Larry. I think what she said about Jackson Kidd is her way of hiding her true reaction to him, sort of a self-preservation tactic."

"Maybe I should have a private talk with Jackson. Make sure he understands I won't tolerate another man doing what that other bastard did to Daphne. I don't think she'd survive being used again."

"Mom, we don't know what Jackson Kidd's intentions

are for sure. And besides, Daf wouldn't like you inter-fering."

"I don't call trying to protect one of my babies in-terfering." She sighed. "But you're right. She'd probably turn me into a toad."

"Be glad she can't do stuff like that," Darcie replied with a smile. "Otherwise, she would've turned all of us into some creature low on the evolutionary chart long before now."

When her mother's throaty laugh faded, silence fell between them for a few moments. Then her mother said, "You look tired, honey. Heavy work load?"

"Not really. And I'm fine," she replied, though she knew that wasn't true.

"Then must be that new man of yours is— By the way, I thought he was coming with you tonight."

"He had to cancel."

"Oh, damn. I wanted to meet him."

Unable to get a word through the tightness in her throat, Darcie nodded.

"As I started to say," her mother said, "he must be keeping you up too late. The two of you need to learn to pace yourselves. Stop trying to draw the sex well dry all in one night."

She nearly choked on her champagne. Dabbing her mouth with a napkin, she managed a crooked smile. "I don't think I'll ever get used to you saying things like that."

Her mother's eyebrows arched over pale blue-gray eyes that twinkled with amusement. "You wouldn't want me to change now, would you?"

"No, I guess not," Darcie replied, then surprised herself by actually laughing, freeing some of the mis-ery she'd felt when she arrived without Quin. Damn Quinlan Jett. She didn't want to think about him. Not now. For the next several hours she wanted to forget the man and what he'd done. Later, when she was alone in her apartment, she'd remember. Then she'd allow herself to fall apart, but not before.

After Jackson bid the last of the guests good night, he turned, his gaze unerringly finding Daphne. All evening long, he'd been aware of where she'd been, as if he had some sort of sixth sense when it came to her.

Under other circumstances, he might have been disturbed by such a discovery about himself, but since meeting Daphne Stoner, he welcomed his newfound ability.

Moving quietly, so as not to alert her to his approach, he headed toward where she stood. Once again, she was studying his latest sculpture, her brow furrowed, lips pursed in a frown.

"Has it changed?"

She started, then swung her gaze in his direction. Seeing him, her frown deepened. "What?"

"Has your reaction to Bliss changed?"

Her gaze returning to the sculpture, she drew an unsteady breath then shook her head.

He studied her for several seconds, then said, "Would you like to have dinner with me?"

This time she turned to face him, surprise apparent in her expression. "After the way I spoke to you earlier, you'd willingly put yourself through more time with me?"

Though the urge to laugh was strong, he managed to resist. Instead, he smiled. "Call me a masochist," he said, lifting a shoulder in a shrug, "but yes, I would."

Her lips twitched. "Masochist, huh? Well, as long as you're aware of the risks, I accept the invitation."

His own surprise at her quick agreement must've shown, because she smiled—the first genuine smile she'd given him, nearly making his knees buckle.

"I know, kind of surprises me, too," she said. "Guess I drank too much champagne on an empty stomach."

"So you're saying when you've had too much to drink, you're not as particular about whose company you keep?"

Her smile vanished. "That's not what I meant."

He stared at her long and hard. Whatever her reason for agreeing to have dinner with him, he wasn't about to blow the chance to spend more time with her. Forcing himself to smile, he said, "I was only teasing. Let's get your coat, then we can blow this place. I'm starved."

Dalton joined his mother, Darcie and Annie in the gallery's main room. "Okay, everything's taken care of," he said. "So we can leave any time." He glanced around. "Where are Jack and Daphne?"

"They left together," Annie said.

His eyebrows shot up. "Really?"

"Jackson asked her to dinner and she accepted."

"You're shitting me?"

"No, dear," his mother replied with a chuckle. "We're definitely not."

"Well," he said after taking a moment to digest what he'd been told, "maybe Jack was right about Daf's reaction to him."

"That's what we think, too," Annie said.

"Then I guess it's just the four of us. What would you—"

"Make that three," Darcie said. "I'm heading home."

When Dalton opened his mouth to respond, his

mother shushed him with a look. "Okay," he said, turning to his sister. "Drive carefully."

Darcie nodded, wished everyone good night then left.

"I need to be going too," his mother announced.

"What?" Dalton said. "Where are you off to?"

"I'm having a late dinner with some friends, then we're going to a party. That's why I drove my rental car to town, remember?"

"Oh, yeah, I forgot. And you're staying in town, right?"

She nodded. "I'll see you at Daphne's place tomorrow evening." She rose onto her toes to give him a peck on the mouth, then turned and gave Annie a quick hug. "You two have a good time tonight."

With a smile and a breezy wave, his mother hurried from the room, leaving only Annie and himself.

"Well," he said, smiling at her, "I guess we've been abandoned."

"So we have," Annie said, letting out a deep breath. While the others were around, she'd been able to forget the impending conversation she planned to have with Dalton. But now that they were finally alone, the apprehension pressed down on her, making her heart pound and her stomach churn.

"Where would you like to go for dinner?"

"I'd rather go back to my apartment."

He smiled. "Sounds like a good plan to me. Should we stop and get a pizza on the way?"

"Let's hold off on that."

"Okay. We can always order one from—" He gave her a quizzical look. "Is something wrong?"

She closed her eyes for a second, then somehow managed the strength to smile. "Everything's fine," she said, hoping that would be the case once they'd had their talk.

* * *

After they arrived at Annie's apartment, she took off her coat then headed for the kitchen. "I don't want a beer after the champagne," she said, opening the refrigerator door. "What about you?"

"Me either. A soft drink is fine."

She pulled out two cans of cola, handed one to him, then moved past him and headed for the living room.

"Annie, what's going on?" he said, trailing behind her.

"I've been thinking about the other night, and"— she stopped in front of her sofa, took a deep breath, then turned to look at him—"we need to talk."

Nineteen

Dalton took a seat on an overstuffed chair, watching Annie sit down on the sofa across from him. He stared at her, yet she refused to meet his gaze for more than a second. A prickle of uneasiness skated up his spine.

Maybe this was the big brush-off, he thought, carefully pulling the tab on his can of cola, then taking a long drink. From the beginning, he'd known this moment would come, though he'd always figured he'd be the one to pull the plug. But lately his growing feelings for Annie had begun to alter his thinking and made him consider the possibility that they should continue their relationship. He wasn't sure where it would lead, yet he knew he wanted to give it a chance.

But now, her obvious nervousness signaled she may have made a different decision. The thought caused a hollow sensation in his chest.

He settled deeper in the chair, trying to appear cool and unruffled. "What's up?"

"There's something I need to tell you." Her breasts rose and fell with a deep breath. "A misconception that needs to be cleared up."

"Okay."

"I've come to care about you, Dalton, a great deal.

And I feel complete honesty is important in a relationship."

"So do I."

"I know, that's why"—she took another deep breath—"that's why I decided I had to set the record straight about the job I took over Christmas break."

Great. The one topic he really didn't want to talk about. "The strip-o-gram job. What about it?"

"Part of what I told you isn't true. I didn't take the job because I don't make a lot of money as a teacher. Not that the extra paycheck wouldn't be welcome. But that's not the real reason."

A muscle in his cheek twitched. "So it was about the excitement. Is that what you're saying?"

"Well, yes, but not in the way you think."

He scowled. "You're gonna have to explain that."

"Let me start at the beginning. A couple weeks before school let out for Christmas, I was having dinner with Lisa and Jillian, friends of mine, teachers at the same high school, and we realized our social lives really suck. So we decided we needed to do something to change that. Something we normally wouldn't do. Something a little bit wild to spice up our lives."

When she glanced over at him, he clenched his jaw, nodding for her to continue.

"Anyway, we made a pact to get out of our rut by finding exciting jobs for Christmas break."

"Your friends are working for the messenger service, too?"

"No. Actually, I don't know what they're doing. I know they found jobs because we got together a week before break started to make sure we all had something lined up, but I didn't ask where they'd be working. And we agreed not to talk or see each other over break until this Sunday night at Gina's restaurant.

We're having dinner together so we can compare notes."

He studied her in silence for several seconds, then said, "So what does the winner get?"

"We didn't do this so we could pick a winner."

"You said you made a pact, so I figured that meant it was a competition."

She shook her head. "We made the pact only to make sure we all found jobs and"—a flicker of an emotion he couldn't read passed over her face—"if one of us wimped out and didn't go through with it, there would be a consequence. Buying dinner for all of us at a fancy new restaurant downtown."

Dalton mulled over everything she'd told him, the slow burn of his temper suddenly bursting into full-fledged anger. Carefully setting his can of cola on an end table, he said, "So all along I was part of your little plan to spice up your life?"

"Yes, but only because you were my first delivery for the messenger service."

"Are you sure?"

"Of course, I'm sure. Why would you think otherwise?"

"Because my museum and gallery specializes in erotic art. Because I have an interest in the *Kama Sutra*."

"But I didn't know those things until after I went to your house."

"So you say."

Her eyes narrowed, a flush creeping up her neck. "What are you suggesting?"

"Maybe you really did know about my gallery's specialty and decided delivering strip-o-grams wouldn't be exciting enough. Maybe you figured you could spice up your life even more by fucking an expert on erotic—"

"How dare you!" Her breath hissing between her teeth, she leaped to her feet. "How dare you say such a horrible thing?"

"I dare," he said, slowly rising from the chair, his gaze holding hers, "because it's probably true."

"It is not true. Our having sex had nothing to do with my messenger job."

He shook his head, refusing to believe her claim. "From the moment I met you, I couldn't stop comparing you to Maureen because she was always on the prowl for excitement too."

"God, I should've known you'd throw your ex-wife in my face again." She made a sound, a mix between a laugh and a snort. "She's the reason I wanted to have this conversation. After what you said the other night, I wanted to make you understand that I am not another Maureen."

When she glanced up at him, a hopeful expression on her face, he remained silent.

She squeezed her eyes closed for a second, then blew out a deep breath. "Look, I admit, I like to have a good time and yes, as you know, I drink on occasion. But I swear to you, I don't go to drunken parties, I absolutely do not do drugs, and I sure as hell don't sleep around."

"Not yet."

"What!"

"Maureen didn't do those things either, at first. But all the other stuff she got into started because she was looking for excitement."

"That's not the same thing, and you know it."

"The hell I do. It's exactly the same thing. You start out delivering strip-o-grams and pretty soon that isn't enough of a kick for you. So then you look for something that will give you more of a thrill."

"Well, gee, I appreciate the vote of confidence,"

she said, lifting her chin, her eyes icy with fury. "At least I finally know what you really think of me. I'm so weak and insecure that my wanting a little excitement in my life will naturally lead to uncontrollable cravings. And then bam, I turn into a lush, a junkie and a slut."

"I didn't call you those names."

"You did by implication. You said I was just like Maureen, and she did all those things, so your meaning is pretty damn clear to me." She crossed her arms over her breasts. "But I think this is a case of the pot calling the kettle black."

"How's that?"

"You claim I'm the one looking for excitement, yet what about you? You were plenty into the excitement factor that night you gave me a tour of your gallery. Or maybe you've conveniently forgotten about what we did in your office. And then there's that night in your car after the hockey game. You sure seemed to like the excitement of having me—"

"That's different," he replied, unable to stop the blush warming his entire face.

"You can lie to yourself all you want. But it is not different."

He scowled, not liking the way she was painting him, but before he could come up with a way to defend himself, she spoke again.

"Not once have I compared you to anyone in my past, especially to your face." She glared up at him, her eyes turning even colder. "But since I'm being totally honest, I have another admission to make. Before we met, I had a preconceived notion about what you'd be like. I figured the owner of a museum and art gallery had to be a stuffy, boring old fogy, who was about as exciting as watching paint dry. Then just when I'd begun changing my opinion, you reveal the real Dalton Stoner."

"Yeah, well, enlighten me."

"Not only is he stuffy and boring, he's also a hard-headed, narrow-minded jerk with a perverted hang-up about erotic art."

"Perverted?" he nearly roared. "You didn't think it was perverted when we experimented with all those positions you wanted to try. Or when I brought you to one screaming climax after another."

"No, but I wish none of it happened," she replied, lifting her chin a notch higher. "Everything we did was a mistake, a huge mistake."

"Well, at least we agree on one thing."

Several seconds passed in strained silence. Then she drew a shaky breath, the ice in her eyes turning to sadness. "I can't believe I actually fell in love with a man who'd rather stay holed up in his house than have any kind of a social life," she said in a low voice. "What an idiot I was."

He snorted. "You said it, babe. Not me."

Her back stiffened. "I think you should leave."

"What, I don't get one last fuck for old time's sake?" As soon as the words left his mouth, he wished he could take them back. He hadn't meant to be so cruel, but the anger, wounded pride and frustration twisting in his gut had provoked him to lash out, dragging him down to a level of viciousness he hadn't known he possessed. Falling in love with Annie had him in— He bit back a groan, swaying slightly on his feet. Helluva time to make that realization. But loving Annie didn't mean shit. He thought he'd loved Maureen, and that relationship went down the toilet. His mother's words about how Annie wasn't like Maureen tried to wriggle their way into his mind, but he shoved them aside. He didn't want to think about what his mother said. She didn't know how he felt. No one did. Unless someone had gone through what he— Annie's voice jerked him back to the present.

He blinked, then shifted his gaze to meet hers. "What?"

"I said, get out, Dalton." Her eyes flashed dangerously. "Now."

He opened his mouth to respond, then promptly shut it. She was right; he had to get out of there before he said anything else he'd regret. Turning, he grabbed his jacket off the back of the sofa and stormed out of her apartment.

Annie stared at the still-vibrating door, fury, shock and incredible pain warring inside her. Damn him. For refusing to see the truth, and especially for saying such terrible, hurtful things to her. She felt like he'd stuck a knife in her chest.

She hadn't been sure how he'd react when she decided to set the record straight about her messenger job. And although she'd acknowledged the possibility that she might have trouble getting him to understand, she hadn't anticipated the painful result.

She sank back onto the sofa, not sure if she wanted to cry uncontrollably or vent her fury by throwing something. Swallowing the threatening tears, she clung to her anger. How could she have actually thought they had a chance together? She groaned, grabbing a throw pillow and hugging it to her chest. *I was an idiot. I never should have made the pact with Lisa and Jillian. Never taken the messenger job. Never fallen in love with a man as stubborn and infuriating as Dalton Stoner.* She sighed. *Like I had a choice about falling in love.*

Another wave of pain crashed over her, dousing

her anger and wrenching a sob from deep in her chest. The anguish too much for her bruised heart, she gave in to the hot rush of tears.

Dalton wasn't sure how he'd managed to get home. He remembered leaving Annie's apartment and pulling into his driveway. But the entire drive up from Denver was a blur. Thank God his subconscious had taken over while the rest of his mind dwelled on what a mess he'd made of his life. For the first time since his divorce, he'd actually been happy, was actually starting to enjoy life again.

Then he'd lost his temper and ruined everything.

He went into the kitchen and opened his refrigerator, intending to find something to eat. After staring at the contents for a full minute, he decided he wasn't hungry after all. Settling for a beer, he opened the bottle then headed for the living room.

After starting a fire, he closed the fireplace screen, then took a seat on one of the couches. Data immediately jumped up beside him. Giving the dog a weak smile, he said, "If you knew what I did tonight, you wouldn't want to get close to me."

Data cocked his head to one side, dark eyes studying him for a moment. Then the terrier jumped down and stretched out in front of the fireplace.

"Great. Now I've chased you away, too." He sighed, then lifted his bottle of beer and took a big swallow.

Jackson let himself into Dalton's house, using the key his friend had given him earlier. Whistling, he shrugged out of his jacket then started down the hall.

"At least one of us is happy."

The sound of Dalton's voice brought him to a halt

outside the living room doorway. Turning, he spotted his friend slouched in the corner of one of the leather couches. "What are you doing home?"

"Last time I checked, I lived here."

Jackson chuckled. "Right, but I didn't expect you to get in so early. If at all."

"Yeah," Dalton replied with a harsh laugh. "Neither did I." He shifted, sitting up straighter. "So, how'd it go with Daf?"

Jackson headed toward his friend. "Great. I had to dare her to get a good-night kiss, but it was worth it." His blood warming at the memory, he smiled. "I've never known a woman like her."

"And that's a good thing? We're talking about my sister, the stubborn-as-hell Daphne Stoner, remember? She chews up men for sport."

His smile stretched into a grin. "Don't get me wrong, it wasn't all roses and moonlight for us tonight. We butted heads a few times, but the fact that I got her to kiss me makes me think she likes me. She's just not ready to admit it. Yet. Too bad I have to leave tomorrow, otherwise I might get her—" Spotting the empty beer bottles beside Dalton, he frowned. "How long've you been home?"

Dalton shrugged. "Don't know. What time is it?"

"A little before one."

"Ah. Then I've been home about . . . uh . . . three hours. I think. I don't remember looking at the clock when I came in."

"Are you drunk?"

Dalton scowled at the bottle in his hand. "Not drunk enough."

Jackson studied his friend in silence for a moment. This wasn't the Dalton Stoner he knew. He couldn't remember the man ever drinking more than a beer or two, and he'd certainly never seen him drunk. "What's going on?"

Dalton remained silent for so long that Jackson thought he wasn't going to answer. Then finally, his friend heaved a deep sigh. "I blew it, Jack. I was a total asshole and I blew it."

He eased down onto the arm of the other couch. "Blew what?"

"Annie and me." Dalton frowned. "If there even was an Annie and me."

"What happened?"

"She wanted to talk," he replied, using his thumbnail to pick at the label on the beer bottle. "To straighten out . . . something that's been an issue between us since we met." He took a long pull on the bottle, then wiped his mouth with the back of his wrist. "She . . . um . . . said some things that totally set me off, then I said some things, and—" He huffed out a breath. "Let's just say everything went to hell in a handbasket real quick after that."

Jackson waited for Dalton to continue, but he seemed to be lost in thought.

"So that's it?" Jackson finally said. "You two are through?"

"After what I said to her, I doubt she'll ever talk to me again."

"Hey, man, I'm sorry."

"Yeah. Thanks."

"Is there's anything I can do?"

Dalton shook his head. "I made this mess, so I've gotta deal with it on my own."

"Okay," he said, getting to his feet. "I'm going to bed. You should think about turning in."

"I will. Soon."

"I need to leave for the airport by one. Will you be around?"

Dalton rubbed a hand over his eyes. "Yeah. I don't have to be at Daf's until four."

"Good. Then I'll see you in the morning."

When Dalton arrived at Daphne's place the next afternoon, he was bone tired, in a lousy mood and still nursing a pounding headache. In spite of the beers he'd drunk, he hadn't slept well—the hurt expression on Annie's face plaguing him every time he shut his eyes—and the pain pills he'd taken hadn't eased the incessant throbbing in his head. All in all, it had been one crappy day. And having to spend time with his mother and sisters, pretending nothing was wrong, was going to make his evening just as crappy.

As soon as Daphne opened her door, he knew the next few hours were going to be worse than he'd imagined. The look she gave him clearly said she was out to strip a hunk of hide off his back. Great.

"I need to talk to you," she said in a fierce whisper, hauling him inside her apartment then blocking the door so he couldn't make a quick exit.

Before he could figure out how to get away from his oldest sister, his mother poked her head out the kitchen doorway. "Hi, honey," she said, flashing a smile. "You're just in time for one of my famous margaritas."

His stomach pitching at the thought of anything with liquor, he bit back a groan. "Um . . . thanks, but not now, Mom."

After his mother disappeared back into the kitchen, he quickly removed his jacket and pushed it into Daphne's hands. "Will you hang that up for me? Thanks." Not giving her a chance to reply, he headed for the living room.

He found Darcie curled in a chair, then blinked with surprise. Her hair resembled a rat's nest, she wore no makeup, and her slacks and sweater looked like she'd slept in them. Taking care to hide his reaction to her appearance, he said, "Hey, sis. Happy New Year."

"Yeah right," she muttered, then lifted her gaze to meet his. "Jeez, Dalton, you look like hell."

Her comment brought his first real smile of the day. Rubbing a hand over his beard stubble, he said, "I didn't figure I had to shave for family. Besides, I could say the same about you, ya know, but I was taught better manners."

When that didn't get the rise he expected out of her, he said, "Darcie, are you okay?"

"She's feeling sorry for herself," Daphne replied, entering the room carrying two margarita glasses, "because the jerk she's been seeing stood her up last night."

Darcie glared at her sister. "You don't need to blab my business all over the place."

"Oh, for God's sake," Daphne replied, glaring right back. "I just told our brother. That's hardly blabbing it all over." She handed one glass to Darcie. "Here, drink this. Maybe it'll lighten your mood."

"Doubtful," Dalton said more to himself than his sisters. Then he said to Darcie, "Want me to find the jerk and pound the hell out of him?"

"No!" she yelled, making the throbbing in his head intensify.

"Jesus, Darcie, hold it down to a roar," he said, massaging a temple. "I was only joking."

"All right, you three," his mother said, entering the room. "I leave you alone for five minutes, and you're at each others' throats."

Dalton managed another smile, though it felt more

like a grimace. "We're not fighting. We were just having a . . . discussion."

She arched a brow. "It was pretty loud for a discussion."

"What can we say, Mom," Daphne said, "we're all such passionate people, that our discussions naturally get loud."

"There's a load of crap if I've ever heard one," their mother replied with a chuckle, then she moved across the room to where Dalton had taken a seat on the sofa. "Here, baby." She held a cup toward him. "Daf was right when she told me you look like you could use this."

Frowning, he accepted the cup and looked at the dark, steaming liquid. "What is it?"

"My special tea. Good for whatever ails you." She took a seat beside him. "And don't say nothing's wrong. I'm not blind."

"Mom, I don't—"

"That's okay, hon. I'm not asking you to tell me anything." She took a sip of her margarita, then sighed. "It kills me to see my babies hurting, though. First Daphne acts like everything is just peachy, when it's obvious to me she's upset. Then Darcie shows up looking like something the cat dragged in. And now you arrive in even worse shape." She took another sip of her drink. "What a way to start the new year."

"Yeah," Dalton replied, carefully bringing the cup to his mouth and taking a swallow of the hot tea. He hoped like hell this wasn't an indication of what the coming year would be like.

Amazingly, whatever his mother had put in his tea did the trick. By the time he drank the last of it, the pounding in his head had lessened, then soon left altogether, and his queasy stomach had settled. A short time later, when Daphne announced dinner was ready, he felt almost normal. Well, as close to normal as he could get considering the words he'd exchanged with Annie still weighed heavily on his mind.

As he took a seat at the table, he looked over at Daphne and said, "You haven't said anything about having dinner with Jackson. He said he had a great time. Even got you to kiss him. So how was it for you?"

"You kissed him?" Darcie said. "How come you didn't tell—"

Daphne shushed their sister with a fierce glare, then turned her narrowed gaze on him, her lips pressed into a firm line. "Did you pump him for all the details? 'Cause if you did, I'll—"

"Take it easy, Daf. When he got in last night, I asked how his evening went, and he volunteered the kiss part. Believe me, I wasn't in any condition to give him the third degree. And this morning, the topic never came up."

"I still can't believe you went out with him," Darcie said. "Let alone, kissed him."

"Me either," Daphne replied. "But I had to—" She clamped her lips shut, focusing her attention on the food on her plate.

Darcie's forehead wrinkled. "You had to . . . what?"

"It's not important. He's gone now, so it doesn't matter."

"Right," Darcie replied. "That's what I keep telling myself."

"Quin's gone?" Daphne reached for her sister's hand. "Are you sure?"

"Yeah, I'm sure."

"Will you tell us what happened?"

Darcie glanced around the table, then gave a quick

nod. "Last night, when he left the message on my voice mail about not being able to make the showing, he also said, 'I'm sorry, Darcie, for everything.'"

"What did he mean by everything?" their mother said.

Darcie drew a shaky breath. "I didn't know at first. But after I left the gallery last night, I went to his hotel. He was gone. From what the desk clerk told me, he must've checked out right after he left the message for me." She pushed her food around on her plate, her throat working with a swallow. "He didn't even tell me good-bye. He just left."

"That sorry son of a bitch," Daphne said in a fierce whisper, giving her sister's hand a squeeze. "Want me to do a reading and find out where the coward is hiding?"

Darcie shook her head. "Absolutely not. I really thought he cared about me. Obviously I was wrong." She paused, struggling to pull herself together. "I had a feeling there was something he was keeping from me, but I figured he'd tell me when—" She took another deep breath. "Anyway, I never figured he wouldn't have the balls to face me and tell me he was leaving."

She gave Daphne a pleading look. "Promise me you won't do a reading. I don't give a damn where he is. Hopefully, a sinkhole will open up wherever he is and swallow him."

"Yeah, we can hope." Daphne chuckled. "If you change your mind, let me know."

Quiet settled over the table for a few minutes, then Daphne set down her wine glass and turned her gaze on Dalton.

"What the hell did you do to Annie?"

Twenty

Dalton stiffened his spine, the heat of a blush sting-ing his neck. "Why? What's wrong with her?"

"I don't know," Daphne replied, "that's why I'm asking you. I called her this morning to ask her to join us. She sounded horrible, like she'd been on a week-long crying jag."

Though he tried not to let his sister's statement bother him, a knot formed in his gut. "So automati-cally you make the leap that her crying means I'm the reason?"

Daphne glared at him. "Don't feed me that line of bull, Dalton. Since you two were together last night, it's hardly a leap to figure you must've done some-thing." She continued staring at him for several more seconds, the growing disdain in her expression mak-ing him even more uncomfortable. "You broke it off with her, didn't you? How could you be so stupid! She was the perfect woman for—"

"Don't start with that perfect shit again, Daf, be-cause I'm not buying it."

When Daphne opened her mouth to respond, he held up a hand to halt more of her reprimand. "Annie told me she made a pact with two of her friends to spice up their lives by find exciting jobs for their break. Did you know that's why she went to work for the messenger service?"

"No, I didn't know that. But I don't see what—"

"She took a goddamn job delivering strip-o-grams just for the excitement. Is that really the kind of woman you think is perfect for me?"

"Dalton," she replied with a sigh, "it's true she took the job, but I happen to know she never delivered a message for the company."

"Of course she did. She called her boss from my house. I heard her talking about the deliveries they had lined up for her."

Daphne shook her head. "Maybe they did. But she never made the deliveries. As soon as she got back from Wyoming, she quit."

"Are you sure?"

"She told me herself, last night at the gallery, when I asked her how the job was going."

He gaped at her, stunned. "I don't understand why she didn't tell me," he said after a few seconds. "If she had, maybe I—" He scowled. "No, that doesn't change anything. She still took the job because she was looking for a thrill. And if she didn't get her fix, she'll just find some other—"

"Dammit, Dalton," Darcie said, joining the conversation for the first time, "you are such a bonehead."

He shifted his gaze to his youngest sister. "And you're the expert on relationships, I suppose?"

Darcie's face flushed a dull red. "Never said I was. But you"—she pointed her fork at him—"sure as hell aren't either. Daphne is right about Annie and you, but I guess you're just too dim-witted, or too stubborn, or—"

"Okay, counselor," he said, "you made your point." He heaved a sigh. "Look, even if she is right for me, it's too late."

"Dalton, honey." His mother leaned toward him

and placed a hand on his arm. "It's never too late. Not when two people care about each other."

"Always the romantic, aren't you, Mom?" He managed a weak smile. "But after last night, Annie is probably glad to be rid of me."

"You may have underestimated that girl or her feelings for you. She's made of strong stuff, and one little argument isn't likely to change how she feels. Oh, she may be mad as hell for a while, but that only makes the making up that much better." She winked. "If you get my meaning."

"Yeah, I get it," he replied with a chuckle, then immediately sobered. "But it wasn't a little argument, Mom. I lost my temper and really went off on her." He swallowed hard. "I can still see the look on her face. I hurt her real bad."

His mother stared at him for a long time, then said, "Well, sounds to me like you must have strong feelings for her. Otherwise you wouldn't be so upset about what you said in the heat of the moment, or how deeply you hurt her."

"Mom's right," Daphne said. "You must love Annie."

"I was awake most of the night," he said, "at first trying to justify the way I acted, then trying to deny what I feel for her. By the time I finally fell asleep, I knew for certain I loved her. And I also realized some things about myself—things I should've faced a long time ago." He shook his head. "But none of that erases my behaving like an ass last night. Or the ugly things I said to her." He rubbed his temple, trying to forestall another headache. "She probably hopes I'll go for a walk in the mountains and fall off a cliff."

"You don't know that for sure," his mother said, giving his arm a squeeze before withdrawing her hand. "If she loves you, she'll be willing to forgive you."

"I don't know," he replied. "You didn't see and hear how angry she was."

"If you want her in your life," Darcie said, "my advice—not that you asked for it—is to give her a little time. Let her anger cool."

"I agree." Daphne gave him a thoughtful look. "But you need to come up with a way to show her you deserve to be forgiven."

"You got something in mind?"

"No," she replied with a laugh. "That's for you to figure out, big brother."

When he frowned, she added, "Don't worry. You'll think of something to knock her socks off."

"Provided that's what you want, hon," his mother said. "In spite of your feelings for Annie and what we think about her, if you really don't want to try to work it out, that's your decision."

"Thanks, Mom," he replied, "I appreciate your saying that." He inhaled a deep breath then exhaled slowly. "But the truth is, right now, I don't know what the hell I want."

After the uncomfortable conversation at the dinner table, Dalton found the rest of the evening more relaxing than he'd anticipated. By unspoken agreement, the siblings' love lives were strictly off limits, but they still found plenty to talk about. Their mother was her usual exuberant self—perhaps a little more than normal because she knew her children were in various states of emotional turmoil and needed the distraction—telling jokes and outrageous stories that kept them howling with laughter.

Dalton hadn't realized how much he missed having his family together, but more surprising, seeing all of them over the past few days made him long for more.

With sudden clarity, he knew what he wanted. He wanted to enlarge the Stoner family. To add another chair at the dining room table, add another voice to the lively discussions. And he knew only one woman who would fit into that mental picture. Annie, with the gorgeous green eyes and golden-brown curls, who constantly challenged him, who roused his temper one minute then made him laugh the next, who fulfilled every one of his sexual fantasies, and most incredible, who made him realize he could love again. Somehow she'd eased the pain and bitterness of his first marriage, made him see that he could find a lifetime of happiness.

But the hard truth was, making the realization and turning it into reality were miles apart—especially after the way he'd spoken to her the night before. From his perspective, a future with Annie hinged on something his mother had said. If Annie loved him, she'd be willing to forgive him.

Annie had told him she'd fallen in love with him, so now he could only hope she truly had and, more important, that her love was strong enough to offer forgiveness.

Annie sat in her darkened living room, the only light the pale glow from her television. She really wasn't in the mood for watching TV, but she didn't have the energy to do anything more strenuous. In an effort to keep herself from thinking about that miserable jerk Dalton, she'd spent the day in a cleaning frenzy. She'd dusted, polished, scrubbed and vacuumed until her arms ached. The apartment hadn't looked this clean since she moved in. Her mother would've been impressed with her domestic skills. The only thing missing was a plate of freshly baked cookies, and she could be a candidate for a little Suzie Homemaker award. If she weren't so miserable, she might have laughed.

She flipped through the channels, finding nothing to hold her attention until Captain Jean-Luc Picard's face appeared on the screen. Damn. *Star Trek: The Next Generation,* and it was just starting. Though the show was a reminder of Dalton she didn't want to deal with, she couldn't make herself push the Channel Up button. Instead, she wiggled into a more comfortable position on her couch, then curled her feet under her.

When Data appeared on camera, she smiled, remembering another Data, one that wasn't an android but a four-legged, living being with a wet nose and wiry brown and white hair. A sudden longing to see both Data and Worf washed over her, making her realize how much she missed the terriers. If only she wasn't royally pissed at their owner, then maybe she would see the dogs again.

No, not likely. Not after the things they'd said to each other. And Dalton, the stubborn fool, couldn't get beyond the ridiculous idea that she was like his ex-wife, and unless he was able to get past that, there was no future for them. The point was probably moot anyway. Because after their heated exchange, she doubted he'd ever want to see her again, and she wasn't ready to go to him—in fact she wasn't sure she ever would be. Sniffling, she reached for a tissue. As she wiped her nose, another thought occurred to her. Once he calmed down, he might want to continue seeing her for the sex. After all, sexually they couldn't have been more compatible, better than she ever imagined, so his wanting to resume their sexual relationship wasn't beyond the realm of possibility.

She frowned, mulling over the idea, then shook

her head. Dammit, she loved the guy, but if all he wanted was sex, he could find someone else. She wanted all of him, a total relationship, and she refused to settle for less. But realistically, she knew the chances of getting the whole deal with Dalton looked pretty bleak.

Another jab of pain pushed at her, slipping through the barricade she'd tried to erect around her emotions. She drew several deep, shuddering breaths, trying to soothe the ache clutching at her heart. Her efforts did little good.

With tears trickling down her face, she sat unmoving, watching but not really seeing the rest of the TV show.

As Annie got ready to go out Sunday evening, she considered calling Jillian and Lisa and telling them she couldn't meet them for dinner. If she could've come up with a believable excuse, she might've done it. But she'd see them in school on Monday anyway, plus meeting in a busy restaurant would hopefully keep her from breaking down in front of her friends, so there was no point in delaying the inevitable.

She'd just suck it up, admit she quit the messenger job without delivering even one strip-o-gram, then try to answer the questions they'd throw at her. But how much she'd tell them was another matter. Revealing the hot sex part wasn't a problem—not that she'd give them all the steamy details—but she did have a problem with telling them the part about falling in love with Dalton and their argument New Year's Eve. Her emotions were still too raw for her to share everything that happened over the past two weeks.

Besides, if she did confess the whole thing, Jillian and Lisa would undoubtedly offer their advice. And at the moment, she wasn't ready to hear whatever they had to say.

When Annie arrived at Gina's, she was told her friends had already been seated. As she made her way to their table, the two women waved and smiled.

"Hey, Annie," Jillian said. "We were getting worried. Is everything okay?"

"Of course. Why wouldn't it be?" She took a seat, forcing her lips to curve in a smile she hoped didn't look as fake as it felt.

"'Cause you're never late," Lisa replied.

She shrugged. "Lost track of time, that's all."

Jillian studied her in silence for a second, then said, "We thought we'd order a bottle of wine, but if you want something else . . ."

"No, wine sounds great."

A few minutes later, Lisa poured the wine they'd selected, then raised her glass.

"Here's to great friends with"—she winked—"great tales to tell."

Annie bit back a groan, obediently clinked her glass against the other two, then took a swallow of wine.

"Okay," Jillian said, scooting her chair closer to the table. "Who goes first?"

"This was Annie's idea," Lisa said, "so I think she should have the honor."

When Jillian nodded, Annie sighed, figuring she might as well get it over with.

She took another drink of the wine, set down her glass, then took a deep breath. "I didn't do it."

Lisa tipped her head to one side. "You didn't do what?"

"The messenger job."

"But you said Charlene and Dan hired you," Jillian said.

She nodded. "Yeah, they did. And my first delivery
was scheduled for the Saturday break started. I . . .
um . . . drove to the house up in the foothills where I
was supposed to, you know, do my strip-o-gram bit.
But that's the day that big snowstorm hit, the power
went out right after I got there, and . . . well, let's just
say, from that point on, my Christmas break wasn't
anything like I thought it would be."

"Well, don't keep us in suspense," Jillian said. "Spill
all the details."

Annie fingered the stem of her wine glass, trying to
compose herself while figuring out exactly what she
would tell them. Before she could stop the words, she
blurted, "I fell in love with him."

She saw her friends exchange a startled look, then
Lisa said, "What! Who?"

"The man who was supposed to receive my first
strip-o-gram."

"Up in the foothills?"

She nodded. "We were snowed in at his house for
five days, and we . . . um . . . got to know each other
and, well . . . things happened."

"Oh my God, this is amazing." Jillian laughed. "You
really did spice up your break, didn't you?"

"Yeah, I spiced it up all right." She frowned, then
picked up her glass and took a big swallow of wine.

"So, tell us about this guy," Lisa said. "What's his
name? What's he do for a living? When do we get to
meet him?"

"And don't leave out the good stuff," Jillian added.
"Tell us what he looks like. And is he a great lover?"

Annie chuckled, surprised to hear the sound come
from her mouth. "His name is Dalton Stoner. He
owns the High Country Museum and Art Gallery.
He's drop-dead gorgeous, in my estimation. All I'll

say about his abilities as a lover is unbelievable. And you won't be meeting him."

"But why?" Lisa practically shouted, then lowered her voice to add, "You said you love this Dalton guy, so you have to introduce him to your best friends. I mean, that's an unwritten rule." She looked at Jillian for confirmation. "Right?"

"Absolutely," Jillian replied with a nod. "So, when are you seeing him again? We'll make sure we're at your place before he's supposed to pick you up. Then when he gets there, you can introduce us. We'll say hi, give him a quick once over, then take off." She sat back, a satisfied smirk on her face. "Piece of cake."

She shook her head. "Actually, that won't work. I . . . uh . . . I'm pretty sure I won't be seeing him again."

"But you just told us you're in love with him," Lisa said. "What's the deal? Do you love him, or not?"

"Oh yeah, I love him. Big time." She drank the last of her wine in one gulp. "But he thinks I'm something I'm not, and my trying to convince him he's wrong ended up in a shouting match. He said some horrible things to me. Then I got angry and said—" She sighed. "Well, I got pretty nasty, too, and said some things I didn't really mean."

"Hey, couples have fights all the time," Jillian said. "They argue, need some time to cool off, then make up."

Annie shrugged. "Yeah, but that was three nights ago and I haven't heard a word from him. It's pretty clear he doesn't want to see me. Besides, this wasn't just a simple disagreement. He thinks I'm an excitement freak like his ex-wife." She heaved another deep sigh. "That woman did some terrible things while they were married, things that cut him real deep. I'm not sure his wounds will ever totally heal."

"Listen to me, Annie," Lisa said. "If you truly love the guy, you can't just let him—"

A commotion at the front of the restaurant drew the attention of all the diners and the wait staff.

"What the heck?" Jillian whispered.

Annie craned her neck, trying to get a better view. Someone dressed like Santa was weaving his way through the tables, heading toward the back of the restaurant.

"It's a little late to be playing Santa Claus, don't ya think?"

Annie and Jillian both acknowledged Lisa's comment with a nod.

"Uh-oh, looks like he's coming this way," Jillian said in a low voice. "Either of you expecting Santa?"

"Not me," Lisa replied.

Annie shook her head. "Me either."

When the man stopped in front of the empty chair at their table and set a boom box in front of him, Lisa said, "Excuse me, Santa, but I think you've got the wrong table."

Santa shook his head, making the white fur tassel on his hat bounce back and forth, then said, "I have a delivery for Annie Peterson." He met Annie's startled gaze. "To show her I'm not a stuffy, boring, hardheaded . . . what else did you call me? Oh yeah, narrow-minded jerk with a perverted hang-up about erotic art."

Too shocked to speak, Annie could only stare at Dalton, his face almost totally covered by the horrible fake beard and the overlarge hat that had fallen forward to cover his forehead.

"Annie, is this the museum guy?" Jillian said.

Still gaping at the man in the red velvet suit, she managed to nod.

"Well, then," Lisa said with a grin, wiggling to a

more comfortable position in her chair, "this should be interesting."

Shaking herself out of her momentary stupor, Annie shoved her chair away from the table and got to her feet. "What are you—"

"You'd better sit back down, babe," Dalton said. "The show's about to start."

Before she could say more, he pushed a button on the boom box and music blared out of the speakers.

As the strains of *Boot Scootin' Boogie* flooded the restaurant, she dropped back onto her chair, too stunned to do more than stare.

Dalton stepped away from the table, then started dancing, his feet moving in steps she'd taught him. But then his hips began bumping and grinding to the beat of the music, making her mouth drop open. She hadn't taught him that!

His gaze locked on hers, he did several pelvic thrusts as he slowly turned his back to her. Then he gave his tush a little shake, glanced over his shoulder and winked. After more bumping and grinding while he discarded the hat and beard, he turned to face her again, his fingers working to unfasten the buckle on the wide black belt. With a flick of his wrist he tossed the belt aside, then reached for the buttons of his jacket.

He quickly finished the task, but rather than opening the jacket, he held it closed with his hands, no doubt in what was meant to be a provocative pose. Then with the grace that would have done a professional stripper proud, he moved his hands up enough to allow the jacket to drop off his shoulders. Accompanied by his hips swiveling to the beat of the music, he let the jacket slowly slide down his arms until it hung around his hips, his hands still in the sleeves.

Annie heard her friends gasp at the sight of his naked chest and thought she heard one of them say, "Whoa, baby, what a hunk." But she didn't want to take her eyes off Dalton to find out who had spoken.

He eased his hands out of the jacket sleeves, dropped the garment on the floor, then kicked it aside. Flashing her a grin, and amid more suggestive pelvic thrusts and fancy footwork, he reached for the fly of his red velvet pants.

"Hold it, slick," she practically yelled, then jumped to her feet again and leaned across the table to turn off the boom box. "You've showed enough skin."

His chest rising and falling with his labored breathing, he gave her a slow, lazy smile. "I'm not naked under these pants, if that's what you're worried about."

"That's not—" She frowned. Okay, so the thought had crossed her mind, but this wasn't the time to pursue the subject. Instead, she said, "Why are you here?"

"I told you why, to show you—"

"Yeah, I heard what you said, but I want to know what it means."

He moved closer. "It means," he said in a low voice, "I was a total ass at your place the other night. It means, I want your forgiveness and for you to give me another chance. It means, I love you, and I think we can make this work between us."

Before she could respond, she heard Lisa say, "Oh God, I think I'm gonna cry."

"Yeah," Jillian said with a sigh. "Me, too."

When Annie sent a frown in her friends' direction, he chuckled, then grabbed Annie's hand and pulled her closer. "You said you loved me, babe. Do you?"

She stared up at him for several seconds, then bobbed her head.

He smiled. "Then don't you think we should give it a shot?"

"Um, can we"—she glanced around the restaurant—"go somewhere more private?"

"Sure." He touched her cheek with the backs of his knuckles, then gathered his discarded clothes and picked up the boom box. "Come on."

Twenty-one

The manager of Gina's told Dalton the banquet room was empty, so he led Annie down the hall then held the door open for her.

Once they were inside, the noise of the restaurant muted by the closed door, he put the boom box and clothes on a table then turned to Annie.

"I want to apologize again," he said, "for the way I behaved the other night. I was totally out of line."

"Me, too. I'm sorry I called you all those names."

"Understandable, considering the things I said to you." He smiled. "I just figured you were lashing out at me. At least, I hope that's the reason."

"Most of it, yeah. But some of what I said was true. As ridiculous as it sounds now, I did have this pre-conceived notion about what you were like before we met. But I guess I was so determined to have fun over break that I wanted nothing to do with anyone or anything I thought wouldn't fit into those plans. Any-way, I really don't think you're boring or stuffy, though"—she flashed a quick grin—"maybe you are a little hardheaded."

"My mother would agree with you."

"Yes, she has mentioned that." The corners of her mouth lifted in another smile. "I guess we're okay with what I said, so what about you? I know you apol-ogized, but do you really think I'm like Maureen?"

He winced at the question. "I did, at first. After the way she made a mockery of our marriage and then threw what she did in my face, I was hurt and angry." He exhaled with a huff. "But until recently, I had no idea how long those feelings would last or how they'd affect my life. I guess I figured once the divorce was final I could put everything behind me and move on, and I thought that's what I'd done. I never realized how much being married to Maureen had messed with my head. Until I met you. When I think about how I almost lost you because of her, it tears me up inside."

He swallowed hard, then blew out another deep breath. "What I'm trying to say is, I know your taking the messenger job over Christmas break doesn't mean you'll end up like her. It was stupid of me to even think it."

She nodded. "You're right. It was stupid. And irrational. And insensitive. But, considering how deeply scarred your marriage left you, also understandable." She arched her eyebrows. "Not that I'm condoning your accusations."

"No, I'm sure you're not," he said with a chuckle, then quickly sobered. "I did a lot of thinking over the past couple of days, and besides realizing your choice in Christmas jobs wasn't a bad omen, I also discovered a couple of other things. One was that everything boils down to trust. I trust you not to do what Maureen did to me, because I love you. I thought I loved her, but in retrospect, what I felt for her doesn't begin to compare with my feelings for you." He lifted a hand and brushed a curl away from her face. "The other thing I discovered was kind of surprising." He laughed. "Actually, shocked is closer to my reaction when I realized the two of us are more alike than I thought. Especially the excitement thing, which I . . . uh . . . I'm embarrassed to admit I'm getting to like."

"And you're okay with that?"

"Yup, totally okay," he replied with a nod, then grinned. "As long as I get my excitement fixes with you."

"Absolutely." She smiled, her gorgeous green eyes twinkling. "We bring out the best in each other, don't ya think? You becoming a little more daring and adventurous, and me finding out I can enjoy the peace and quiet of the mountains."

"You do?"

"My visit home for Christmas turned out to be a lot more than seeing my family again. For the first time since I was a little girl, I actually enjoyed being on the ranch. And the isolation was no longer a big deal; in fact it surprised me to realize I truly liked being out in the middle of nowhere."

She gave him another smile. "Anyway, at the time, I didn't understand why I felt that way. But then I remembered your mother telling me it takes falling in love to discover who we really are. Since I got back, I've thought a lot about both what she said and my visit home, and I realized she's right.

"The reason I hated being on the ranch when I was younger was because I wasn't happy with myself. I should have figured it out sooner, but falling in love with you made me see things with a whole new perspective. Where a person lives isn't the key to being happy. Happiness comes from the inside. When you're happy with who you are and what you're doing in your life, then where you live really isn't all that important."

"Do you really mean that? Because if you don't, I can always move closer to town."

"Don't you dare even think about selling your

house. It's beautiful and I know how much you love living in the foothills." She lifted a shoulder in a shrug. "So we don't live close to each other. No big deal. At least it's not a true long distance relationship, right?"

He stepped closer and pulled her into his arms. "Right, babe," he murmured just before settling his mouth atop hers for a long, toe-curling kiss.

When he pulled back, she drew a shaky breath, then said, "When I came here tonight, I never figured I'd end up kissing Santa."

"Play your cards right," he replied, "and you'll be doing a lot more than kissing the guy."

A burst of laughter exploded from her. "You're not suggesting we do anything here, are you?"

"Hmm, could be really stimulating if we did," he said, giving her nose a quick kiss. "But I'd prefer complete privacy so I can have you naked, spread out on a bed."

Heat sizzled in her eyes. "Sounds like a good plan to me."

"Then let's go." He loosened his hold on her. "Did you leave anything at the table?"

"The table! Oh God, Lisa and Jillian are still at the table. I forgot all about them."

"Yeah, I do have that effect on you."

She swatted his arm. "Gee, I hope you can get that swelled head of yours through the door."

He flashed her a crooked smile, a laugh rumbling in his chest. "We're really good for each other, babe."

"I know," she replied, lifting her face to his and pressing a quick kiss on his lips. "Funny how we both thought we were wrong for each other, and it turns out we're really perfect together."

"Can't argue with perfection." He took her hand and tugged her toward the door. "Now, come on, let's

go say good-night to your friends, and then we're
outa here."

Six months later

Annie entered the gallery and immediately spotted
Dalton at the base of the staircase. As she aproached
him, her heart did an odd little flip in her chest, the
same reaction she had every time she saw the man
she loved more than she'd ever thought possible. She
still couldn't believe how wonderful her life had become since meeting Dalton Stoner. Smiling, she said,
"Are you ready to leave?"

"In a minute. There's something I want to show
you first." He held out his hand. "It's upstairs."

She moved closer, took his hand, then walked beside him as they went up the wide staircase.
Surprisingly, they didn't stop at the second floor but
continued to the third.

When they reached the top floor, she noticed lad-
ders, drop cloths, paint cans, and carpenter tools
scattered everywhere. "Did you decide to enlarge the
gallery?"

He smiled. "Come see for yourself." He opened a
door, then stepped aside to let her enter first.

Annie walked past him, then came to a halt. "Oh
my God!" The walls had been repainted, the floors re-
finished, and across the room, through another
doorway, she could see what looked to be kitchen
cabinets. She moved into the center of the room,
stunned. "Dalton, what's going on?"

"I took the advice a really smart woman gave me
not long ago, and I'm turning the third floor into an
apartment. For us."

She turned on her heel to face him. "Us?" Her

brow furrowed, she glanced around again. "I don't understand."

"Remember when I told you I don't go out in the evening very often because of how far I live from the city?" When she nodded, he said, "Since meeting you and discovering I have a—what did you call it, oh yeah—a more daring and adventurous side, I realized how much I've been missing. But even in good weather, it's still a long drive to my house, a drive I don't want to make at all if I've had a few beers. And then there are Data and Worf to consider.

"So now, once the remodeling is done, staying in town after I finish work won't be a problem. On days when you and I have something planned for the evening, I'll bring the dogs into town with me and leave them up here during the day."

"Then you'll spend the night with them here."

"No, we'll be spending the night." He moved closer and took her hand. "Turning these rooms into an apartment is my wedding gift to you."

"What?" She blinked, certain she'd misunderstood. They hadn't discussed marriage, and given Dalton's first miserable experience, she understood his hesitation and didn't have a problem with not taking their relationship to the next level. His bringing up the topic now had thrown her for a loop. Giving her head a shake, she said, "Uh . . . would you repeat that?"

"Can't say as I blame you for being skeptical," he replied with a laugh. "Though, aren't you the one who told me I shouldn't let a single mistake ruin my life?"

"Yes, but—"

He pressed a finger to her lips. "Uh-uh, watch those buts," he said, giving her a tender smile. "What I said is true, babe. I want to marry you. I want this to be our home in the city. Just like I want my house to become our home in the mountains. We can split our time between them. Weekends at the house, week-days here, or whatever combination you want. I don't care, as long as we're together." He moved his hand to push a curl off her cheek. "So what do you say, will you marry me?"

She stared into his blue-gray eyes for a long moment, love filling her chest and pushing up to clog her throat. Touching a fingertip to the cleft in his chin, she smiled. "Absolutely."

He let out a whoop, then started across the room, waving for her to follow him. "Come on, there's something else I want to show you."

Curious what else the man had in store for her, Annie followed him into another room, this one with furniture—well, one piece anyway: a massive bed with a beautiful carved oak headboard—then continued to what she knew was the turret room.

As she stepped over the threshold, her breath caught. The space had been transformed into an el-egant bathroom, complete with a bathtub in front of the window. She took several more steps, stopping in the center of the tiled floor, then slowly turned to take in the entire room.

"Oh, Dalton. I can't believe it." She drew a deep breath, hoping to slow her pounding heart. "This is going to be unbelievable."

"Yeah, it is," he replied. "But then I had it on good authority that it would be."

She smiled. "That really smart woman you men-tioned a while ago?"

"One and the same," he replied, returning her smile.

She moved to where he stood just inside the door-way. "Well, if she's the one who came up with the idea for turning the third floor into an apartment and for putting a bathtub under the window over there, then don't ya think she deserves a reward?"

"A reward, huh?" His lips twitched. "I think I might be able to handle that." He trailed his fingertips down the side of her neck, then rubbed a curly strand of hair between his thumb and fingers. "You got any ideas about what she might want?"

"Hmm . . . actually, I think christening that bed in there might be just what she wants."

His eyes widened, their color turning a deep, rich blue. "Ya think so?"

She nodded. "Oh yeah, I definitely think so."

With a deep chuckle, he scooped her into his arms, carried her into the bedroom, then dropped her onto the center of the mattress.

He started to join her, then suddenly straightened. "Almost forgot," he said. "I've got something else for you."

She watched him stick his hand in his pants' pocket, then withdraw a small envelope and hold it toward her.

"What is this?" she said, taking the envelope.

"Another wedding present."

"But that's not fair," she replied. "I don't have anything to give you."

"I'm about to get my present"—he gave her a knowing look—"so hurry up and open yours."

Laughing, she turned the envelope over and read aloud, "Colorado Avalanche." Giving him a quizzical look, she opened the envelope, pulled out the contents, then gasped. "Are these—" she drew a deep breath. "Are these what I think they are?"

"Yup. Season tickets. Your favorite section. Fifth row from the ice."

"Ohmygod, ohmygod." She scrambled to her

knees and threw her arms around his neck. "Dalton, I love you even more for doing this, but you didn't have to."

"I know, but we both love hockey, and the games are more fun in person. Besides"—he gave her a fierce hug—"now that we have a place in town where we can stay on game nights, I figured we should indulge ourselves."

"Indulge, huh?" She gave him a sizzling glance. "How about we do a different kind of indulging right now and get back to christening this bed?"

"Don't have to ask me twice," he replied, reaching for the hem of her knit top, then pulling it up and over her head in one fluid move.

She made fast work of unbuttoning his shirt, then unbuckled his belt and unfastened the hook at the waist of his slacks. As she lowered the tab of his zipper, she said, "I just thought of something."

"Yeah? Well, I'm thinking of something, too." His fingers released the catch on her bra. "How fast I can get you naked and bury myself inside you."

"Yes, I'm sure you were," she said with a smile. "But what I was thinking was, you never told me what you were wearing under the Santa Claus outfit that night at Gina's."

"No, I didn't." He tossed her bra aside, then started to work on getting her out of her capri pants.

"Come on, slick"—she shoved his slacks down his hips, revealing the hard ridge of his erection pressing against his briefs—"tell me what were you wearing."

He huffed out a breath, then grimaced. "A thong."

She removed her hands from the waistband of his underwear and sat back on her heels. "You're kidding?"

"Believe me, babe. Thongs are nothing to kid about."

She laughed. "God, don't I know it."

His eyes narrowed. "You've worn one? How come I've never seen you in it?"

"Because I only wore the damn thing once."

"When?"

"Remember the day we met and you asked if I was naked under my red velvet outfit?"

"I'll never forget it."

"Me either," she replied, her heart doing that same little flip in her chest again. "Anyway, I was wearing a red satin bra and matching thong panties."

"Seriously?" When she nodded, he said, "Do you still have them?"

"I guess. After I quit the messenger job, I think I stuffed 'em in the back of my underwear drawer."

"Daphne told me you quit the messenger service right after you got back from Wyoming."

"Yes, I did. Even before I went to Wyoming, I was pretty sure I'd already fallen in love with you, so the idea of taking off my clothes for someone else had really lost its appeal. I gave my boss a flimsy excuse for why I couldn't make any of the deliveries she'd lined up for me, but when I got back from seeing my family, I knew I'd never be able to go through with the job. So I called her and quit."

"I'm glad." He smiled, stroking the side of her face with his fingers. After several seconds, he said, "If you . . . uh . . . can find those red undies, will you model them for me?"

"Model . . ." She blinked, then burst out laughing. "Listen, I'll make you a deal, slick. I'll show you mine, if you'll show me yours."

He grinned. "You got a deal, babe. Just pick the day."

"Well, let's see. I think our wedding night would be the perfect time for a little fashion show."

"Hmm," he replied, pulling her back up onto her knees and pressing a brief kiss on her mouth. "Perfect time for a lota other things, too."

"Uh-huh," she whispered against his lips. After a long, mind-boggling kiss that left them both breathless, she said, "How about we practice some of those things right now?"

With a laugh, he quickly tugged off the rest of their clothes then took his sweet time obliging the woman who drove him wild.

Suzanne would love to hear from readers.
Send an e-mail to: suzgray@myway.com
Or write to her at:
P.O. Box 563
Comstock MI 49041-0563